FAKE FUR

Also by John Fraser and published by AESOP Modern Fiction:

Animal Tales
Behaving Well
Best Friends
Black Masks
Blue Light / Starting Over
The Case
Confessions
Down from the Stars
The Ends of the Earth
Enterprising Women
Exploring the Clouds
The Future's Coming Everywhere
Happy Always
Hard Places
An Illusion of Sun
The Magnificent Wurlitzer
Medusa
Military Roads
The Observatory
The Other Shore
People You Will Never Meet
The Red Bird
The Red Tank
Runners
'S'
Short Lives
Sisters
Soft Landing
The Storm
Strangers and Refugees
Thinking Scientifically
Thirty Years
Three Beauties
Tomorrow the Victory
Wayfaring
Wisdom

FAKE FUR

John Fraser

AESOP Modern Fiction
Oxford

AESOP Modern Fiction
An imprint of AESOP Publications
Martin Noble Editorial / AESOP
28a Abberbury Road, Oxford OX4 4ES, UK
www.aesopbooks.com

First edition published by AESOP Publications

www.johnfraserfiction.com

A catalogue record of this book is
available from the British Library.

First edition 2021, revised 2024

ISBN: 978-1-910301-93-7

CONTENTS

THE WAY BACK 7

ELEMENTARY EXERCISES 89

THE WAY BACK

Shérine

THE VILLAGE main street is our river. The stream of life. We indigenes, at our window, peering out, watch the explorers wandering past. Us: circumspect and bored.

I'm the primitive: – history forgotten, hanging on to junk, cosmology busted, rusted out, my head a jumble, too much dope and booze and suicide. Unloved, unlovable, a lush. Too far-out to be sexy.

Village life: the settlement, the long house in your head. Digging. Weeds.

Some visiting families paddle by, old-time mums and dads with squawky kids. Gawping at us banal oddities.

They don't appreciate our demotic architecture, the rare plants cossetted like cats.

There's single women. Not following the map, but curious, looking for a hook to hang on. Curious and wispy. If I asked, would one come in?

I'd love to talk, explain why I'm here, alone. My little house? Me, a female, an alien, a trap. Foreign. I had a reputation once – maybe someone's found it lying in the road?

I think ... those who'd come in would be terrified, and think it's some commercial trick, or else they've misunderstood – the invite comes from someone who doesn't speak their tongue. And tongue is what they absolutely wouldn't want to show or have it used, as a toy, a sweetener, a token of love or lust or both.

Or – they might be a thief. Or mystified, quite unafraid – to see your scruffy interior, thinking no harm can come from me, a woman seemingly alone, and maybe there are pickings of something, a posy or a recipe, or just nothing, a trip around the curio shop: – 'I'll think about it ...' they'd say, sidling out. Not specifying what they might have wanted or what kind of thinking they are capable of.

Perhaps when I'm not here, or I'm asleep – someone comes in ... a sneak, not thieving – leaving a presence, a whiff of somewhere else. Police? Landlord? A nemesis?

*

Speculate. Don't make a sign. They've corrupted you, generations back; nothing is left. Other people? – know nothing, call you an Indian. Where's India? Here or everywhere.

*

I'm lonely, always have been, a consequence of not enjoying company, still less intimacy, and carrying on a kind of symposium in my head, of questions classic but not resolvable – deep questions but not immediate, can easily wait for you to die before they're raised again, and you know all the human talent goes in practicalities and running squads of people; making plans that are not read, or disregarded, even not written down. Plots, conspiracies, in-the-know – and blow-them-up. Or, making an analysis, preparing a report on sexual improprieties in some big corp – people enjoying themselves or others, too extreme, or overstepping, causing misery in offices ... creating pseudo-slavery...

You need knowledge, that's for sure. And there's creation. It's supposed to grow from knowledge. That's what knowledge is for – knowledge in the sense of knowing what you want, which means knowing what other people may have wanted. Is there a way of going straight to creation? Knowledge ties you to the ancestors, their thinking, judgements, and the stuff they've left.

You invent a tank, a bomb – for wars interminable they carried on, and we inherited ... our faces the patrimony ... us drawn in every cave and on every boulder. Warriors, stick-men.

Let's be reasonable – creation with the slightest scent of knowledge.... Would this be the naif, the spontaneous – already experienced and now dull routine ... copied out ... surrealism, always starting a club to share the mystery ... the prodigy, plays, invents nothing new, just possesses youth-fulness – so what? Creation – must be recognisable – a copy. Or a fake.

*

Creation: 'as if you knew, what it was worth, creating; and how it will play out'. .... You create: into the spate it goes, becomes the future. Could it all be different, with you a skeleton, a ghost, gesticulating from the past? God? On the beach, dictating rules, a book, unseen, a miracle, a void.

I'd want 'Creation with free-flow', not guessing what might happen. I, God, would be absolutely unknowable and indifferent. I'd be the *fabbro*, making the shoe – then it's all up to the horse, where it goes, its adventures. I'm not on its back. Create a universe. See what happens. If it grows.

Then stepping back, not being in it: – a has-been: the father, mother ... Not a fit, not a part of it or anything.

*

'It isn't like it was,' says Tiva. 'Oddballs mooning round, wondering what to do. Now, it's urgent, and there's no good results. There's something precise anyone can do, and spend what time they have at it. The result's uncertain.'

Her house – my inspiration. A bare kennel.

There was a little cloudy window, up high ... While we talked and speculated – there were awful wars, campaigns, starvations. All going on while ... we looked for the Word. Up there.

An interlude, when we knew reality is a parody and laughter disarms dragons. It wasn't good, and ended bad. Loving each other – means there's no children to be created. Tiva's acquainted with the vacuum. There's a pause. She says, 'Bad people scheme; the rest are spontaneous, follow whims, the flickering lights.'

It isn't relevant. I say, 'Near where I come from, the women are so beautiful, they have to wear not veils, not burkas, but a plaster carnival mask. In the souk, the husband can't distinguish his woman, trailing a distance behind – so he loads her with bangles; the *tin-tin* of bracelets and anklets identifies his wife ...'

To be a sound. Be a mouth, an ear: be a tiny hammer on a drum.

*

When I leave, I think, 'the fawn presses its nose on its mother's fur – "What am I, mother?" he asks. "You're food," she says. Maybe she cries. "What are you?" he asks: "I'm sex," she says.'

The fawn's the missing link. The food chain.

The Buddha. Maybe that created something from nothing.... No sons left dangling, no laws on stones or golden plates....no book.

The Buddha, possibly? – and all the company of bodhisattvas, the reincarnations of your big thought, before and after you had it shaped, typed in the lemmas and *postille* .... Although, an idea can never ever be a 'you', and so the Buddha is right for us to replicate; to make into multiples, duplicates, hordes of saints hung on a '60s gallery wall, cutting you in on something brilliant, for sale from a world a little tawdry, like cups and saucers mass-produced, silk-screen prints after everybody did them, and they all seem false as wallpaper .... Imagine an original painting, a unique God – yet an idea which is not common, shared as water – wouldn't even be an idea.

Troy

The doors and stairs are brown, shading like browning leaves. At the top, they're chocolate: below, like mottled scabs. The ground floor – a family of dwarves. That's what they want to be called. Not circus people, but proud of being small, smaller than me. A borshch a-bubble, and merriment always on the hob. Once they'd have been called mechanicals – they move stiff, precise, like machines that's always thinking how to be beautiful, conserving energy.

Then there's the gaming school – you hear the ball rolling, could be a scimitar drawing a circle on the ground with you in, round the track, and a crack and snap as someone opens a new deck and bends and shuffles – most of the pack dies unseen, unshuffled and unplayed, like they are wolves in penury. Hollow guys go in, and hollow they come out. Up again – and the street sounds dwindle, make more sense – shouts loose, up the stairs, big motors, V8s toiling and some flat 6s, old cylinders: aluminum blocks.

There's couples up a floor: two facing doors, all misbelievers, but the women stick to foulards, men to black beards, clinging sweetly to their jaws like swarming honey bees. They scheme, for and against everything, passionately.

Up and up, there's a guy – a guitar, but quite refined, maybe six-stringed, or even more, an oud, or something in between or previous, he's skilful but the plectrum flavours over the sound, plastic twang .... if there was a woman, would do better, but women have to sing or dance – his body shapely, maybe too much, women want a lover angular, without an inkling of breasts, and lots of hair, on the back, like on a boar, they say it's ugly, and it is, but still – it's not a thing you choose.

And up I go, now the brown on rail and door is hardly fingered, but the smell has risen, dirty bodies, cheap disinectant like you use but in twenty-litre cans, not for domestic use, but what for, then? This. Dirty bodies. A stairwell – down you look, it's narrow as a weasel trap, a rhomboid, and you think of suicide, but you would hit and bounce all the way down, be smashed before you reached the concete floor, so you can do better – maybe a place where everyone is stranger to the rest, and so your fall disturbs them more and brings them all together.

'I'm up to see king Ouf,' instead, it's Troy, he calls himself. Troy after king Troas. Probably he's once a Turk who knows a tiny piece of history, Syrian maybe, or from Iran: – knows that Troy citadel is an immense piece of history, a fantasy for many here, though less for those Moldovan dwarves. A place they had to build, invent, from scratch. The diggers found a village, but no sign of walls or horse, no attributes of gods .... as though divinities would champion any one of us, all are punished indiscriminately, for trivial peccadilloes, adultery, a sex-theft, not even love ... Gods have little else to do, seeing they all believe in sin, original and going on, and free will, so they keep out the mess, mortals are all guilty wantons, ignorant and fey.... but gods need their stories, some fall-guy mortals fleshing out the tales, being blinded or impregnated, worth a small digression on Olympus....

Poke around the vulnerables, make them rich, or dismember them.

*

'Troy! What's doing?'

He's for ever unemployed, and could be plotting, on your side or not, a gang, a sect, secret society – maybe you're a cover for him, or he may be one for you... Terror? Yes, he frightens me.

*

An act of violence. Can't make a stir these days without ... You expect it from a beefy bearded guy – unjust, for sure ...

'Love for the people,' Troy says. 'When I have sex, I put on this plaster pig's head.'

I say, 'It's a joke. Not funny. Not with me, Troy. The overtones – you'd be straining to hear them all .... Not worth it.'

My judgement is much more severe, not only about the sex. Am I here for that?

*

I have been wrong about everything. I've been moderate when the massacres were descending from their ancestors; over and over, lookalikes.

You must be extreme, give no quarter, above all to yourself. Don't be thoughtful, be clean; don't expose a doubt, a trace of failure or of weakness.

*

'I need a coup, Tiva,' I tell her. 'At the tables, or finding a fortune, my old reputation. A cure or a disease.'

'Not to give money to Troy, I hope,' she says. 'You say you're not with him, but you're always going to that house. Those people ...'

'To get away, Tiva,' I say. 'I'm tired of being the only sane one in this place. And yet not even being ordinary.'

'Everyone says that,' she says. 'What will happen, happens. Be content that it's not now.'

'That's so,' I say. 'Exactly. This is a low day, that's all it will be. When *it* happens it will be in the big field where there were animals. Or the room is quiet, peaceful, because no one comes to it, home. The rest – is in photos.'

'I'm an actor,' Tiva says, 'so I can make it happen when I want. It won't stop, because – I'm an actor. I act out.'

'It's safe here,' I say. 'It's dull. The money will stop. That's the way – the motor can't run without. Remember when there started to be nothing – no cash, no food – what to do? No one could tell.'

I was beautiful, I was a butterfly, I had six legs. They had me in their mouth. I gave away some legs – now I have only two, I walk on them, like everybody else. Another disaster – we who are left, we who've recovered.

*

'Suppose it happened again here,' says Tiva, 'Or worse. How would we ...'

'I'd give another leg, I guess,' I say. 'But no more than that, not more than one.'

'You had your war,' Tiva tells me, questioning: deflating quite politely. 'It would be unlikely you'll be here to survive another. And after all – you weren't there. You watched it like we did. You might have been there if you had not been here ... but it seemed more your war than ours. That's the flaw – in your life, your story. Surviving.'

'Yes, Tiva,' I say. 'I lie. Or – I dramatise. But I'm in bad shape now.'

'It's true,' says Tiva. 'I grant you – you're as bad as if you'd lived through your experiences. The past: goes for everyone, wherever you were or weren't. The past has gone – except it lives inside you, all of it. You could try to kill it. And what's the good of being dead? We want stories, not atrocities....'

It's a movie. I say – 'People used to know all that was around them – it made a picture ... the donkeys, the calls to prayer, the geese, the markets ... wise men, the mad ones shouting in the streets, shadows of the women.... Now, it's all in pieces. What can I claim to know, to want? – truth? Death? Both; or, it's the same. Each with a toy theatre, a big square stage that stretches round the world and in a warren underneath.'

A small, black lacquered box, hi-shine, on a small table –

On the stage – a showman – could be a punk, a situationist – but evidently it's not. Wears a worn 'smoking', a monkey jacket: smells of ingrained sweat and secondhand and cleaning fluid.

Shérine and Tiva stare ...

'What's in the box?' the showman, magician, asks the world, his public. 'What might be inside?' It's head-size, no opening, no lid that you can see. 'There's no key, and if there was – who has it? What's inside? Irony? Satire, caricature – or parody ... a travesty, the world turned up and down? No! I see your faces – *you're* inside this box. Can't let it go, can't leave....'

'He means – concentrate,' Tiva whispers. 'Screw your mind up like a fist ....'

'When you explain,' I say, 'you spoil it.'

'No, Shérine,' says Tiva. 'You're slow, that's all.'

It wouldn't be a drama, being slow. Tiva goes on, 'Men want what we've not got, Shérine. There's no answer to a hopeless want, not even concentration.'

'I know,' I say. 'I'm Helen. I thought it would be fun. And Troy.... I know it's just a village, lots of goats and sheep... You must invent. If I was disappointed nothing happened, it would have no consequence.'

Tiva looks sadly at me, says, 'If I loved you, Shérine, you wouldn't feel a thing.'

'I might,' I say.

'You could find work,' she says, 'even some part of a humble job. Work isn't you, you understand. It's ephemeral, not your identity. You think you sell yourself – but no: the next day you are all there, as you were. You even gain. Not much, but day by day.... What you do is different from what you are.'

'It isn't so,' I say. 'Most places – you are you by glance. By colour, how you wear your clothes and walk, where you go and where you live: – your work is the "tin-tin" that follows you and sleeps with you and has your kids. Another skin.'

'Maybe it's so,' says Tiva. 'After all, your food is you. So is your work – it's how you stay alive.'

'I can't,' I say. 'I can't fold up and take some work. I am perverse, perhaps. Your work's another skin, you're right. It's transparent, you slip it over your original one. See, Tiva, I can't forget ever what it is I am.'

'What you are, Shérine,' Tiva says, 'is a collector. You're not a you, you're what surrounds you, what you hear ... you're fastidious, you like the forms, the curiosities you've stacked up, but keep your distance. All faiths, all monsters, the pleasing, the baroque, the rusted, faded, the grotesque, the yellow books, foxed prints … all you have gathered, collected, you preserve, gloat, enjoy. You'll never accomplish anything – it would mean not collecting, but being part of the immense collection that all the rest of us are in. ... the squirming spaghetti of the species ... noodles or snakes, or tapeworms? A puzzle, a sacred knot, the pit of vipers, the gods' gift to their misbegotten ...'

'You riff, Tiva,' I say, laughing. 'I don't understand you, not a bit.'

'Beware,' she says, laughing too. 'Beware the towers of Ilium.'

*

She's right. That house, tall and brown and tottering, its feet uncertain, the underground dug out, made into little houses for some mousey people, who nibble on corn stalks all the day; at night, they leave the dark rooms, out on the dark streets, peddling – their bodies and their pills....

It's amazing how quickly it comes down, an old house been standing, dull, for ever, older than a dolmen, a pyramid, necropolis – welcoming, digesting, excreting its occupants, living, dead and moribund, generations of them, renting, squatting, living together, apart, by the day, the hour, the lifetime, till....

Down it all comes. Troy the man – hammering down through the planks, into the fundamentalists, Sunni backsliders, fearing for their souls, into the purgatory with them all, Troy the transgressive, misbeliever, *takfir* – the neighbours, all of them, embraced .... dropping like a bomb-case into the shell game on the floor below, plaster and laths on to the types in brown demob suits, ticket-of-leave men, slick slackers, florid sharpers – Troy, half dead already, centring, hitting the wheel of fortune, smashing it down, down through the floor into the dwarves, who scuttle, scatter, like a nest of squirrels, baby badgers – all, everyone, borne down into a pit of their own making, heads and feet the living shovels, spearing the dust and clinkers, the faith, the lust, the hope, all the familiarity – mulching like a stratum of Russian salad that some master of the cold table buries, covers, slapping on the final slice of steamed tan loaf, or here a wholesome red-brown roof – making a sandwich of them all....

The impish bearing of the roulette wheel goes bouncing down the street, breaking the news ... there's not much other noise – a tinkling of brick-bits, the cement crumbling down – could be thick paper tearing. Not a cry.

Guess what the last wish was ... Not this!

Nothing, no response. Be content. Physics is the law most trustworthy, and buries them, will bury us.

*

'That's terrible,' says Tiva. 'Poor you, Shérine. Poor Troy, of course. The rest too, apostates, I bet – those poor little folk .... Time, my dear, time did for them, indiscriminate – all blameless, or at least – unjudged and uncondemned.'

'I must do something,' I say. 'Be an engineer: – inspector of old houses. A poet – on the corner of the boulevard, set out my sorrow, anger ... street singing, a punk waif....'

'Beware, Shérine,' says Tiva, deepening her sombre mood. 'We tend to madness. We're obsessive. If we aren't King Ludwig, we admire him, we aspire ... to understand, share, cheer on, and then complete the quest ...All quests, his too, of course.

'We're clever monkeys, and we want to be the cleverest. Maybe being cannibals is worth a try – dismembering the greys among us, or the ageing females. Artistry – to be super – be versatile.... Paint the portrait of the sallow lady with the swollen mouth – over and over ... make it a factory, a band of sorcerers' apprentices.... You're a wonder, you can invent a tank, an aeroplane, and mustard gas, hurrah! hurrah! for artistry ... obsess, write a sonnet – make it hundreds: variations, and sonatas, don't stick at dozens, twist and twist...more cards! – a play that lasts for days, a movie starting over, over six hours without movement, man sleeping, squirrel up a tree for days. No – months.... Hear the applause, we watch with love, the creativity! The daring!

'Ford and his trained ape workers? Make work obsessive too, a screw, a screw! is yours to tighten all your life, then you can see some actor screwing on your screen when you go home, until you sleep and wake to .... endless travel, prickly heat and cancelled flights, writing, musing – plotting and vendetta – all vanity, Shérine! Processions, cheering, play your trombone, listen to yourself on tape and clap until you almost burst, and shout 'bravo!' as if they didn't know they were ... Stendhal's syndrome in the aisle – the beauty! Makes us swoon – the demon bride has won our heart.... Bequeath your money to the magus or the conjurer....

'Those who can't be geniuses – as we all are born – must die of frustration, emulation – whatever folly we get up to, there will be a following, a competition ... in fours and fives , bass drums and kilts.... What do we reach? A devastation. Our aspirations are a suicide – obession. A compulsion....

'On and on, until we break our nature and the nature of the beasts. Exterminate and discipline.

'The reasoning response? Quite unavailing. All on a diet; walk and run, then into the balloon and see ourselves from high and higher up. Obsession leads us on until our love of madness is normality – and we have dug our hole, our trap. A tragic paradox – we seek our happiness – and arrange, carpenter, our misery. That former revolutionary, Marx, now in an attic penning books that drop off into obsolescence as he writes The End.... We remember his first dream, the faun beneath the tree who dozes into fantasy – the revolution! Instead – think of those grey books, 'the outlines': volume four.... A ground-plan of eternal capitalism. We follow folly, can't digest an argument. We obsess about the greats' obsessions....

'There you have it, Shérine. It's a paradox. We must escape, but breaking from the cage we lose ourselves in forests where we starve and burn.... We have to struggle, intervene – or all our houses will fall down,' she says: 'And yet, and yet! They *do* fall down: our houses sink like galleons in sargossa seas.....'

*

Am I convinced? Well, yes and no.

*

'All this vehemence, Tiva,' I say: 'Is it love, perhaps? A passion? Us two? Or a frotting, spiritual or not?'

'And are you interested?' she asks.

'Interested – in a general way,' I say: 'But not enthusiastic.'

'Enthusiasm is a vital part,' she says, looking disappointed. 'Maybe you lost it, like you seem to lose your nationality, religion, family too, I'd bet – you're what they call "free radical". No roof, no bed. No income.'

She puts her arms around me, feels my shoulders: 'Some types who've lost their substance find they have acquired the wings of augurous birds, who dine on death and spiral up to spy down every chimney, tower of winds, each flat roof, its sprawling occupants, and from that height, let drop a maleficent clod of evil excrements....'

She laughs. It was a joke. Another joke that doesn't make me laugh.

*

'It's our fragility,' I say. 'It makes us sexy, so they say. A breath – we croak. A drop in sales – we're on the street. Some torrid days – the rivers dry, the oceans boil. And yet – without the pheromone, the scent, the taste, for human flesh, communion, conjunction ... the hug – we're unfulfilled. Embrace, a cuddle – whatever catastrophe occurs, still we feel a hug will ease it all – the pain, anxiety, the trembling and the fear.'

'It's too bad,' Tiva says, rubbing her hands together, moving away from me. 'The gold price is too high. The miners – down those ant-holes – the sun, the rain – loosens the cladding on the shaft, silently, the men, the kids, the women, disappear....'

'It moves fast now,' I say. 'It's speeding up. There were slow wars, intractable – Sudan, the Yemen, the Sahel, Ukraine ... meanwhile we moved around like filings round a magnet.... We swirl, there's water, sand and cops – everyone infected everybody, solutions came, then there were more.... You can be anything at all, what you want or what you don't. Your soul is small, and getting smaller, your body large and swelling....'

'What do you think about, Shérine?' asks Tiva. 'It should be serious. Last things. Did Troy pay you, by the way?'

'Oh. not for sex,' I say. 'He was bristly – an aloe! You couldn't touch.... Paid not for sex – before and after, for other things, perhaps. And now ... full stop!'

'Now, it will all change soon,' says Tiva, encouraging. 'No one counts costs, or wonders where the money comes and goes....'

'The funeral...?' I ask.

'They'll paint the ruins,' Tiva says. 'Stones. Grey crumble is the grave, they'll paint some angels on it – just wings, like the big mosque in Constantinople....'

*

'I thought, when the house came down and we saw Troy's wooden legs come careening in the street, that I was the last person left, left in the world,' I say to Tiva. 'What a blessing it would be! All the despoilers and the warriors gone – all at a blow, by accident. But no! You and I – we two must be the last. Unless you believe in virgin birth, my dear – there'll be no more! We're the last one, extinguished like the rhinos and the hippos, those pigeons and the Buffalo Bills....'

'Whoa, old horse, my love, Shérine,' says Tiva. 'More will probably arrive: our riders. Not the best, for sure: those that held on, trampling their fellows so's to make a ladder, rise up out the silt. They have survived. And they'll come rampaging down the street, looting and yanking flowers....'

'We'll have to make a plan,' I say. 'Five years at least, to multiply our food and drink.... Statistics: – that's the key, I'm sure....'

'We could use artillery,' says Tiva. 'To knock some other houses down, free up the scene, let us all breathe.'

'That's not serious,' I say. 'Things happen much too fast to be philosophised. To be quite frank – it's not just we can't, we don't react – we don't make sense, don't grasp what's happening. The idea used to be: catastrophe was all our fault.

It may be so, but now some power has hold of us. A power that's not benign, not from our pantheon.

'We've lost it, Tiva, the initiative. The houses – all of them – are falling down. Effects are multiplied, a chain reaction, sucking us all in – men, soil and butterflies – our nature's changed....'

'I love it, Shérine,' Tiva says. 'I love to see the bossy guys strung up and twist, eternal values crumple up like paper party hats. Into the bin! I say. The new – not, as they used to say in ignorance, what we would love when it came at last. Now – we see it is a monster. It stalks us, snores beside us in our bed, crawls in our blood and dances there in 5/4 time. Nothing. It brings a nothing that we know or can foresee, no laws, no mineshafts full of gold, no ruins underground, no charming kids, reforming tsars. Chaos, my dear. Nothing. Nothing we can do, no hope to save ourselves. Completely unpredictable. Disaster....'

Gus, Marvin, Amelle and Nadine

Up the street come Gus and Marvin, Nadine and Amelle, bombed out and freaking, blood in their eyes and jaws.

'How good to see you, pretty things,' says Nadine, raising her lacy bonnet, curtseying.

'We lost everything,' says Gus, lisping with his short tongue. 'Then we lost our way as well. Now we are completely lost. We find you – does that mean we are not lost...?'

He's full of messages – his skimpy clothes, his long furrry arms, all written on: a curriculum, a picture book, a naval code of signs and ensigns. Flags of the nations, rules of engagement and of promises breached and reneged.

'Marvin's house fell down,' says Amelle. 'I never had a house. I'm with these three by happenstance – and with you two now –' and she points to me and Tiva '– that's five. No one knows where that will stop – it's common, universal even – but it's odd. It gives a clue to all the mysteries that we wander through....'

Maybe she's Bolivian. I wonder – Nadine for sure's from Homs.... After a while, it seems it isn't so – but it's irrelevant – they've both been here for years, and now, like Gus – are homeless. Just like Tiva, and like me.

'No mystery, Amelle,' says Marvin. He's tall, scrubbed white, all the original colour lost, maybe from birth – never an albino, bewitched and feared – but pale as a dawn mist, no tattoo, no pictures on his skin, as if he despises us, who see ourselves as sketchbooks, pattern books, as if someone will choose us for our beguiling, our design, instal us as the decor of a kitchen or a lounge; a feature. Or duplicate us like a tile, linoleum or carpet squares....

'These houses,' Gus says, pointing round – 'They fell because they're jerry-built, for guys like us, the marked ones, losers, poor and struggling, or just struggling.... Every two months, everything in life falls down for me, love, sex and friends – as if I cannnot hear the shout – "Change partners!" Change everything. And now there's nowhere safe, unsafe even, we can live....'

'I said it,' Marvin says. 'No mystery. Just ignorance.'

'There's six of us,' says Gus. 'We need some cash. If we work hard, we'll beaver out some scams, three at the least.'

'Gus,' says Tiva. 'I'm all for scams. And maybe we've no cash. But – here, there's nothing left, nothing to spend it on, no one to buy, nothing to sell.'

'You're a fine woman, Tiva,' Marvin says. 'It's well-known. I love Russian broads, and you're the best, the top cut, sirloin even – but – you're talking like a movie script. The point of cash is not to spend, it's to have it make more cash. Invest. It's when there's nothing you can gain the most. It's economics, stupid, like they say. Now, to get the cash, we have two paths. We find a guy with lots who wants to make some more: – we cut him in. Or else we do the politics, become a state, and tax not only him, but everyone, and start up things with money we have coined and credit that we give ourselves.

'People who don't agree – too bad for them. There's jail and guns and wars – they'll even vote, vote for our pals....'

He's fascinated. So are we. He does a circle of the world: – we are his stardust tail, we trail behind, diffusing sparks.

'The problem is,' says Nadine, who rarely intervenes, 'there's only us. No city – so, no citizens.'

I think, the problem is, we know what's wrong before it happens. And when it has. We know what's wrong with Gus and Marvin, and why Nadine and Amelle are eclipsed by them: but knowing what is wrong, it doesn't change a thing, and leaves me wondering if I'm right, and though I know I am, how can I go on, pushing my rightness to one side, and behaving as if it doesn't count? I'm not a genius for being right, as everybody knows exactly what I know and we all think 'what can I do to have some peace, do something different', although....

And then I realise – it's all gone bad, stayed bad, just like I knew it would.

*

'It's all decided,' Gus declares. 'No bridges, explanations. No 'can I?' 'should I'. No 'if'. Bridges are doubts. 'This side or that. Which country? Which people?' Forget it! Amelle will be president for twenty years, Nadine the Vice: then turn-about. I shall be Intelligence and discipline. Marvin – the finance. We're good together.'

'We'd need some people,' Tiva says.

'What do me and Tiva do?' I ask.

'"Do"?' Gus says, with a rich laugh. 'You do all the rest.'

'When you get tired,' says Marvin, lighting up a yellow thin cheroot, 'other people will come. They're hid in cellars, under the stairs. When they get hungry – they'll scratch a way out. Meanwhile....'

'The problem is,' says Gus, 'when other people come. Until then, we six are legendary.'

'It's Shérine's fault,' says Tiva, snarling towards me, 'Anyone who went with Troy was greatly disappointed, almost no one made it back – they're all there, in the ruins.'

'He was a monster, but he gave me hugs,' I say. 'Gus is right. We need more people, doing work....'

'You didn't understand,' says Marvin. 'Gus didn't say anything at all about them working. More people work to feed themselves and have the bosses boss. Money – it makes itself, it reproduces. The Austrians told you – money breeds on wants, not needs.'

'We have to keep the people quiet, and tax them hard,' says Amelle. 'But Shérine's right. However we get cash – there's nothing we can buy. Power's pleasant for a while, and so's doing nothing all the time – and yet it palls. If our wants aren't satisfied by buying things and having people play the lyre and having sex with us for cash – what is the point of being rich? We might as well be tough and puritans – except there's nothing we believe. One thing's as good as any other thing....'

She is near to tears. and Nadine weeps, and cannot stop.

'We must be radical,' says Tiva – and I see she thinks that Gus and Marvin, on a social scale, are far far down below us two. Are vulgar loudsters on the fiddle, Amelle and Nadine only good for saying 'yes' to all the dirty deeds the guys propose....

'Maybe Shérine would like to reel it back, go to where it hadn't happened, pretend she didn't know it would,' says Marvin, blowing smoke from one side of his thin-lipped mouth, this side and then the other, like in a fairground, a whistling giant, or a Popeye, only sinister. 'Have reality unwind in quite a different way, more pleasant, measured, with leaders intellectually spruced up.... As if her civil war had never happened and never would, or maybe postpone it till you knew you'd win, and all the powers conniving decide to see their interests differently, in quite a sweeter way.... And Troy, forever present, buttoning up his pants and paying her, so she could go on working in that peculiar way, of "not working", not doing what we all must do, the grafting....'

'Yes,' I say. 'I would. I'd like to try it all again, and make it turn out like I want.'

'Collect, restore, repatriate. No empire, no colonialism, no fear and patronising of the different multitudes,' says Gus. 'So – how would you collect? Museums, documentaries? Beauty, moral superiority? How would you know that other cultures were more developed than your own, more beautiful, more skilled, more spiritual? You have to steal and loot to get your knowledge, shoot the ill-armed with your gatlings and your thompsons, hang and decapitate. *That* way you get to know the evil, and make restitution. You might call it your "stage two": repentance after massacre. Perhaps they will sell it all; their treasures – all back to you, so you can put the stuff again on those empty labelled plinths? And on and on....' He laughs. We all laugh.

'Oh Gus,' says Tiva, laughing still, 'That's black! You devil,' and she laughs, and nudges me, as if we have some plan we're following....

*

'It seems it's up to us,' I say, 'to save what is most valuable. Forget the rest, and show how we can appreciate the best. Except ... who are we to do all that? What basis has our judgment?'

'You're a bad example,' Tiva says. She can't stop laughing, straighten up and think. 'There's Troy. You and he – a dirty duo ...' And she laughs some more.

'And you love me,' I say.'I don't go in for that, my dear. And Gus and Marvin – what can we learn from them who's over us, or expect they'd take from us?'

'Courage!' she says. 'When humans waver, other species raise their heads – if heads they have.... There is profusion.... You told Troy the house was condemned.'

'If I knew, I should have gone down with him,' I say.

'If that were so, the words to say it wouldn't have survived. Once, I had a pet goose,' says Tiva. 'I never told it anything. And – it didn't ask.'

'Wants, Tiva,' I say. 'You think you will arrive at them through other people – like wishes granted with a wand.'

'We summoned them,' says Tiva. 'Gus and Marvin. Our fates are there right from the start. We don't come in, our feelings....'

'I don't believe in those,' I say. 'They're all we have, but who'd believe in them?'

'All houses are condemned,' says Tiva. 'When they're built, they have a time to last. Then they come down. But who's to see it's done? Everybody knows, just see the documents. It's what we know, like my goose knew.

'He was a boss, though he was slow, slower than the rest. Those oblong bodies cancel out the advantage you'd think the neck should give.... It isn't so. The body's clumsy and the neck too long.'

'You never had a pet, Tiva,' I say. 'You never went into an old house; said you loved someone. People like complexity in others, so they say – it's rarely so, but you, you are a labyrinth. If ever someone reaches whatever's at your heart, they must escape, find the way out, and back.'

'Gus is bad skin,' she says. 'You scratch and scratch, it bleeds, and spreads all over.'

*

'We want to leave,' I say. 'Escape, resist. Liberate – who? Us? You don't believe in it, and I believe it in a different, an impossible, way. Assassination? Or maybe having Marvin make us both a fortune. You from slaving, me from building those freed slaves a bright factory to work in....'

'Buns!' Gus shouts. 'Eat the buns. No meat – it's putrid, probably embalmed and waiting for its brother to identify what's left.'

*

'We left it too late, Tiva,' I say. 'We couldn't pull it together. We went down the side-alley. We followed the piper, into the mountain. Ourselves, that was the problem. And everybody started talking about saving the world, themselves, their children. Putting a brake on, turning it around. 'Capital'. Living with it, putting a bridle on it, letting every honest Jo take a ride on its soft back. Humanity and order, the good guys trying to convince the bad guys. And now – it all fell down. We knew it would, and we are two, and they are four, and there is Gus, and there is Marvin: making new rules.'

'This is just the first day, Shérine,' Tiva says. 'There's been lots of laws and exhortations – we'll take some time to read them all. We'll be prepared.... Don't worry ....'

*

'Martians,' says Marvin. 'Remember them? They had it all. A life. Mynah birds. Leggy ladies in white frills. Never got ill, not one of them, and lived a thousand years. Then – they asked too much, protests and transgression. Not satisfied – and lo! they lost it all. Everything became extinct.... You don't need me to draw the lesson, ladies! Lose it – and it's terribly hard to start it up again. Meanwhile, some crude guys will have come and started digging up your gold ... they'll drink a cobalt soup, and light themselves like deep-down fish, and blue and green – they'll make their body glow all night so's they can dig bright while you sleep....'

He ends his warning with a laugh. We smile – no more than that.

*

'The only way we can escape,' I say, 'is take a row boat. There are heavy ones, like those they use for rowing tars out to the tall ships in the port. Each of us would need to take an oar

– alternatively we plunge them in, and veer to right and left, but very very slow we go ahead.'

'The sea, Shérine,' says Tiva. 'Does what it wants. We might not find a progress in it, or in us.'

'Mechanical things,' I say. 'Attract Gus, delight Marvin. We must be physical. Gus has his goals, imposing them on us. Marvin restrains him: Gus can have only what margin's left, once we have worked all day.'

'We could wait,' says Tiva. 'For a second day. Times pass, quite speeded up, like in the books. Time is talismanic, but the heavy boat, the tender, is slow: wait till we might find a skiff, and train, and dress our part. Be real waterboatmen, on the meniscus, and away, away....'

'Of course,' I say, 'We've not decided where we want to go.'

'Relationships,' says Tiva. 'Not real ships. That's what are supposed to be the jewels in life – we could try those. You and me – it could be anyone, but we're at hand. Art and commerce – those rely on holding hands, and bed, and looking into other eyes. Ideas? Those are ephemeral. And accidents, like all those that fold the landscape in on itself: we must accept.'

'Food is a problem, Tiva. We have none,' I say. 'That must fit in your cosmology. The cheesy moon, the sugary stars....'

'We should invite them, Amelle and Nadine – since we don't intend coming back....' she says.

'I don't like them,' I say.

'Then we'll just ask Amelle,' says Tiva. 'Although – I hate these fawning bosses. Wanting votes. Offering jobs.'

'If they gave us work, they might have food as well,' I say. 'Before we put to sea, we could eat those biscuits with the bugs inside. A feast, on the shore.'

'I don't like adventures that you don't know how they end. None of us is magic. Nadine is overdressed. We need someone to steer, share out the biscuits and put the dead in shrouds. It's a lot to ask of Amelle. We'd do better by ourselves,' says

Tiva. 'Your hand – it's blistered! and we haven't even run a rope....'

'It's the anticipation,' I say. 'My whole body knows – when there's to dig, or if there's heat.'

'That's useless,' Tiva says, paddling my lumpy palm. She is exhilarated. It shows we're going to leave, my blisters.... 'I guess I'll have to use both oars. It's how humanity begins.'

'That's deep, Tiva,' I say, squeezing her hand and pulling away. 'Every country needs a President – but we're a crew. We don't need anyone.'

'Something rather than nothing, remember,' Tiva says. 'There's language. It expands faster than any universe.'

'My head's full of it, language,' I say. 'My skull's still boxed. It won't expand. You haven't made your point.'

'There's no point,' she says, impatiently. 'The owl and the pussy-cat – they got married and danced. No point. No probability. No possibility. Wisdom conjoined with instinct – it doesn't work.'

'They had honey, and the colour of the boat: green peas. I'd die for bosnian bean soup,' I say.

'If there's no bees, honey can be synthesised,' says Tiva. 'Irradiate your head, and see how your brain works. Those are two wonders. On the sea, we'd look for islands – land has nothing to do with sea. Don't look for contradictions on horizons – they're in that box under your feet.' She points.

'Hooks?' I say, pulling some out, then trying to get the barbs out of my hand: 'Esses? Kill the poor fish? Because we didn't bring our food?'

'I say this for your good, Shérine,' says Tiva, ignoring hooks and fish. 'You're culturally shallow. When you lost ancestral faith, you emptied out your skull. There's scraps is all that's left, scratched up from somewhere else.'

'You're glued on to shadows, Tiva,' I reply. 'It's true – my village had no clubs, exotic groups were not around, no avant-garde – and yet, the world was mine.'

'The fishy world,' says Tiva. 'We have to make ourselves acceptable in it. Respected even. It's a society we prey on and which lives by eating other citizens. They scoff the differents. We're safe, Shérine. *We eat the fish!* Only once, with Jonah, did one side break the pact, and then the fish – it gave him up. Though – it was dead by then, of course....'

'It's quite precarious,' I say. 'As if we are afloat in air, on the top floor of a tall building, with the fish below, indifferent. All else is sea. And is there love, I wonder? Even there?'

'Oh yes,' she says. 'The mothers. It's as if they clone themselves. Mother love – is just a splitting. If you love yourself, you love the kids. They're you.'

And us?

'Tiva – we're not in a propitious spot,' I say.

Gus and Marvin

'Stay calm, Marvin,' Gus says: 'We know everything Amelle and Nadine don't. That's what will count. What others think of us, and where we get the cash....'

'What others?' Marvin asks.

'There must be, or we'd spend our lives at funerals,' says Gus, using a pinkie to clean out a tooth:

'And we have learnt from the catastrophe.'

'Self-knowledge?' Marvin asks. 'It's said to be quite crucial – but I'm not sure what it does. Or how you can be sure that what you have is right. Or is enough. Maybe counter-productive – to something else productive ... which could be anything, anything at all.'

'I meant – 'don't live in houses' .... Not made of heavy stuff, at least,' says Gus: 'Don't make real friends. Don't trust people who elect you, whatever it is for. Learn the lesson: – don't trust anything, anything at all.'

'Learning is personal, it's true,' says Marvin. 'We have to know what everybody knows – and just a touch more, giving us an edge.'

'We're ready to take on extra people, when we consolidate,' says Gus. 'We must be – "the little fathers of the people". We're the king-pins, charisma ever-ready, like hot broth. No one new can challenge us. Amelle and Nadine, though – they'll need to make their plan.'

It's all destroyed. Marvin buys the names, the shells, of enterprises. He bids, he wins: he is the auctioneer. He pays with sacks of tomans, dinars, sterling, dongs. Potentially, he's rich. There's no activity.

*

'We'd be crazy to wait here,' Tiva says. 'The very best that Gus can do, is make this place like all the rest. There'll be more catastrophes....'

'If life isn't hard, there'd be nothing to improve,' I say. 'Marvin says that. The working poor: ... they'll sign up.... They love a bargain.'

'Going to sea, we're sure not to meet anyone,' says Tiva, ignoring me. 'We have identity cards. We'll swap them. You take mine. Each one is black and white, white and black.'

'Troy can't be found,' I say. 'But the fall of Troy – is certain.' We laugh, and I let Tiva take my oar, try a few strokes ... and I take hers....

'Maybe we'll find survivors,' I tell her. 'People not crushed, who lived in lighthouses.'

'Vanusa,' Tiva says, ignoring me. 'That's a name I'd love to have. Perhaps we'll find a Vanusa, clinging on, *à fleur d'eau.'*

'She might be disagreeable,' I say. 'Aside from the cannibalism, and the eyes – poached and salted, the dark tongue, seethed.'

'And she might be a warrior,' Tiva says. 'We'd have to rescue her, of course. It's the law, but instinct too. Even if the Trojan war was the fuck stupidest even Gus could have thought up ... instinct and reason say that you must fight.... They told Gus he must start a war.... They'd all been fought.

Everybody had fought everybody else. Even the divinities were tired of it.'

We don't find Vanusa, but – the tall guy dressed in red, leaning on a long stick on the shore says: 'Vanusa is a ship. And did you see her?' we say 'no' – and he tells us here, they live in light houses, losing them it doesn't hurt a bit when they collapse, ha ha, but there's no food.... It was on the ship.

'Why did Vanusa pop into your head, Tiva?' I ask.

'It's written on a plank I saw, floating as we rowed,' she says. 'There's lots of them around – all feminine names. There must be a curse....'

Ants

'Sometimes it's penguins, sometimes – here, with us, you see – it's ants,' says the tall guy, Aaron the lookout. 'They take it over. Totally.' He's tall, tall as a Masai, wrapped in red cloth, ants can't stand red: his legs with knotted knees like knobkerries, the arms articulated like he's come in a box, or on a card, the long bones in weekly instalments, you press them ball into socket – there you have it. *Ecce homo.*

He goes on, desperately, 'Ants ate the food, then the ships, and then the timbers of the houses. We watch each other, ready to brush them off – an ant. They're growing. They stand up, waving their arms, their mandibles – they're hoplites. Fearless, and busy. Here, they've beaten us.

'You can't stay here. Leave a memorial of what you've done and want to be remembered for upon our shore – then out to sea, the endless sea where no ant scurries and infests....'

'I don't know that we've anything to be remembered by,' I say. 'Even Amelle, Nadine – they'll have done much to be recorded, but they should be ashamed of everything. We're .... nothing. Big ants. Solitary.'

Tiva looks appalled – but there is nothing to be done. If we were dead, we shouldn't know we were insignificant. We are alive, we peer around to see if there are insects who have scaled us, made a foothold on us, on our boat; a line of black or red invaders on the gunwale.

'This is an archipelago,' I say. 'We can row on and visit all the other islands, see if they have catastrophes – algae, scabies, high water, no water, everybody in the soup together – ants, of course, the biggest crisis, though there'll be a cure, a powder, a genetic tweak that makes them impotent or females all.... And we'll find food....'

'Yes, yes,' says Aaron. 'Hope. You must hope. And come back when all's tranquil, you'll sleep with us in the long house and when you leave you'll find both of you are pregnant, gravid with warriors....'

We row as fast as possible. 'Farewell!' we hear him cry, 'Remember me, oh, remember me....' And that we shall.

'Courage, Shérine,' says Tiva, urging me forward, though the boat is heavy and cumbersome, waterlogged. 'We are good. We have solutions, we shall survive. We are not furies. The furies are archaic and crude, they play the evil part, yet I know there is no sin in us or them – instead, it is the root, the bone, our beginning.... We inherit, we will crumble, but we're bright, we're not to blame – we're limited. The furies are older even than we are! Evil is their business. We identify good and evil, but we cannot choose, or else we swing from good to bad.... The dark birds are everywhere, they are like a legion of viruses, evil is inevitable. That means there's no escape. Sin is in our constitution. We're not guilty, we're like snakes and tigers – we kill, we eat, we lie in wait. We're a pack of good and evil. Kings, queens – and knaves. We expect, we want, we obsess – with judgment. And couldn't care less. It's right, everything is: good, bad – all in our nature, in us. We attempt now one, now the other: – incapable of settling in the one, or in the other. Nothing to be done.

'Row, Shérine; visit every island and in the end – we're beyond, and inside, simultaneously: good, evil; not concluding; choosing neither; being nothing of the sort, nothing definite, unstable, indefinite in choice. It's beyond us

– we talk about it, being good or not, we take our sides, backslide. It's just philosophy, we know we can't take control.'

'Food, Tiva,' I say, my arms weakening. 'I know we can't go further, being decisive, good or evil. I know that would be too much, and we are destined to be a species which doesn't make it, does not prevail. Maybe on earth no species is adequate, probably we, the humans, are not lasting. Our religions duped us, gave us our airs. We vacillate, we're opportunist. We're the best there is; we failed. We choose, but haphazardly, and indeterminate. Our arms tire – rowing the boat, our back to where we're heading....

'I need food. I must eat, even if it means that I must steal....'

The Eumenides

'We should visit every island, Shérine,' Tiva says. 'They need to recognise – we're not the Fates. It all began before we came, and goes on after we'll have left.'

'Of course, my dear,' I say. 'It's not enough if we deny our role. The Furies come before it ends, the Fates are there when it's got under way. They visit, tour, and listen. The Furies bring – not the disaster – but a further one. It's justice. I'm not sure I feel adapted to bring that – justice – although it never influenced the Fates, the *Parcae*. All in the same firm, though what if they should socialise? Do they sing? "atishoo, 'tishoo – all fall down"? Eat dumplings, chicken wings and guts?.... They're old deities who underlie the modern ones: they saw it start. They have no second thoughts, the first ones were quite stark enough.'

'It isn't so,' says Tiva, laughing despite seasickness, and her hunger too. 'It's judgement that we bring, not punishment. Justice is made like that, in two parts, two sequences, administered by different guys. The judges – fragile, in cloaks.The punishers are goons....'

'Well, even so,' I say. 'A judgement isn't quite my thing.... And those Eumenides – they didn't eat, it isn't in the book. They are divine – maybe we should learn to be.

'There's no food in the boat, and little left that's in the sea....'

'We started off,' says Tiva. 'Being tough on the politicos: – Amelle, Nadine: accomplices. And turn and turn about – either the agents or the tools, they're the spanners for Gus and Marvin....'

'Marvin was sweet,' I say. 'Even quite stupid, in his way.'

'Unfeeling, ruthless – those are other words for what you think,' she says. 'Suck on some stones – they make the hunger less.... There's stones on board – maybe some other Furies rowed in it. Now, don't let's argue....'

'Oh, I'm sure they did,' I say. 'The Furies must have valued differently, quarrelled among themselves; or else the chariot wouldn't make that roaring rushing sound....'

She laughs: 'The people fear us, but there is no punishment to come. Either you take it now, or else – you're free!' she says.

'Those ants,' I say. 'They are not quite a punishment. Aaron – a paternal paradigm. Ants are a force – like us: doing their thing. And humans are just unstable; an impediment to the little ones, the running up and down and carrying eggs.... perhaps we're not even guilty of attempted species-cide....'

'These islands,' Tiva says. 'Are all afflicted in some way – with animals, their parasites, their appetites, the instablility of sand, stability of rocks, the lack of fish, excess of sea – or vice versa. All the rest – the crimes, the punishment – they seem banal and trivial, or even without a proper fit and consequence....'

'We'll have to sharpen up,' I say. 'As Furies, we're too scattershot!'

We laugh. It makes the hunger less.

*

'Fates, Furies,' Tiva asks, 'Are they the same? We did all this at school, but I forget. At school, we're saviours and royalties. Then – it all falls away and disappears. We row – we do not spin or knit like Fates. We don't rush around like winds, like Furies do.'

'I can't respond to this,' I say: 'It's clear – fates and furies are the same. The level of the sound, the speed of vengeance – justice, if you like – is different. It's all a question of the time: ages of stone and bronze, and then electricity and air. Faster and faster, but more silently, more flexibly and light. Yes, they're the same, the Furies and the Fates.'

'Then it's a fix,' says Tiva. 'First the punishments. The natural, the disasters. Then they change their smocks, and they're the fates – quite unpredictable. You live, you die: snip snip – they cut your thread without a care for what you've done.'

'Well,' I say. 'We've not done any of all that. You mean, though, we'll get the blame? Worse than Gus and Marvin – they'll think we bring infection....'

'Oh much worse,' says Tiva. 'Gus and Marvin are admired – hated too, and a bad joke. Compared with us – they're popular.'

*

We wake, tumbled, on the strake of our boat. 'Who were they, Shérine?' Tiva asks: 'Bankers? Explorers? The Convention....'

'Yes,' I say. 'And, you know, I think we're pregnant.'

'Oh no,' she says, jigging up and down. 'I know you have a piercing eye, and apprehend such tragedies. So, were we drunk?'

'For sure.' I say. 'If we can't remember. The Fates – it won't be logical for them to have a child. The Furies – you'd have thought they wouldn't need a reinforcement. Their children could be nameless ones, or questing – carrying a potion or a sword ... not taking up the family trade....'

'Mine could be banker, yours an explorer – some guy who risks his life and opens up a dell for tourism....'

We laugh. It's a disaster. We want at all costs to avoid the world of tales, of fables, of genres that no one reads.... Of warriors with no cause, maidens more distressed than we ourselves.

'This pregnancy,' says Tiva, swaying hers from side to side, a medicine ball of potentiality unwanted.... 'These fated islands – some are uninhabited except as spots for orgies, raves, conventions – palavers of the powerful – oh dear.... We might see Gus and Marvin... They might even have impregnated Amelle, Nadine by now .... there'd need to be a crèche.

'Life transforms in an instant, Shérine, quite wilfully. A flash – a memory blanked out – and your tale takes other twists and wags '

'I guess this will mean children,' I say. I'm shocked. 'What do they say to you?'

'Open mind, Shérine,' says Tiva. 'We don't know what the outcome is – of this, or anything. It's unexpected – like an embolism ... mythology gives no clue, and if we weren't consenting, there's no law, no lawyer here. In fact – there's nothing much at all. The people, residents, will have moved away – their sheep all died, the water stank, a great wave or a freeze ... then it was restored, and became a centre for the risky guys. I hope my whatever's an explorer – true, they end up on a barbecue, but bankers – some – they end in jail....'

'Yes, Tiva,' I say. 'But – if we bond? With what is in us? Those pregnant ewes, sacrifices to the Furies – did they lament their roasted lambs? I'd much prefer we farrowed, then our life went on, without encumber, no offspring. No ties, no love. You, Tiva – already you insist, you pester, want love or some complicity – and if I give, what do I give? What can I gather back?'

'I know,' says Tiva. 'We don't know if we've been cloned, or if we're heavy with a spare. A spare for ourself when we switch out. It's all most worrying. Something from stock movies, horror, sci-fi – not our kind at all....'

'I suspect,' I say. 'The generation-in-waiting inside us is just a new model Fury: more drastic, up to date. These island places are nests of judgement. The more of us, the better. That's the decree. At all events, our objective is the good, not sniffing out the bad. Creation, by definition, is all good. The bad sneaks in – a fault of the design.'

'We'll find out all about our bodies,' Tiva says. 'And gender. Suppose we bear another something. Inspiration: not our own, but maybe quite unseen till now: unknown. What will it do? Does it have toys? On afternoons – especially Saturday, what will it find to do? Do we broach God with it, and transubstantiation, bilocation and matryrdom; not eating lobster – all that stuff?'

'It's really up to us,' I say. 'I only hope it doesn't hurt. Something must have crept up unobserved – unless of course we're virgin birthers. Useless to speculate – what was the booze, I wonder? Or – maybe a pill, a smoke?'

'A clubbing on the head?' Tiva speculates. 'I don't feel good. My head's weak as an egg....'

'We're pregnant, Tiva, but it may not mean there'll be a progeny,' I say. 'Maybe – it will go away.'

*

'If we don't assume we know,' says Tiva, 'what's supposed to be, how the future might turn out – it might be what we'll produce is damaging. Hostile, even murderous, to us.'

I say: 'The evidence goes all that way. For every Moloch, every Kronos they evade, the younglings seek their Lear. And are not merciful ....'

It's all a puzzle: what's been implanted, what we should do with it.

'I'm sure the pregnancy will have been the Aquavit,' I say. 'Tequila leaves a taste, sometimes a worm. The same with pepper vodka – I can tell. Pure spirits – those are what did for us,' I say.

We laugh.

'It could be universes, Shérine,' says Tiva, pretending to be incredulous.

'Like us,' I say. 'But don't do science fiction. You can hold universes in your head – but materially, the one we're in, it can't be caught and plotted. So – a universe, as material, can only be a shadow in your head....'

'Yes,' says Tiva, 'but we don't know if a new-born universe is new. It could be a copy....'

'Oh,' I say, 'you go too deep for me, Tiva. What concerns me is how'd a new universe, already in our head, come out? How'll it be done? Through our eyes? Maybe we'd be blinded. Or our mouth...?'

'It's quite obsessive with you, dear,' she says. 'The Word. That would be a universe quite tiny, spoken just once and fleeting through the void. Expanding, running, escaping – never still – for ever? Yet – I'm quite swollen up – I'd bring forth at least a paragraph. Or many millions of words, of verses – universes!' and we laugh some more.

I guess it's nervousness, the giggling. We row on.

*

'One way or another,' Tiva says, 'we must decide about our pregnancies.'

'We're in the dream, Tiva,' I say. 'Look at Dacca. At the Mekong, or the Amazon – and think: 'the mystery of nature'. No longer so mysterious. As they say, the end of life – is it to forge a soul, or forge a blade? Or is the end of life the end of life?'

'You think there's options?' Tiva asks. 'We could postpone the outcome of our gestations. What next? Science? Fiction? Or some endgame, where it all goes on, but it has already concluded. Like a movie – there's an end to come while you are at the start, but the end is fixed, defined, unchangeable. Everybody knows. The knowledge ... everyone suspends it for their pleasure or their resignation. Like the farm – you love the animals, you make them fat and happy – if you don't they're turned back at the abattoir, and you and they live on in penury.'

'We could pretend it's genre,' I say. 'Turn it all back. Everything that happens – these islands that once were continents – the water and the plagues, us – are we pustules or the earth, or...?'

'I'm still hungry,' Tiva says. 'That isn't genre.'

'*Chercheurs d'or*,' I say. 'It brings your bankers and explorers into the same scene. The mercury, the poisoned water, the residents sniped at and raped.... *Dune* in a single, frozen, frame.'

Out of shot – the universe

It's all happening everywhere. All's been happening, somewheres it's not begun, often it's finished. Point of view. You can't not believe in this, it's science, not fiction – it's not that here you're living and somewhere else you're dead, it's that once you're dead, that's it. The same with planets, and with stars, forests. Cut through the paradox: *it's all a question of the position of the observer. Who is this observer?*

'It's not that kind of question,' Tiva says. 'Position and observer are hypothetical. Or universal.

'Look, Shérine my love, we have to eat. Then we can decide about our pregnancies – how they transmute, bear us along, make a real narrative, bear more people you can sympathise with. Graves to weep over, graves to fill with throttled slaves ... the newborns, for luck, cemented in the temple basement.'

'I'd be down to earth,' I say. 'Hang on – there's no alternative. There's base foods in that corner-store. Now – don't say there is no corner, so there's no food, no store. There's a store – be happy with that. Things are and aren't – you start with a book, a movie, then there's no book, no movie, no cash, no budget, just a storyboard. But then you have the Incal, something quite different and yet offsprung. That explains why you don't go, are afraid to go, anywhere at all because the story is immense, the end of everything, which would stop any expedition going anywhere, like where those explorers went – or didn't – up the Essequibo, and where we were, the valley of lost ants, Aaron with his living stick, the snake of resurrection, its double head of good and bad, though mostly bad for him.... Make a story, a movie – or you don't, you conceive it, you put an end, and when it reaches there it stops. Sometimes it doesn't even start.'

We laugh. We're breathless with our gallop through the scenario of everything imagined, nothing set down ... set down, instead, as the story of everything of quite another everything.

We gobble down the food. 'Well,' says Tiva, 'We have to decide – are we pregnant?'

'Let's see how it turns out,' I say, and so we shake on that; and that's the way it was, will be.

*

You must believe that Gus and Marvin are real people, because they are, and you can vote for Gus, sometimes, and if you don't, he'll win by millions anyway; if he stands of course. Maybe Nadine and Amelle aren't quite real, but you can certainly vote for them, or people very similar.

'Here, we can say: we feel free. There's nobody above us, or below. It isn't natural,' Tiva says.

'When we go back,' I say. 'We won't find anyone whose life we recognise. Their tastes. Is there anyone back there that you know, Tiva?'

'Not what they call an intimate,' she says. 'To think about it ... no, I've no one.'

'There's no one here,' I say: 'Or rather – there is everyone. Everybody's needy, everybody lacks: – or spins the tale. No one is comfortable, and secure.'

*

'No one is looking for us, Tiva,' I say. 'Not until we find the money, the corpse, the guilty ones – or we are guilty, rich, or armed. Until then – would anybody like us? When you're grown up, you're branches on the tree, not lively imps, delightful, unencumbered.'

'Let's build a house,' says Tiva. 'There's no one here. Then we can decide if either of us wants to live in it. We must do it quick.. Nothing is any good, if we die. We must plan the future while we have one. Find a law that holds for something we might write.'

We laugh – 'Write?' I say. 'You know me, Tiva, you know everything I might have to say. No one else has a glimmering. Besides – there is no paper here. If there were bottles, I could write on leaves and sail them off.'

She nods. It's not enough. 'I love you, Tiva,' I say. 'In my way, of course. But – it was your idea – the boat, the islands. The cosmology. Just for my company? My desperation? For the off chance?'

'Look!' she says. It's a tall cage with two birds – tall grey hussars' plumes, yellow feet and yellow voices ...

'Is this all?' I ask? 'Someone abandoned them ... and how can we...?'

'Oh,' she says: 'I'll take you to the general.'

He has a machete – looks about eighteen, with cut-off jeans, and a straw hat like stage Mexicans wear, only this is far gone....

'What do they want?' I ask. Tiva must know: I've been a communist, and hung around with mafia people. I got disillusioned with them both, when I discovered what they call 'human nature' – how people are and what they'll be, and how they excuse themselves. There's money, lots, in communism and in mafias, but also lots of risk. Capitalism is about the same, I guess, but I have never joined.

'Want? Nothing,' she says. 'There's an installation – too dirty that anybody wants it. The birds are its guards. It's their hostage. If they want something, they take it, and if they can't, they don't.'

'This is nothing,' I say. 'There's nothing for me. The cause – it isn't just, it's habit. A secret society everybody knows about. Protecting what you can't have.'

'I built the house,' says Tiva. 'I loved that. Yours fell down, Shérine. I give my small heart to a small cause.'

'Why are you angry? You could cut me out, abandon me: – it wouldn't take a day,' I tell her. 'Go it alone. Be a guerilla's moll.'

'No,' she says, 'you're right. It wouldn't take a minute. It'd be over quick. Anger is bad for you: I'd feel rage for an hour at most.'

'We move the boat so well,' I say. 'We don't pretend our personal oar can drive it in a single way: each of us pulls to right or left. You hate me because you can't have me? Can't have all the things I know....'

The general listens in, and says: 'We were immortal once. We asked for knowledge, and in exchange got death. I have a plan to turn it all around and start again.'

I think, therefore I know I am not what I am

'You can't be double, Shérine,' says Tiva. 'If I steal from you, or make you my slave, I must know I have it all, all of you. You can't be one thing, and think of being something quite quite different.'

'Yes I can,' I say.

These guys are useless – the army. They're many, but they wave old guns, nowhere to put the ammunition, no discipline, no plan. I'm not involved with them – it's rhetoric, they'll lose, be dragged behind a truck, put into oil barrels, left out, sealed, in the sun.

The army is one: all are children of the same fear, same desire: – in this case – poor, thin. The soldiers are always similar – running forwards, running backwards. One: a Moloch.

'If I trivialise, Tiva,' I say, 'it's to give me more room for feeling.'

'History is made to miniaturise, and possibly to make us laugh. If we don't laugh, we wonder,' she says. 'It all goes in the dustbag: everything. Troy disappeared, and it was hard for him, for all of them. We grasp each other – it's good for understanding, but there has to be a plot, one that we follow through, willy-nilly, and that will have us shooting down through laths and plaster, cement and tiles, into the street without our arms and lgs, then winched up, high on a wall to rot inside a box, a box of bones, named and dated, so no one bothers to contest.'

'You have the gritty eye, Tiva – it's evident,' I say, 'but you're eager for this fight parading here – and should I be?'

'Justice and power, Shérine,' she says, pirouetting. 'Can you resist? And patience, concentration: forming threes, joining processions, obedience....'

'None of those is me, Tiva,' I say. 'But I'll keep you company....'

*

We run. We wait, we crouch. We eat some stuff they bring, we fill in forms, a snapper sets us up and down. Someone stands and falls, is carried off, a crowd protests and scurries off.

'I see,' I say. 'I see how it is all connected up....'

'It's terrible,' she says. 'We lost so bad. Throw away – everything you can. Into the bushes – then we'll get back in the boat.'

'I thought we'd done so well,' I say. 'The crouching, though....'

'You're best at that, Shérine,' she says, pushing me towards the sea, 'You're dumpy, with short legs – those are the best ... Most things fail, all things don't meet your hopes. Everything organic rots if it's not eaten, or maybe it seeds before.... The theorists of the cosmos – really, only observed the world. The world – it goes this way and that, my dear: the cosmos has no mountain ridges – the world has lots. The world has *pi*, who cares if the csmos does as well? You must get used to be forever wearing out, threadbare, the brain covered in dark spots. We'll take the soldiers ... the boat will be much heavier.... The general won't row – it's not his job, and all the rest are wounded, maybe tired or suicidal....'

'I'm not sure, Tiva. You shake me up,' I say, 'with your stark tales. They're all mementos – but you've never known what I am, what I am like....'

'Oh,' she says, 'what you are like – that's easy. What you are? That's all in your imagination, your imagining. To get in there – I cannot see a door, just sand and footprints leading here and somewhere else....'

There's shouting, but I don't see anyone. Then – there they are, a raggedy band.

'Off we go,' she says, leaving me standing silly on the shore. She pushes off the boat, full and wallowing with the fighters – broken like pheasants after the shoot.

*

Tiva never lied to me. That's good. She never told me anything. We conversed. I told her everything in my mind, my doubts, my desires, my wants. The same from her. They call it intimacy – it may well be: it doesn't mean a thing. Everyone's the same. We had no goods, nothing to divide. Troy fell from the topmost storey, and disappeared. No one has ever found it, though it's been constructed everywhere, even in California – much better than you'd imagined it.

On the shore there's a line of naked people. They dance, *butoh*, the choreography of ugly truth. The shoulders hunched covering the ears, front on they make two cheeks, the head-top is a black hole, a mouth.

The master of the dance is shorter, dumpier than me, wearing a forage cap, with a blazon – deserter from a Walloon army, lost, unrecorded, certainly not paid.

'I understand that truth, if you want it so, is difficult; but does it take so much effort to be ugly, to show ... the limit?' I ask.

'Yes,' he says. 'It's all difficult, until you just let go, tell lies, relax, and slummock.... That isn't dance! For that, even the angles must be precise, and held. You watch the dancers make the art, it doesn't make you better, make you worse. For us – for them – it is just difficult. *Butoh* dancing brings out everything you are, what you want to be and what you don't, and everything you've been before your birth, and when you're dead. It's very very hard.'

I believe him. He could be Hijikata. 'No, I'm not,' he says. 'That's the first ugly truth. I'm someone else you hadn't heard of, when you believed the dance had mutated, fallen out of fashion. *Butoh* – comes, goes, and spreads like lichens, or like mushrooms. The dance itself – you cannot do, but you'll be troubled by its meaning. You must go everywhere, Shérine, and often you must not return. Except – you are not beautiful, not desirable. People don't lie to you, you have no cash. Maybe you are shadow, an old root: nothing, a past. Then wild, frenzied. A face afire with spasm. A house that stands for centuries, and then in seconds – it falls down, the skulls and skeletons – they burst out and plug the road.... The ghosts come woken in the dust and shards, and start to leap, make faces, put out long tongues, and wave their sex.'

He jiggles up and down, excited, pawing at me.

'I know,' I say. 'Where does it lead? I lost my lover; then, my friend. All normal. No one expects that you will make a face.'

The choreographer begins, 'I came to Africa ... the last place we hadn't danced, and they'd just stopped here....'

'No, no,' I say. 'This is not a continent. It's islands, all different. We fit in. Colonists and colonised, rider and beast, stones for stepping on. You can take ship between them, or ride across the straits on dromedaries....'

'It seems there's no place for judgement here,' he says. 'Remember that, you won't go wrong.'

Tiva'd said we're here to judge, and then move on. I haven't started judging, but already I am moving on.... Every continent terrifies – being in one, moving to another. Fates and furies hovering. These are islands, but they're on a shelf, like pottery cats and bonzes' bowls.

'We all migrated from somewhere,' says the Master-dancer. 'Or we were born into a place we knew nothing of.... We made a fantasy of origins. Now, we have an idea of how it will end. Mostly they thought it would go on, until there was a ceremony, or a fire. Where we thought there was a cosmos, full of different beings – now we know there's only the one creature that talks and speculates – it's us. There's no hell-beings that is different. It's all us.'

'I could stand much taller,' I say, not following him, but recognising words. 'I'd be tall and serpentine.'

'You'd need someone to see you so,' he says. 'To me, you're a figure buried in the sand, no one will touch you, dig you out. I dare say you're harmless. You show there was once a civilisation – not only here, but probably ... in many places, many ages, around where there's a river.'

'There's civilisation everywhere,' I say, 'but you don't need know where it comes from, or who's in charge, and what it's for.'

'I know,' he says. 'You think of Mali. It's your place, and there you'd look like all the sculptures, crouching down or rearing up. No one would touch you because the stuff you would be covered in is made to be repellent. The blood and spit and mucus puts even the faithful off. You're special, so no one knows what might happen to them.... Empire after empire – ah!' he sighs. 'One of the centres of the world..... But now – we're far away. In my dance you can be thin and tall – emaciated, lofty. But – it's a dance. You couldn't live in it.'

I could cry: 'You sketch a life for me, then say it can't be had.'

'Oh, that's just a shadow of a cruelty,' he says. 'What you can't have – is nothing. Cruelty is when you have what you desire.'

'I don't have anything,' I say. 'No presence and no absence. I don't seem able to accumulate.'

'There's Providence,' he says. 'Or – you might want to shake a leg. Join with us. Otherwise – you must sit quiet throughout the piece. Then you applaud or boo – it's all the same to us.'

That's disappointing.

Some islands are laid waste by winds. Some slowly sink. The Furies and the Fates – I had no hand....

A Spacious Hive well stock'd with Bees
That lived in Luxury and Ease;
And yet as fam'd for Laws and Arms,
As yielding large and early Swarms.

'It's not my favourite lyric,' I tell Horst, 'but it keeps coming back. If you are solitary – through choice or rejection – you don't achieve. But if you're social – you're driven by others, by the instinct and the interest....'

Horst was in the dance. To do well at it, you must be flexible – a contortionist, in fact. Classical theatres, in the East, require you to learn another way of moving, of being in society. He knew 'what'; could not do 'how'.

'You're unreal, Shérine,' he says, 'as well as unrealistic. No one can be one thing – unless it's mad, or shut away. You have to turn it on and off – you can't believe in just one thing.

It's crazy. Your dilemma – it was fashionable half a century ago. Being or not being you. Now – it's dull. People aren't interested in uncertainty – you must go ahead, achieve excess, then stop, or take another turn. Even if you switched your brain, wired it into Tiva – your orphan body would be desperate; and all the rest, the thinking you, would be the same.

'But – you would suffer infinitely more – for nothing. A bad choice. In blackjack, it will change your life, taking another card on nineteen and winning. Or – it may just be a game of cards. But either way – usually, it's stupid and it fails ... because you wanted something exceptional, except it wouldn't be exceptional – just lucky.

'I can carry you, Shérine,' he says. 'Or – there are wild camels in that stand of palms: – we could ride across the straits....'

'But, I'm looking for some substance in my life,' I say. 'Crossing the straits from one island – unexplored – will take us to another one the same, that's all.'

Horst is tall: he sports a ginger beard. 'I'm waiting for a friend's wife,' he says. 'I can't spend long with you. I'm not into exploration. I don't trust my judgement – that's why I'm waiting for someone else's wife. Someone has made a choice. I'd trust them more than me....'

'Oh, wives!' I say, laughing. 'There's no judgement there. It's like the blackjack tale – you hardly ever see him and enjoy his spell – the dealer shuffles and he's gone again.'

I laugh, and Horst doesn't understand, but laughs.

'Workers! Wives!' I say. 'If you want to humiliate, insult – what would you load a person with? Work! Wives! A kit – slotting in, or making kids from plasticine, a tube of cobalt, makes them glow like bluebells in the dark. Their eyes! They must be blue – no other animal has blue eyes.... The rest of us – all went through the fire: we're brown and black. Scorched and toasted, singed rice-paper, mulberry, lambskin. We're wasted, Horst, what they call men and women, young, old, thin, bearded – russet like doormats: their potential's all reamed out, consumed, right from the start. Mostly husks, some bloated....'

He uses the backs of his freckly hands to make the gestures: brush me away. I shout at him. His friend, the wife, people of every colour, gender ... none of them, none at all, shows up.

'We were gold,' says Horst. 'We were valued. All of us, in the Party. It imploded. What a joke!'

'I was not worthy,' I say. 'They wouldn't take me. But I know tragedy. All on the stage – they died, no one's left to carry them off. So what? It wasn't necessary to use the tumbrels ... now, just handcarts bring them on, and wait to lug them off....'

China too?

Breaks when it drops – whatever the design, they say.

'You're rubbish, Shérine,' says Horst, striding past the stand of palms. There are no camels.

He's angry. That's good – so am I. Love and hope – what monsters, buried in the wood, erecting like deathcaps, up through the coat of leaves.

*

There's nothing to eat. I eat nothing. I grow tall, thin, thin and supple as Aaron's rod. Very desirable. Who desires me? A lion. A lion with a tarbush. He sleeps, waiting for an appetite. I wait to be saved, I wait to die – the beach is full of people waiting, hoping to be turned to bronze.

It isn't fashionable, not worth a cent, all this. All the people, the characters, if all rolled into one, would be striking, egocentrically exotic. But you can't coalesce them, not in life: each is singular. Each is like us humans are; one-dimensional, each striving to consolidate a single character, which becomes a characteristic, that's all.

And all I experience with them, from them, is passive. What would be active is everything I could feel, if only what came before me had been different, more intense. And yet –

what's really intense is what you fear, know will come. That terror will be the last, and you try to avoid it, but what you remember is what could come again, and again, and never has. You remember what's not happened: remember it for being not repeated, non-repeatable. You remember what perhaps has never been – a landscape under cloud, laughter, a confession. A betrayal, a void in someone you've much valued. An escape, a betrayal, a void.

*

They closed the factory, drove off the geese, cut the benefits, maced us, put us under surveillance, took our children, poisoned the river, outlawed us, closed the clinic, wrote our history without us in it.

In three days, I know it all – how the world is. The future doesn't look so good. I'm hungry – it's my fault. There's inequality? – it's hard to tell, I haven't met the rich ones yet. Most things are my fault, but hardly any account for what I have experienced. I need a Tiva to explain. The past is over, and it's within us – like everybody's pregnancy, there, but never coming to term, an ache.

And we're full of metaphors, wound round the foetus, even – surely you can't live like that – a long white worm consuming all you eat, growing, down to your toes. Very intelligent, *sympa,* like an absent lover. Useless. Try to shake it out – the dance! Rock! Twist!

Erwartung

'Tiva!' I hug her: 'Where did the soldiers go?'

'Detention. Like bad schoolchildren. They'll have the choice – a beating, or get to join another army,' and she grimaces. Her hands are blistered.

'Life, Tiva,' I say, desperately. 'Let's leave out sentiment and history. Help me make sense of all these guys on beaches, islands – try to pull it together. Find me a context. Rice, manioc, couscous, *pommes paille.* Something basic.'

'Sometimes these beach shacks are for animals,' she says. 'Then, they're quaint, and tourists use them, then once more, they're back, back at the start. Our start. We won't be surprised when things look difficult – the sea, the sky, the winds, the rain, the droughts – all changed and changeable. We know all that, and it will come, or maybe we shan't notice it. We must make a life here on the shore – we've nowhere else. And look – there's cavalry!'

And so there is. In the Sudan, and with the Masai – they ride out on horses – and it seems that almost all armed states have troops of horsemen – cops in Chicago, French guys in cuirasses, Cossacks all over. Threatening. Magnificent.... The horse, the horse! Its time come round again! Fantasy countries – they display in armoured dune buggies: – the regular guys have cavalry. We watch them, their plumed lances, the animals worrying at their saddle cloths, longing to be naked.... Riding past, horsemen, jiggling up and down.

Our shack – we paint it blue and red, like Pierrot le Fou – it's hot, it could explode. It's waterless around, but sometimes a tide brings brown water in the doorway. 'Fish!' says Tiva. 'Nuts,' I say. 'Crabs.'

You can find nuts, and bushes like huge cabbages.... At first, we grow quite fat.

'Is that good?' we wonder. Fat? No one replies.

Wants and needs, that's all it is, explains the system that makes rich or poor. Can we be friends, despite these transactions, through the handshakes and the shaky deals? How to turn a ton of corn into a ton of steel? That's all the economy, all economics. Production is exchange. How? That puzzle comes with the gesture that defeated Wittgenstein when he was on the train with the economist. A gesture from Naples can bewilder philosophy, Naples and production is gestural: all style.

A glass of our sweat turned into a bunch of coconuts.

'No fish!' I tell Tiva. 'No killing! Not just my philosophy: – it brings a hex.'

The white caparisoned horses of Libia: of the Maghreb: of Tlemcen – a posse rides past our hut at night.

Communism should have made everyone a friend – exchanging sweat for corn and iron. Maybe if it didn't work, that communism was something else?

'We're not appreciated here, Shérine,' says Tiva. 'We're beetles burrowing in ironwood. They hear us buzz, but when we reach the light, you can be sure a squirt of chemicals is waiting, and we'll be gone....'

My wants and needs – bigger than a hundred tons of corn or iron.

'Try this,' says Tiva. 'Call it "coconut bouillabaisse".' It stares at me. The eyes....

'This is just the first day,' I say. 'That's always hard. Maybe....'

'I think this is how it's going to be. Unless the riders take a fancy to you ... or to me ...' says Tiva.

Vesna

'Vesna gives protection,' says the louche guy, lounging outside the bike shop. Bi, uni, tri – all cycles, round and round, for sport, not enlightenment or use. 'Keep coming here and asking, you two – and one day....' And he points across the dusty street to a wall – there's a glam face, arching brows, a beauty spot, a sequin or a jewel – hair à la pompadour.... Dark clothes. Dark significance. 'That's Vesna?' Tiva asks.

'That's how someone thought she is,' the guy says, not bothered. What's the difference?

'What can we be?' Tiva whispers to me, giggling. 'We're too frumps to be bar girls, too finicky to do the mattress duty in the back....'

'Mediocre people, Tiva,' I say. 'I'm tired of them. But of course – it's the cavalry. I'm terrified.They're people,when they stop – they rape and skewer, tear out the unborn, burn the hut.... The horses and the guns – they come from far away, clean-shaven countries. Rich. Liars. If you're rich, why do you need to lie?'

'It's habit, Shérine,' says Tiva, drawing away. 'If there's a thing about you turns me off, my dear – you're quick with your contempt, your judgment.... There's your theories that don't matter. Yours are a century old, all listed in the manuals as unavailing. Futile. Then there is life – a hill you have to climb, and no one does it by themselves, or even with a team to push and pull them up ... and we all know – you reach the top, the other side's a cliff, a drop, a *gouffre*. You play the pretty lady, play the knowall snob, but all you want is someone saying what you should do and want, and then you tire of them, and suck out their sweetness or their bile, and shake them off; "fuck you!" you say. Maybe that's right.'

'Am I like that?' I ask. 'It makes me out a box of mahjong tiles: dragons and winds. No person, though.'

'I'm sure there isn't one,' says Tiva. 'You try so hard to be enormous. Now you're destitute. Let's find a saviour: Vesna looks a smart sort, with a gang. A gang of painters, anyway.'

'Let's be careful before we give ourselves to Vesna, Tiva,' I say. 'No one has touched us. No one has even noticed us specifically, even people saying that they hate us, love us – we have seen terrible things, nothing happened to us except what is normal, ordinary. Just normal suffering, Having no money and no house – our fault. Most people are blameless like we are – we are responsible for everything. Is there a plan, Tiva, a larger plan?

'Maybe making the houses fall – that takes organisation. You had your life, a place to be, observe things from.... *You* had a plan, even if others were plotting against you, your sort, or had a goal, or just – things falling down. There's no intent. There is intent, but not that everything, everything, the lot – falls down.'

'You're right,' she says. 'People intend a little thing, and little things add up, and down it comes. And there's a mass of plans with limited intents, that add and add. And then there's more intent, and goals: what happens appears improvised, but you know that if you frighten people, shoot them, put them in jail, in camps – you reach the state you want. That is the strategy we know. It's when it's personal, it shakes you most, Shérine. Happens precisely to oneself. That's why we need protection, why we need a Vesna.'

'The banks come,' I say, 'and give us money, then take more. But we don't have anything, Tiva. So – for us, it'll be the politics. Horse-riders. Be them? Escape them. That's the plan. I'm sure Vesna has a way – if not to make a victory, then to do a deal.'

*

'We'll try,' says Tiva. 'But, there's really only one possibility....'

'I know,' I say. 'We must hide our bodies. It's been tried. In Paris, the rue d'Ulm – it was notorious. Theory after conflict, denying the past, its existence. A present, a future? All screwed up, I fear, at history's conception. But that was long ago. Now, bodies come in – everywhere. You can't forget – yours, other peoples' ... bodies: their potential. Doing exercises? ... catch the essence before the body ages, putrefies and falls down stairs.

'We'll suffer if we take that path, we'll be exposed. Nudity – it makes you vulnerable. Tattoos and hex signs – they make visible where they ought to hide, protect, defend: and don't. And in the end – we die, the ashes mixed with asphalt for the roads, or in the vase of dust pole-vaulters use to get a grip....'

We cling together, and we weep. We break apart. How can we hide, escape the cavalry?... Slough our skins, hide the bones, and wind the parchment round the tree, make them a binding; velum – for books.... Books – what on? Concordances – but of what? What text do we make accessible?

'The long bones – stack them in the rack with billiard cues – no one will use them – they curl, they're knobbly, so we're safe. But skins?....'

'Kites,' says Tiva. 'We should fly them high. Our fingers – as the tails of kites.'

Of course, it's useless.

Vesna ... at last....

The louche guy, Nikolai, says – 'You could sell – or even rent – your bodies to the boss. To Vesna. Have them work for her, then your brains are free to roam, or lounge around all day.'

'That is the least we might arrange,' says Tiva. 'Oh, and incidentally, Shérine – I know more about your Troy than I have said. It's true – Troy is a fiction, has no existence – but the story, it was totally about me. I'm the heroine, not you, my dear.'

'It's not the time, Tiva,' I say. 'What is your story? Rape, elopement, abduction or an infidelity? We're treading on the clouds. We all risk being cancelled out. Those twins? the mind and body? For us, our mind's an encumbrance, it's that part that feels and suffers. And you and I – we're a duality. Losing the other – it would be an amputation, a separation. Alas, our better part, immortal mind, is blowing in the air, invisible and almost always – it's switched off, or "unavailable". Meanwhile – yes, let's see how much our minds and bodies fetch. See if we've a contract on the one or other, or do we just hope that Vesna, our dear unseen sister, will treat us well....'

Vesna: boss? Or star? Comet – without a tail, just dusty rock and roll...? Her face, enamelled; the scumbled hair castling and dissolving like flocks of crows around ... she wears a tiny matador's jacket, over a bodice, arabesqued, a pair of alligator pumps, and pants – tight, but then, she's no intention of sitting down, and losing height to you. She's a smart cat: they size you up – how tall you are, how broad ...

they do the sum to see if they should fight, or saunter past and bristle up.

'What can you do, Tiva?' Vesna asks.

'Oh,' says Tiva, pretending to think and put her skills in order. 'The sea, the sea! All hands, all ports ... Low level military stuff. Emotional defence in court for awful crimes – not mine. Frescoes and tiling. Last suppers served, tombs robbed, and resignations accepted joyfully....'

'And you, Shérine?' asks Vesna.

Modesty's the best: 'I can feed birds,' I say.

'That's excellent,' says Vesna, 'I'll give you both some binding work. I've golden pheasants – they must sleep on perches in the warm by night. I need a person who will call them in – *brrr brrr*'s the sound you make – and shake the bushes where they lurk by day, use iron tipped sticks if that's required.... And a cashier's needed too.

'It sounds to me as if either you or you,' and she points to me and Tiva, 'Could do both jobs by turn and turn about.'

'And you'd protect us?' Tiva asks: 'From cavalry and hurricanes?'

'Of course, of course,' says Vesna, backing off.

*

'If anyone can save us,' Tiva whispers, 'Vesna can. You know – she's Malgache, from a village near the Namoroka – each year, it burns – the *massif* is ridged karst and caves.... It rises to perpetual clouds – the rock is sharp as knives, all's calcified – the trees, the weapons.... When the island broke from Africa, all the armouries, sharp objects, floated off. The lemurs once were sailors, the originals. And Vesna – we should stay with her. Why, she could even give us happy lives. Here, there are no houses to fall down: no sexual mysteries, no dealing, and no kids.'

'And are those pheasants really made of gold?' I ask. 'It's clear they're special, needing a particular keeper....'

'Oh, no one suffers, that's for sure,' says Tiva, twisting away fom my odd questioning. 'She stands for bars, not brothels. Even if she has us work all night – the day is ours, to have us fill the time with joy and dance.'

'And the patrols? The state? The clash of wills? The degradation of the world of animals and plants?' I ask.

'Of course, there's that,' says Tiva. 'But we can live our lives in peace.'

*

'Tiva, already you seem to resemble me, and I'm the same as you. There is no drama, no contrast: – we're almost like we're one. Childless proletarians. And somewhat stupid,' I tell her, bewildered once again.

'Well, you're the brains, Shérine,' she says. 'I am the action faction,' and she punches me, my arm, in fun.

'You sorted out the soldiers, Tiva, that's for sure,' I say.

'Yes and no,' she says. 'Some wanted to fight on, and some were sick and wounded and got dumped. You use the common sense that comes to you as inspiration – you brainy guys, you're brought up evidence-based. Mostly, there is none: no evidence. Only the phenomenon itself, believed in or unbelievable: or irrelevant. You need use common sense plus some credulity; fear and paranoia too – that's never out of place. Or else your reason takes you from one imbroglio to the next. You are a super-sheep – they fleece you once, and there's another fleece already sprouting out your head ... brain floculence, it might be called.'

'This Vesna ... can we...?' I ask, shaking. 'I know that in the past for paradox, I've said some slavery is better than paid work.... I give offence, I'm sure. But now we have it both ways – paid work with slavery. What should we do, my dear? Give more offence? Run, despite the danger we'd escaped?'

I know, though, that there never are two heroines in anything, a movie, an invention, even when the male lead comes flying down a vacuum dismembering on the way, and then it seems his namesake, his goaty village, Troy, hasn't been discovered in two thousand years ... though replicas abound, the wooden horses, they go galloping on every roundabout.

'It's a fantasy come real,' says Tiva – 'I found the message on my screen: "Vesna gives protection, just type in...." And this time, just for once – it's true. "Send no money" – that's what it says, because eternal bondage is required and can't be monetised, still less insured.'

'The horsemen – they are round us like the sea, the waves,' I say, 'And we, the birds, and Vesna too ... we are the complement, the *Geist*. It's all cosmos, Tiva. It all is: everything. Statues and temples, barracks and stations – they all are miniatures of entirety, they're cosmic maps. There is a doorway that brings it down to size, that's all. You have to bend and think and crouch to enter, then once more – you're in the universe. You always were. I'd like to know, though: is there a bad cosmos, Tiva? Are we in it? Might we casually drop in ... fall, as in Troy's cataclysm?'

'Everywhere is cosmos, Shérine,' Tiva says. 'You're right. But knowing that, it doesn't help a bit. The part is always part, component, of its whole, whether you can see that, or you can't. Anyway, it doesn't matter, the good or bad: it doesn't matter, not at all.'

'I'm depressed,' I say, much disappointed. 'I thought I'd found the answer....'

'Yes, you have,' she says. 'The trouble is, the question and the answer – they're both easy, and don't resolve, reveal, at all.'

'Vesna does business,' I say. 'Here and in the other islands. I can't say she's a crook – she's beautiful, of course, and probably there's no law here that anything obeys, and if there was, it would protect her, that's for sure....'

'The fall of Troy upset everything,' says Tiva. 'It's like a paw stuck in an ants' nest. It makes a scurrying. We are the normal, though – we don't suffer for our colour or our sex, or our vocabulary: or because we don't know physics' laws....'

'Speak for yourself,' I say. 'Most things about us change. We change, of course – the light ... the fancy ... distance. Colour, sex, size.... But – I did physics and chemistry: it never did me harm, though I admit, I'm not respected, not for anything I know.'

Tiiva laughs: 'Oh, that's just street philosophy! Except – there is no street here. There are paths – people have made them, they take you anywhere....'

'Of course,' I say. 'Vesna can't protect us from everything. Not from her, not from the people in her service. And some things we don't mention – they don't fit: the fall of cities, people driven off, into the desert ... abductions! The classics are full of them, passed over quickly, taken as the norm. Those were their stories, not to be dwelt on: – the damage and the details. Slavery, Tiva, like we've known – it doesn't fit the tale we want to tell; ongoing, educational. Full of fear, no doubt, but....'

'We're still here,' she says, 'So we can say exactly what we want. And leave the parts out that don't fit, that, anyway, everybody knows, remembers. Every age must have its way, I guess, of telling, leaving out, what is and isn't characteristic. Enslavement and cities falling – it's not us. If it happens, it's a classic, put in to help the teller pep things up. It doesn't matter, not a bit, if you believe or not. There's no merit in believing unlikely, incredible, phenomena, just as it's up to us what we describe. The house collapsing. Did it make you sad, Shérine?'

I say, 'Troy must fall, and bring down all the rest, all that lies beneath – except, they never found the city, all its slaves, the abducted and the runaways. Everything that happened before and after. If it's a story – what are we, our feelings...?'

'If it's an invention, what's its point?' she asks. 'And since we know things similar have happened, happened to us both – we can ask, what is the point of real things happening all round? What happens to us...?'

We leave it there.

*

‘It’s funny,’ I say. ‘We think Vesna has a god’s powers, is a god – protecting us, giving us food. Making us suffer these crap days, the types we must accommodate. The fear, the dearth. And yet – it seems Vesna has a god herself! Maybe that god has a god – and on and on. Or up and up.’

‘No,’ says Tiva, ‘I’m sure having a god makes you feel big. A small god needs a bigger one. It’s just our stubbornness that makes us two so sceptical. A god forgives and scolds, but comforts you when you are sick, and when you die, it gives you paradise. If you’re a depressive type, it makes you sweat, and gives you guilt, anxiety. Best worship one that drinks a saucerful of milk: likes flowers; and mends the roof.’

‘How we take advantage of it, this religion? I read the book, of course, “the elementary Forms”,’ I say. ‘I know why we do what we have done; and now we don’t – what do we do instead?’

‘Nothing,’ says Tiva. ‘We wait: just like we did before. Ants make a termite palace. What for? Why, for the anteaters, that’s what for.’

That answer’s good for ants, and we don’t raise the matter any more. Vesna’s a snob, it’s right that she should have a god: she must have made her cash, a lot, during her career.... Presenter, songs and dances, wearing clothes and subsidising causes ... bought the island, and the people ... the wrong place, it turned out, but she has protection ... pays guys off, or payrolls them....

‘Why did Vesna become a gangster, Tiva?’ I ask. ‘She was a star. She fell, though that’s a metaphor. Stars implode, burn out – she did not – she’s bright....’

‘She doesn’t go on show,’ says Tiva. ‘She’s dependent on chewing *paan*. It started on a set in Bollywood: – it stains teeth black. In olden times, the cameraman could have the faces turned away, the mouth kept shut, and it was anyway all black and white. People played an instrument, they didn’t sing.... But now – you can’t be a celebrity with black teeth. Not anywhere.’

'Then all the rest – the husband, the young cousin wheedling in, the cold lyric of the marriage; singing Tagore's song, the suicide, the frozen shot.... There's ice and melt: which does a creator choose? In any case,' I say, 'Vesna has no story, and no doubt. The movie, though....'

It's a deep part of my life, it should be part of everyone's....

'No, none of that, says Tiva. 'Only black teeth. I don't believe she saw the movie, Charulata. Things have changed: – if you're rich, or political – you have to be a gangster too.'

'I love you, Tiva. You're my arms and legs, my muscles and my blood,' I say.

'You cheat, Shérine,' she says. 'We are not one. I'm separate. We're independent. I think. I suffer: it's not only you who do. If I could leave, I would.'

'We can, of course,' I say. 'Be separate. And leave. There's nothing in the other we could covet – my brain, your body ... not transferrable. But there's the risk. The horsemen, always circling round.

'And as for love – it's only what you feel. It doesn't lead to anything, it doesn't guide us. We both know, if it wasn't for the risk, we would be far away, and have our lives ... once, I'd have said in Istanbul. Paris, perhaps? Where reason once upon a time – it had its seat, and then ... and then.... Too bad.... If we weren't confined here, what would you do? What would I do? I can't do modern things, not now....'

*

'Vesna,' says Tiva, bold as ever. 'Do sing for us!' Our boss – she's never sung, opened her mouth – she's statuesque, in white and gold ... those elephants suffered for the white, the miners for the gold ... Their reward, if they were around to savour it, would be the silent spectacle.

Vesna – she grins – and then she shows.... Teeth black, black as a king of Bihar's – and she sings ... an awful yowl.

Emotion, sadness – is it possible, the lyrics of a narcissist? Vesna's a boss, but in the song – how she laments, self-pity, solipsism....

'Usually,' she says, closing her mouth, 'I had someone else to do the singing part.'

'You're magnificent when dressed,' says Tiva, and I add, half a wink thrown in – 'And without ... who could forget.'

'Well,' says Vesna. 'Flattery is always well received, and you are champions. Now, for one of you – I have a better job. Lieutenant, with some bouncers under you.... You'll cream off the pilgrim tax from those who seek a refuge here, and those who come, from curiosity, to catch a sight of me – exercising with my dogs, my archery, dancing for rain....'

'What is the test to get the job?' asks Tiva – 'Choosing a suitor, extracting a sword, guessing a name, proving paternity? Both of us are excellent at all of those.'

'Oh, all of those plus common sense,' Vesna says. 'Shérine, you're taciturn – maybe you're bruised. Or thoughtful. I pity you, natch, but they are your demerits. Tiva's a warrior, one of the boys.'

Dominion

'Nothing has changed, Shrérine,' says Tiva, fluffing out inside her uniform, waving her pace stick: bags of swank: 'But of course – I need some time to show I'm boss. My guys must die for me, of course – be raped and hung up by the flesh, be mutilated, buried alive ... Of course, we're still friends, dear Shérine, but I must win some trust, so that the guards will follow me and take the bullet that is meant for me....'

Nothing is the same. To make an empire, you must make the ice, freeze the surroundings, bring down the temperature, so that dominion will last until all melts. Then, there's heat until it all cools down again. I'm on my own, and it is good, except there's always people waiting to climb up on your back and ride you off....

The stockade

Here on the periphery – we're a centre. We're at the extreme of the empire, yet the conflict here is central to it. We're a fort in the desert. Are the horsemen our liberators? It's hard to think it's so. But Vesna – arms, money – it's all come to her from a real centre. Which side are we on – victims, protagonists?

'We need more soldiers,' Tiva says. 'And aeroplanes. We're in the front line here, and Vesna doesn't talk, the teeth...! She nods. It's not enough.'

'I've suffered much from battles, Tiva dear,' I say. 'I'd sooner move away....'

'That isn't sensible,' she says. 'Your fear is here. Your job as well. We need more capital – the roads....'

'I know all that,' I say. 'The soldiers and their base, and working in big shops, losing my job if I protest – there's nothing new. I read the books – I'm sad that you, Tiva, should jump over to the other side because you have a uniform, and in the end, I shall be screwed because of fear....'

'Well, who will help you?' Tiva asks. 'Horst, Gus and Aaron? Chancers and mediocrities, you've forgotten them, and if they stood for anything.... Often our pasts are terrible – who preserves them? Forget. You pay for your security like all the rest, and I'll defend you – if I have the means.'

It's all too trite. I wonder if the guys, who live rough in the caves ... they're not on any side, they say, but being on a side is what we're said to reason out....

'Tiva,' I say. 'I must escape. Dilemmas and threats – I've lived with these before, and come off bad....'

'The boat we came in,' Tiva says. 'You'll find it hard to row. It's made for many rowers ... you are weak. And, worse, you'd be a renegade, if you desert....'

'I know, I know,' I say. 'I lose your sympathy; your friendship has already lapsed.... I have no answer ready-made. Flee, freeze or fight.... Fighting you is undesirable, it's not my thing, and it would fail. I'm looking for a way, return – a way back to where I didn't want to be.'

'You might try something radical,' says Tiva, patting me. 'Join a lemur gang, like the primordial sailors did – eat fruit and scrap with other gangs, and wave your bottle-brush, your lovely tail.... You'll be in Vesna's entourage, her spectacle, her claque....'

We laugh. It's hard.

Leaving the empire

Whose empire is this, I wonder. Who runs it? Am I the right – a good – colour, and do I speak the right language, or speak it with a funny accent? Do I fight for it, this empire, and what happens if I don't? Tiva will know, and maybe, like me, she thinks old empires are quite glamorous and enterprising, but no doubt we're differing about this one, the one we're in. Is it I'm a coward, lack the vision, want the unattainable, the undesirable, and if I manage to find a place that isn't part of where I am right now – will I be vulnerable? Or very very poor?

'Write to me, Tiva,' I say. She looks big, bigger and more muscular, wearing the uniform. 'Send me Vesna's records, Tiva,' I say, to win some favour, though you hear Vesna – someone – singing loud, all over. Wakes you before you go to work, if you have some, naturally. 'Plangent' is the word ... not a criticism, but it's intrusive, certainly.

Vesna: arriving in her boat, the island bought unseen, her audiences remembered, rippling like corn – the cutting stones of Namoroka her waves. A scene on film, on coins, on souvenirs, as if you would forget. A noble barge, powered by her phonics, her backing group, her managers and agents.... Glam exile. A journey you don't repeat.

A frozen shot – her hand is stretched out to us, to hold, to squeeze, but – she can't be the empress.... Not with those teeth. I don't take the hand.

Breaking with Tiva – gives you the chance to go back, start again – but how far back, and what will change? Nothing, of course. The past that you don't want is always there, a curtain hung over the screen, and on the screen there can't be anything – just light, and shadows. Nothing. A blank surface, past or future.

Life once went very fast and careless – now it has no particular rhythm, as if different instruments are tuning up, being taken from their cases – as if to play some vast symphony everyone has heard before.... And the people around before I ran away, they must be mostly dead and serves them right for what they did to me and all my brothers, sisters – as if the dead care about the right or wrongs. That caring is the one luxury you can have for certain when you are alive, but it can make you sick, and where it's gathered no one know; the rights and wrongs.

Tiva used to say, 'Shérine, you're here – it didn't happen to you. If you saw, only saw, you're over it. Things happen to the others....' And I said, 'Seeing is everything, the confirmation and the imprint. Seeing is having something happen, happen to you, indelible.'

There's an earth rampart you must climb up – a dyke or a bulwark, bastion, to keep the water out or keep us in. Then there's the boat, the tender. It's very heavy, and the oars are leaden too, even using one at a time, a long awkward paddle, but I'm lucky, and the tide takes me away, to where I am to land. In the empire? Or on the edge, not in, not out, but with all the consequences....

Every movie is about me, but I'm in none of them. Why, now I'm about to land, why should I hope I'm not in empire?

In empire, you have a number, and a tomb: you can be mad, addicted, dissident – and there you are – on the record.

Not in the empire: physically, you can be a nomad. A pirate, or any sailor, a bandit, a guerrilla. Not speaking the language, not graduating from anything – even not picking up your analysis, not going to the interview, giving a false name, not having one. Not having anything.

But, outside the empire – you are thin, a shadow, misnamed, already a defender, an attacker, buried somewhere in your leather shirt under the hill-fort; lost: lost at sea, in the desert; Russian, Austrian – your regiment left off the roster, overrun on the front – maybe you'd long been a hero, or deserted from a non-existing unit, in no battle. Rounded up or rendered down ... a bounty on your skin, your ears, your scalp. Illegal through the border: out again: a field hand, a slave when slavery's been ended ... worker in a phantom factory making fake goods....

There's no one on the beach.

I can be any one of these, the shadows – grease on the wheels. One of the people not in empire yet its contemporary.... You can be anyone, see anything, your skin scarred like a lino cut with imperial maps – except you can't have the madness, addiction, poverty and sickness that's logged when you're in empire – you won't, you can't, have them, not any one. You're a shadow – you can't lose that....

That won't work. You may be a shadow only, but it's a shadow of something, has to be.

The enemy of empire? – probably *jihad*, the most successful; iconoclast, ephemeral, pure and cruel – and so the first pillar of every newborn empire ... the circle's joined up again, its revolutions never stopped, and maybe it's not at all your doing, you needn't exist, or think – it happens to you and you glimpse it – a break in the celluloid, the empire, its sequence hiccups, fades – there is a second of you seeing, doing nothing, deafened and compressed, the blast that you don't hear, the buildings cancelled, like the landscape dissolved by acid on the copper plate, then to be cut again, bigger, deeper incised, until it disappears and is etched again, another state....

You don't have history? Vain thought – everything changes just the same.

'Hey!' I shout. Maybe I hope this is the empire, good and bad, inevitable, another branch with sweet-sour fruit hanging on the history tree that when I ate, it made me gripe and scour and bleed and hollow out. I think – therefore there must be empire. Am I sceptical of it? Or of myself.

*

'I'll push down back,' says a man, I'll know he's Bulat.

'No,' I shout: 'Let me say if I want to land.'

'There's a family here for you to join,' he says. 'Maryse has made some children – you could have the same. No commitment to anything beyond the people that you know, even that you have conceived. I can't see if you're a critic of where you come from, or just dissatisfied. Do you want change, so you can go back? Or make something entirely different here?'

He could push me back, into the sea, whatever I say. I say, 'I differed with my best, my only friend, Tiva. There is a mass of things I see dividing us: not trivial. Maybe they're necessary, or inevitable. I won't know, until I've moved outside. Where do I think to finish up? I'll be old and incapable, younger and imprisoned. That's usually the choice.'

'Empire,' says Bulat. 'It is a serpent, wound tight around your brain, a serpent. A snake that holds you tight, can sting, or find you warm. I don't think about it. It's there? Or not? Maryse is here. We quarrel, fight a lot. Everybody does. There's burials constantly – but there are children too – you grow attached to them, they're bright, they see all that you see, and much much more.'

It's a bad start. Bulat's a creep, a waste.

'Where am I, Bulat?' I ask. 'I know for you, the answer isn't simple. Even if I know exactly where you say I'm at, that's just the start, although....'

'Although it's no more difficult for you to know than it is for anyone,' he says. 'However, this shore's disputed territory. So, whether you are really in or out – here it is just the same. Appearance is everything, for once....'

'Some places are quite different,' I begin.

It's ridiculous. Of course they are, everywhere. It's rules that I must mean.

'Here,' he says. 'I make the rules, and Maryse adds, and rules are common sense.'

How does it all work? I wonder. I scramble out the boat, the land goes up and down. I give up the project – empire, system. I start from Tiva – what do we differ on? What happens after Vesna? – Tiva and the palace guard? An autocracy that really is a fief ... part of a tower of overlords, topped by a thundercloud....

I don't fall over, I lurch and yaw. Conquest and debt – that's what I mean, that's what has made and holds us; that's what I resist. I have no credit – maybe Bulat will give me some.

Scientific killing. That rests on engineering principles. Lending money in return for work and buying stuff. That is my time, my era, my universe. It sounds banal.

Bulat holds me vertical – it can't be done. I am a sapling in the breeze.

'You look tired and dirty,' says Maryse. She wasn't asked.

'I've lost my colour, lots of it,' I say. 'I like to think I am Malian, but like you, I'm African in origin. Then came the long walk, the sun grew pale, the eyes – some turned to blue, the skins were matt and indeterminate....

'You and Bulat are white potatoes – I still have some patina, I didn't scrub myself, like I was fixated on being pale....'

'That's precious,' says Maryse. A double meaning, she stands on that.

So be it – she's a sharp knife, a walking razor.

She walks away brusquely, then turns, not sparing me: 'You're a wanderer?' she asks. She knows.

Imperial history

'It's broken,' Maryse says. 'Broken centuries ago. China, India – ravaged, reduced to poverty, and poverty became their sole resource. Being poor, and being many. Slavery all over, on an industrial scale; the workers – made into a machine ... a melting one, made monkeys: a sloppy force.... Disaster. Poor Russia, half and half – part colonised, part coloniser.... And remember, there is no return.

'Wars at the center – then by proxy, into the periphery, here, where we are ... the edge.

'We're small and flickering: we're mayflies, we live, die in a flash – we can't turn into ants or bees and find our place, try to hold on. Evolution is cumbersome, it doesn't seek a super man or person: only survivors. Not intelligence – just adaptation. If you screw up – no second chance.

'I see you, Shérine, like the other wanderers and strollers who drift up on these stony shores – you want the answer, but you know it. It is simple. We made a mess of it, and can't redress. Empires, then Empire, based on conquest. The losers; screwed.

'The sceptics and the curious – you romanticise the places that were overlooked – abandoned, inhospitable ... unstable grasslands, deserts, sparsely populated so you don't see the human catastrophe we – you – brought on ourselves, perpetuate ... a monstrous error, spreading like a weed, a virus that we make, then try to extirpate.... That is the task, you think. But – we live by our complicity, Shérine – we make catastrophe and wring our hands, try to undo what we have done and justified, and make more catastrophe....'

It's true, the truth that makes the answer obvious, a truth I know, hide from myself.

'Your children, Maryse,' I say, pretending to ignore the history.... 'Oh,' she says, 'They're wanderers like you – except they were too small to think.. Feet are the way they are so you go forward – another species might prefer reverse.

'The eyes, Maryse,' I say. 'The eyes. They don't relent – we only see, we think we see – the future. In front. Onward, upward – it's all we countenance.... There must be better, must be a reparation....'

'You mean – like women strive to be accomplices of men?' she asks. 'That is the plan…. Imagine you are different: bury the history, forget the philosophy, of being equal or superior. Our intelligence revolves round that – it's self-deception. I expect you'll ignore the truth I've laid out, Shérine....'

She's said it all, but I intrude – 'The powers – they made a desert where I was ... the despotism – was their solution, not ours....'

'Being a victim isn't smart,' she says. 'Rich places, poor ones – are full of people crushed, deluded ... that's empire, Shérine, that's what you're trying to avoid.... Look at our rocks – see, the termite hills are all around, and we live poor ... this place, remote, abandoned, not sought out, hard to romanticise....'

'And so,' I ask, 'apart from dig and hoe – what do you do?'

'Keep silent,' says Maryse. 'Avoid complicity. I don't seek equality, not with the oppressors, the warriors ... no casino, no bleak reserve, no representatives, no hi-tech campus – just the truth, just like I told it to you ... you, eternal wanderer, a simpleton ... on, on, to your next disappointment, your next halting place....'

'At least,' I say, 'I know the story. I was right to leave my dearest friend, dear Tiva, servant and probably resented chief ... accomplice and deceiver.... The truth is puzzles, now I see....'

'Exactly so,' Maryse says. 'Puzzles that don't give solutions that you'd like ... just puzzles ... that's the truth.'

'Why Bulat?' I ask.

'I wanted a bully. Bullying helps me define myself,' she says, 'but it's like your bully Tiva – you see what they are: they don't. They don't let you play your game with them. They let you go, your need is unresolved. All my children – not mine, of course, he's quite indifferent – they can't fly. They have no instinct to grow up, leave me alone. You have to sick up awful stuff to feed them. Or – you could say they are sick plants: he waits to pull them up or harvest them.

'Others: that's what they are. All in the balance.'

Maryse is honest. Is that good?

I say, 'My story starts among the Arabs of Iran, down South. It starts among the Syrians, that's where I'm from. It starts in Germany, starts in Iceland, where I was born, re-settled: where I had to trek. Attila's Huns – they came in luxury, compared to us. They founded Europe – we begged.

'I'm the wrong shape, I fit in anywhere. I have no characteristic that makes it hard to melt into a pattern.'

'And so you're here,' she says, 'because you can't row a boat.'

'There's other things I can't do too,' I say: I'm sure she knows.

'Half of you is dead, Shérine,' she says. 'That half is here. The live half's left somewhere along the way. Bulat can use the dead part – he likes the curious, the questioning, you zombies who've been told and seen what's what, and still you prowl around – dead people round dead meat.'

*

'Help me lift these slabs,' says Bulat.

I'm not sure if I shall stay. It's ten years since I landed here. It passes like a week. Perhaps it is a week, a day.

This field is full of stones: 'We carry them,' says Bulat, 'And lay them over there.'

'What will you plant?' I ask.

'I've no idea,' he says. 'I'm not a pessimist like you. And Maryse, another pessimist – as though she knows what happens next!'

A stony field – made pristine, just the wormy soil and weeds – and lo! a field of stones, created over there. Creation. The stones are like the sea, you pile them up in waves, there's grey and grey, brown, and slatey blue.

'And is this art?' he asks. 'What would it mean, and if it's art, would I be an artist then? And if I am – what does it change?'

'Where I am from,' I say, 'and that is almost everywhere – you can't be classified. Maybe – an optimist?'

Bulat surveys the field of stones: a critical eye. 'It could be a cemetery,' he says. 'Without bodies. There's many Malians, many Syrians, many many like you and me, died at sea, trying to get here. Trying to get somewhere. Land. This would be their cemetery – they didn't make it. But – here's the field we cleared, potential – you could plant anything there. That's optimism.'

'This is heavy stuff,' I say, crying a little. It's very cold, and there's nothing to eat. I miss Tiva, and the pheasants. I miss not being able to go back to the beginning and start again – without Troy, without Venus butting in, without the horse – an early tank, stuffed with those sweaty cavaliers, Troy destroyed like Carthage, Dresden, Stalingrad ... and I wish Bulat, who seems a good, a taciturn, man who surely can't be profiting from me arriving here with nothing – I wish Bulat .... But he can't. He won't. It's up to me to make my habitat.

There's always a mistake, once made it's irrevocable. Just one, unravelling everything else. I should have gone to fight, fight for the gods, the myth: for the destruction of the shining towers, the massacre of all the animals, piling up the warriors eviscerated, and me – the plague: turns you black and stinking, black blood from every opening, the eyes, my navel swells like an avocado and when it bursts, out I pour; into the pit with me....

My error, me: it was asking what he'd plant. Wondering if it might be me. What did I care.

'Your sea is hollow, Shérine,' he says. 'It should be full, a sea of love, populated and rich.'

'Well, Bulat,' I say, 'the boat, the oars, were heavy. The air was heavy – it must be, so low down. It stifles you. Sea level? That's wrong. The sea is never level, it tilts against you.'

'And these children,' he persists. 'Are they yours, Shérine? Silent, demanding, crawling from the sea and up the sand like turtles, or down from the hills, slithering toward the water they need and can't drink....'

'That's poetry, Bulat,' I say. 'That, I won't judge. You're wrong – I have no children, those are other people's Maryse feeds. Only the dead remember whose they were. I have ideas, instead: silent, demanding. Never young, never dependent. Completely useless and unfinished, sterile. I don't know other things. You can't teach me what you are, Bulat – if you could, you'd lose what makes you special, different.'

'Your boat is here,' he says. 'And you're too weak to face the waves. Patience.'

Not what I want to hear.

*

'Bulat wears you down,' says Maryse. 'Calling us pessimists, what we've been learning. Pessimism doesn't save you from disappointment. You can hardly call it wisdom. Superstition? We could do the dance. Cut ourselves and sacrifice. Baloney. What happens – you can delay it. Then it happens. Time is on the side of all procrastination, time is always there and ready. Any fault is yours.'

'You mean,' I say, 'Troy will be discovered, re-assembled?'

'It could even be. The problem – or the blessing – is that Aphrodite isn't there,' she says. 'Not even with her other passport, aka Venus. She is in the sea. When you were sleeping with your Troy – did Aphrodite smooth the sheets, put on the porno videos?'

'If she was there,' I say. 'We didn't see her. Maybe with Tiva, the goddess could have lent us helping hands. It's fleeting, Maryse – the magic of romance. You need white witches, conjuring with smoke and coca leaves. Keeping it up with chants and fancy. Those white faces ... underneath the mask, the clay – they're black, of course. Like me, like you. Appearance – all we have to go by. Look: submit to what seems the reality. There is no other way, no reasonable course. Spells are hit and miss: use them, but don't expect they'll work. In the end – you'll see – the bones of everyone are white....'

She keens, she rocks. To and fro. I don't join in.

I find Maryse depressing, Bulat too bland. There's not enough to eat. For me, hope is a slow horse. The slowest in the race.

One of the staves we use to prise the stone slabs up ... it makes me a strong leg. With three legs, I manage to climb up the hill, and set out for the hinterland....

*

There's villages. Some burnt, some burning – all built centuries ago, for doing other things, some in the front line, new people always, looking the same. They don't want help, they want a difference. A difference might make them good, or better. I can't pay for anything.

My hunger's stronger than my fear. I keep going. Going on's a risk.

It's all empire.

Melons

I've never seen so many melons. Fields of them, like breasts on a Guro figure, and a beauty, two Guro breasts of her own, holding up melons to a camera on stilts.

'Let me hoe,' I say, 'for a melon – though I'd prefer a stew....'

'This is an ad,' she says. 'Get out of frame. Fuck off. Besides, the rind is thick – these melons must traverse the world, chained in containers in the dark – your teeth won't penetrate.... The rind is nature's packaging....'

My mouth throbs, the teeth dance. 'I need a knife....'

'These beauties go to the New World,' she Bouchra says. 'They are our best. What don't go abroad, we sell on line.... We're poor, it's true, but richer than we were. The rich are richer than they were, more numerous – take this path, and then the road, and then the super-road you can't walk on, and you'll see it all. We shall be richer, all of us, so long as we're obedient. If we were rich, we'd have a plan, a manifesto – but there's been a manifesto, and a plan. What, anyway, do we say? We grow these melons, foreigners invest.... That's mostly what there is to say....'

'I'm just hungry, Bouchra,' I say. I hug her. She's a beauty, perhaps she hugs me back. We eat our melon soup, it's excellent.

'Of course,' I say. 'It's empire here....'

'So what?' she asks. 'Over there, it's empire too, except there's more "each for themselves". Their money goes into melon fields, here, where we are sitting, in this house....'

'It's small,' I say, 'but better than a shack, and there's tv. My dearest friend and I – we had a seashore shack, without tv.'

'You notice everything, Shérine,' says Bouchra, laughing. 'You'll like my man, Asmat.'

'Why would you think that, Bouchra,' I ask, amazed. 'I cling to you, you tell me everything I need to know.'

'Asmat is full of things to notice,' says Bouchra. 'When he sees how you're attached to me, he'll be attached to you as well.'

'I'm not sure that's what I want,' I say, thinking of confusing nights.

'We here,' she says, 'we are coordinated. We have a future, have it in our heads. Where you are from – they've different dreams, and different chiefs.'

'I know,' I say. 'My friend, my Tiva – she's a warrior. It's unacceptable – all puff and pomp.'

'I see you are the brainy type, Shérine,' says Bouchra. 'But neither brains nor body tell you much. If you know what I know, dear – how many melons should we grow, the price, and where they go – you'll know all you need to know. It's very complicated, if you do it right,' she says. 'It is the root of everything....'

'I like the soup, Bouchra,' I say, 'but generally – I don't care so much....'

'You cretin, Shérine,' Bouchra says, quite kindly. 'It's all to do with melons, and it's also nothing to do with them at all.'

Annick

It must be years I've stayed with Bouchra. Learning nothing, except a hatred of the melons, and breasts like those on Guro fetishes.

'Asmat won't last,' she says. 'His lungs is playing up. Besides – maybe I should have said – I have a dear friend – over there,' and she waves, 'Annick. You're so stuck up, Shérine, you two together wouldn't do at all.'

'I call that a deceit,' I say, 'However kindly meant....'

'Oh, that's not it at all,' says Bouchra, not kindly meaning at all. 'She needs someone who's destitute like you to work for her, that's all.'

'You mean,' I say, angry and tearful, 'you'd sell me to her? Instead of melons....'

'You'd go spin wool,' says Bouchra, unflinching, cool. 'Subsistence living isn't good. You need a wiggle now and then. We have a subtly different line....' And she opens up a little barn – could maybe hold two goats, and on the backside of the door there's pinned a grinning corpse – quite hairless, pink and white as Bubbles in the pic, or might be Fragonard – as healthy as a corpse can look. It's Asmat. 'Bouchra,' I shout, 'there was no need – we could have driven him away....'

'No, it's not him,' she says. 'It's Asmat's pig. They were attached, almost symbiotically. Now, since they can't cure Asmat, comes the time when we must cure the pig....' and she laughs. 'You must keep quiet, Shérine,' she says. 'We specialise in melons, we're not allowed to keep a pig – though, I suppose, a dead porker might not count....'

'This is not at all how I thought to go on,' I say. It could all finish here.

'I'm not a factory, Shérine,' Bouchra says. 'I can't have a court of people, husbands, lovers, friends and counsellors.... You've nothing, and you're not a slave – take what is offered, or refuse it – no one can advise you differently....'

*

I crouch down in a corner. Many invisible roads have ended, come to terminus. Philosophy – petered out.... Religion – cloudy post-stations along a misty road, totems and tabus you tiptoe round. Don't tread on either one, they're Guro melons, many people live on them. Science: – useless, when there are pork chops to be cleavered out. Art? Maybe sculpture is the key – it's all an engineering trick, making proportions cohere ... caress out the delicacy of the trotters, and the wistful grin. How to verticalise the whole cadaver, make the components: jive – that is the trick. But here, it's crucifixion, but the head won't loll, it stares, straight, quizzical; 'well-met' the message, a guy across you in the pub: – to speak, or smile, but not suggestively?... Offer a drink ....

There's Annick – uses a little blowtorch, singes off the golden bristles, wipes the corpse.

My spirit, *Geist*, kicks in. I take a pole, a bill-hook: made for snagging up and down, perhaps, or just an implement, a multi-use.... I hit her with it, sweetly on the nape. An improvisation – not thought out at all.

She kneels, she slumps. A stolid trunk. The pig grins, unamused.

I feel dread.

There's a saying, 'no story is the truth'. It's true.

It's time to go. For once, only the truth is here, apparent. No story: best keep schtum.

They're all in the fields. How's Annick? We – no one, will ever know.

Can clean people do a dirty deed, and after, continue clean? Removing a problem – must it always make a bigger one?

*

Art, a tale – a distorting mirror to reality. Ourselves – another mirror, distorting our reality. I haven't told a tale, untruth. All the tears are mine – no one else need feel involved. Everything I say is true. In all my life, I never told a lie ... unless, maybe by mistake. That doesn't count. If I had taken work – I wouldn't have a tale, I'd have a carpet. Woven from my life, there'd be the designs, the lives, of all the rest. The slum, the cat-house, the back kitchen or the camp. It might make outsiders cry. It wouldn't mean a thing. Emotion is for guys who buy the tales. Fictions. Crucifictions: except the pig was real.

I tell the truth: – what's happened to the rest, the others, who kept me, persecuted me, ignored, or touched and rammed – I just don't know. Don't ask, don't bother empathising.

Rok

I'm right up against him, he and I engrossed in my commiseration – the old sage, sitting on the fence.

'All I say is true,' I say. 'Trust me.'

'Yes,' he says – and maybe he's not so old. Not so sage. 'The age of reason's over. It never had a chance. Now is the age of truth. What's yours, Shérine?'

'I start from what I am,' I say: 'All quite exact.'

'I'm Rok by name, and not by nature,' says Rok, the sage. 'Think of me as an ear eternal – a shell. You hear the sea in it, in any shell. And any sea, now, once, or never. *There's* a truth! The sea would hardly lie!'

'We are agreed,' I say: 'Seas don't lie. They swash.'

The job

'You're smart, Shérine,' says Rok. 'And careless for your future, and your life. What we need here – is mediation. On one side – there's unrest, on another – info. We need a hand that finds these two a common need.... As for you, be selfish, and be prudent too.'

'Someone to put together guerrillas and the cinema? An impresario?' I ask. 'Movies and manifestos? Chaos in cahoots with disorder?'

'Is information chaos?' Rok muses. How slow he is! 'Maybe you're correct. But the rebels – they used always to be in the right. In the right and on the left. We loved them. What's happened, Shérine? Are we too old? Is everything falling down and disappearing? Seeking order, did we wind the timepiece up too tight, and break the spring? Gun the motor, over-egg our madeleine?

'What I mean, my dear, is: you can steal from the producers. Your cream, your fee. They give you cash to buy the bearded guys more guns. Besides, guerrillas, insurrectionists – they don't do accounts, they've millions stashed on pallets ... maybe planes dropped all that cash; maybe they found the matrices, stopped the right truck? Money makes you live, long and well. We all know that – it's late, but you too should discover that....'

'I'm Voltaire,' I say. 'Except I don't take his risks. No playing games with sovereigns – with gold ones, perhaps, not in the flesh. Rok, that flesh is vicious.'

'Was there order where you've been, Shérine?' he asks. 'I feel you live on happenstance, monstrosities and ghosties, close shaves and shaggy dogs. You've wandered into real worlds. Stop! Find your stage!'

'Perhaps,' I say. 'But that's not what I want.'

'What you want,' says Rok, 'is not available. Everywhere is hot and wet and smoky now, unless it's cool and dry and ash.... The menu's much reduced, and baked alaska is a speciality....'

He laughs at his small *mot*.

'There's patterns in a chaos, Rok,' I say. 'Science is indifferent to that, to everything. Never still and never satisfied. Reason was a rusty passkey, fitted every lock, but that is all. Reason's a major domo, what the butler saw and cannot do.... Reason opens boxes. Science watches magma. There's patterns. But there's an enigma. Design. It's fierce – horrors unending, with fake clues....'

'And death is very orderly,' he says. 'Be very careful. Don't exaggerate with cash. Skim, don't scam, be moderate, and don't get caught. Seek order, avoid death.'

'The cause,' I say. 'It might be one I can support. If so, I shouldn't steal, take money from it. I'm a progressive. There's no progress, though.'

'It's not necessarily so,' says Rok, impatiently. 'And we all have sympathies. But we must all get paid.'

*

It would be work. A go-between. Guardian angel, a fixer, ambassador, mediator, enabler. What percentage am I supposed to steal? Will anyone show these interviews, all lies filmed ... all of the representatives, all filmy, once in security and special forces, bedroom warriors and genocides....

Where are the old causes, I ask myself: justice and freedom, where did that end up?

'You'll find me warm and loving,' Rok says. 'But opaque.'

'You've nothing in you but experiences. You're all yourself,' I say. He seems satisfied.

We are all narcissists, we have to be, but some are all yolk, no shell. Dictators brew their self-regard, pour it on their flocks: a concentrated narcissism.

Remember the Trojan war, first fascist enterprise....

Rok: he's rubbish. A character. I have nothing inside myself, no qualities – certainly not a me. That was eaten long ago, or lodged in a bank no one would think to rob.

'One day,' he says. 'You'll find Tiva. This is her kind of place. People who look for power, new kinds of it, new places where they think they'll get the power they want – they end up here.'

'It's past,' I say. '*The* past. I know about countries, and ideas that don't have countries. Nations and Islam. Islam goes beyond the nations and in the end, it is the nation of Islam.

'I know all that. I know all this old stuff, it's in the books, and when Tiva does an interview, if it's not lies, it won't be interesting, and if it's false – well, she's rather slow and limited. I wouldn't bother with her. Things disappear and people talk about that – it's a mystery. And yet it's not: if there is Troy, there's Troy. If not – there's not. No mystery. People are the same, people are Troy – banal, aggressive, begrudging everything, especially love and loyalty. Then disappear.

'And the cause: it might be one I can support. The old-time ones. But then, I oughtn't steal their cash.'

'That isn't necessarily so,' says Rok, impatiently. 'We all have sympathies. and everyone takes money – openly, or steals. We all know that. Your cause: is Chaos, dear Shérine. Information. Truth. Remember that, you won't go wrong. Chaos: not disorder leading to new order – chaos. Truth is not order, so it can't be disorder either. It's just chaos. You agreed.'

'Minds change, Rok,' I say. 'These are slow-burning issues.'

'I've fixed you up,' he says. 'Tomorrow you begin.'

*

They are all renegades. They have to be. All did the training – the movie people too. I never see them, neither party, no credible participant. From neither side; not one. We're all on the take, all intermediaries – I'm probably the best. They're all afraid of being traced, of telling truth. All want to bring order – and yet ... they don't. Don't want, don't bring.

I'm pleased to be for chaos: I don't need do anything at all, it's there, and I'm the truth, we know.

The rebels want recruits. The cinema, TV, has far too many guys.... Rebels negotiate, make friends, use massacres to make a deal, are massacred in turn and need a sympathetic counterpart – transmitted before you as you eat your pasta, mortadella, your stale bread. It's not for you, the news, unless you're militant or relative, *compaesano, patelin,* or co-religionist.

Rok takes a cut – I'm sure. Mine – I'm frightened of it.

One day a rocket blows away most of both the sides – the casing, the shrapnel, gun down cameramen and pierce the rebel bunkers. I'm terrified....

The cause. Should I have one, and should I stay on here, risking the second strike? Maybe they all think I called in the explosion....

*

'You have dark ideas, Shérine,' says Rok, approving.

'No, no,' I say. 'I'm sceptical. I see a mass of people switch beliefs, up comes a fascist God – down on their knees they go, exalted: suburban angels, at the summons they sprout wings and height thirty metres tall – await the call, these fathers, warriors, their golden swords ... and rifles, naturally.... It's myth again, the world. We're off to Troy, if it exists or not, the gods enrol ... and on we march.

'I cling to what they don't believe, and clinging's not belief.'

'It's too contorted, dear,' says Rok. He whittles. Stick men, brigades of them, and lines them up in fours and fives.

*

No one pays up. Why should they? Everyone will promise, no one settles. 'Rok,' I say. 'The job is fine. But doing it – I'll starve.'

'Shérine,' he says, 'I told you. Warm and loving, that is me....' He tips a wink. I shudder backwards. Sex, the universal coin. Where do I run? Towards the rebels or the movie men?

'If hens could talk,' says Rok, 'they'd talk like you. As if you translate yourself as you go on. Cocks and eggs is all you need to know – but on you chatter, same as everyone, but never listen, ever, that the sound of chickens everywhere's the same. You shrink, you are superfluous: you have no skills. You think – one day they'll pick you up, the big guys, and you'll be off to fame and consultations. But no! It's festa time, and yours has come. You'll be the centre-piece, but you won't know. Your severed head's outside, the cat plays football with it, and you're full. Of stuffing up your arse....'

'Be wise, Rok,' I say. 'Don't try to be a wise guy, though. Sex with you is not at all the joy I want.'

*

'Think, Shérine,' he says. 'See how ridiculous it's been for you. You're charmed – think of the others when their town fell down: refugees, nowhere to go. Really incredible, nothing to believe in, no destination whatsoever. You – you are lucky, marvellously lucky. Still, it's been tough, a disappointment, a privation. Circling the periphery; doing bad, for sure. Looking. Seeking a nub – a hub. Not everything must have a centre, and you never even found the rim. Not everything must have a rim.

'Tiva was your best thing, and you gave her up. I can love you, you're like me; we're all like that guy's cat: somewhere dead, somewhere alive – even immortal. They say you're dead for ever, so for sure you can live for ever.

'Look at me – my precious unique self and body. I'm the worst, and I'm the last. It's over, Shérine, and it hasn't finished, it's still travelling; you are a shell, an envelope, and you're still voyaging although you have no eyes and there is nothing you can see.'

'They fought the war, such triviality! – and then they left, like me, like I keep doing. There was nothing, no ruins, no rubble, nothing. As if it had never been. Just them,' I say: 'Then they too disappear, and let us make up tales about them.'

I'm much cast down. It's all true, everything I've seen and everything I said. What's to be made of that?

Topping-out

I can't go back, return and ask somebody 'how did it go?' 'How did I do?' If you've a character, you don't do that – everybody has their tale – you were once in it, in theirs: they in yours, marginally ... don't exaggerate. Onward. If you know which way that is. What you are on, it might be circular: you might be on a globe. Or tracking round a star. A fly around a bulb.

I've built my tower. The shining tower. What goes on top to finish it? A cock? An arrow, a pointing finger? Or a ceramic tile: round, like Pinocchio's clown hat. A finial. For a monument, made specially to a standard design.

*

'Well,' says Rok, 'If you stay here – I'm here too. Common sense, I provide – and questioning. With my aging mortal body, all over hair. Then all the rest. The physical. For ever, into you, all over. You could do worse, Shérine, much worse than me.'

ELEMENTARY EXERCISES

Fire

It's my first work. It's her first big gig. Entertaining the people's choice: – the redneck soldier – an ogre in the ogreworld....

Amina sings a little – a little voice is all she has.

She has a dress, shimmer and melting glass, strass and fake fur, but you can see her, all of her, light against light, a body like blue gas in a sheath of gas.

The President – he sits and stares, chats through the show, deals and wheels, shows off. It's all performance, everything is, and he's the show, always.

'Master of ceremonies'. Our spectacle was poor, the impact I made quite adequate, and so I got the title.

'You won't get her, my client, my Amina, President,' I say, 'Unless you take me too.' And so he does.

*

This used to be a court. A court of customary law. It's still a court, it's his; bedroom and kitchen: rumpus room. Now it's a dormitory, and a mess-room. Over the world, despots and champions – they all set up brief monarchies. Some pass the torch on to a generation, mostly they're roman candles, entertainers; stale jokes, short lives: short shrifts.

Me – organiser of the ceremonies. Master.

Master of the horse – there is one, but I've never seen the horse. Mistresses there are, of the bedchamber: – mistresses by chance, without a contract.

The keeper of the privy seal, the purse. The seal is in the zoo – the purse ... is carried off, its many folds, by anyone who can. The privy is for everyone.

The master of the rolls – there is a Rolls.

The household cavalry is on the gallops, some on duty with the cops. Is there a master of the self-propelled?

If you're in, you're precarious, if you are out – you dangle....a monkey on a rope.

Amina's not mine to sell or give – she's a loan. Everything is free will, all up to her.

*

The chief needs people round him. He can see everyone, but they're dull. They're terrified, except – if you are dull, you don't feel terrified, it's an ache, like knowing there is tomorrow, and wanting to be there, despite what you may have done today. In auctions, there are groups of porcelain pugs and chimps, playing cards or violins. These guys are pugs. You can break the set in seconds, stick the wrong heads on bodies. They're wrecked, the value broken.

*

Amina is a greyhound. You can train them to race round corners, that's how tracks are made, but all dogs – they're made for the straight. A bitch will sometimes start to bite the other runners when they're in the traps. Owners are used to agression, but casual biting – they don't stand for that. She'd be warned off. Is she fast? She's moody. She's independent. under contract, legal slavery. She knows what she must do, why she's taken to the track, why winning keeps you safe till the next time.

*

The chief – he's fixed, baroque. He loves a good time that's a bad time for the rest: – in costume, drunk or duelling, on horseback or in a tank. Making mockeries.

Babak. The name reminds me of a carcase made of papier-maché, dragged on a cart in carnivals, lampooned and burned: something of Ubu Roi. Something of Babar the elephant. Something of Moloch. A colossus, astride us all.

*

'Your gang,' Amina tells him, feeling cheeky and invulnerable – 'You boys: off into the woods, to camp. Do you never feel an urge – those summer nights, the adolescence?... I know I should....'

'Only we males,' says Babak, putting an arm around her, pressing her against his silver waistcoat, accoutrements – like the Scotsman's skian dubh: ... arms in his socks, his pants: a button to call for bodyguards.... His pistols and his frogs....

He says, 'Only we males know what it is to share a tent, a puppy tent, head to toe – with a dear friend. Sure, there is the urge. Resist, it's good and you can boast of it. You yield at times – and they are yours for life....'

He takes her down to where he keeps his line of women – not his bimbos, but huge earth mothers, made of clay, terracotta grotesques, clefts deep as mortal wounds, breasts like unsteady cornices, threaten to crash down on humans gawping up..... 'That's art,' he says. 'The only kind worthwhile. Shout loud, don't flinch. Assert ... They're terrible, and they're inert. Respect your origin, and store it in the dark.'

*

'I can go out,' Babak says, 'out to the end of the longest pier, past the circuses, the human pyramids – I can do all that, and be alone, exposed. Then, there's the sea. I can't do anything with that. It's beyond my power, my wish to clean it up, or dirty it. Performance, Amina. You should know that. When the music stops, the clockwork pauses: – the dancer droops, a crocus in the wind.

'Those blind giants, Iskandar, the Great Khan, up they rear!... and then you see – those mounds of skulls they leave are progress, destiny. Without them, there's a hiatus. There's a stop to burning cities, heaping up those bones – the world, its history, all goes back: – to being fruiterers, trunk-makers, letter-writers. Without me, nothing would move, move on. If I'm gone, an absence.... There's been a mystery, and you'd all be left bereaved, to die without me....

'I dance, Amina. I can tire you out, I twirl for ever, make the rules and break them, promulgate, rescind – I'm there when you have dropped with tiredness, with amazement. When you're silent – I shall eat you, every one. And if I stumble – take your knife and try to slice me up – but watch it! Don't be deceived! You'll bleed. I am your lives!'

*

'He's not deep, Amina,' I tell her. I think she knows.

I say, 'He's schematic. Useful. When he talks purity – everyone sees how he's a libertine. When he urges massacres – we know he's indifferent. Anyway, we two are here to please the people, the more the better. It's our work, and if we don't work – we must abandon art, find something else.'

'I know what I do,' she says, 'but what do you do, Parviz? It's not art, for sure.'

'I give out the presents from an empty sack,' I say.

I'm sure she knows.

*

None of this is true. Neither of us would say what I've written here. We schemed to get our jobs, we'll fight to keep them.

This country has no past: no underground – no burial mounds, nothing. Small change someone dropped, not much. No hoards. Few monuments, much restored and pillaged, nothing written. Some of us look like we're from the East, and others from the West. Our language comes from somewhere distant, and people there don't understand us. We're herders, peaceful, and we're warriors.

With all humanity, we have in common – shamanism. What shamans tells us we must do, we mostly do. Where do they get it? Dope, malignity and madness. Amina says, 'They get it from the dead. We pass it on, then we're the dead.'

*

'My sex means I can't be a griot,' Amina says, 'so I'll be a shaman, and play the gravikord – and I'm in love, and not with you, Parviz. A groom – a horsegroom, not a bridegroom, and he's right, exactly for me – people who aspire, or who seek their origins, are sure to be deluded ... a groom's exactly right for me, I've studied. Of course, I still have vacancies for love in different categories, but....'

'Being in love, Amina,' I ask. 'What does that mean for you?'

'A getaway,' she says. 'A quick horse that won't be tracked. All I need do is learn to ride it. That's where Musafar comes in.'

'Enjoy him, Amina,' I say. 'We have nothing to fear, except accidents. We're insignificant, we've no one to blame. Ceremonies? That's life. Where to sit, what to wear. When to stand, and when it's all over. Then, there's long sits – the music, the plays, and longer still – the opera. The audience with foreign guys.... Yes, we are all the audience: silent, watching an exchange of views, hoping it all ends well. Foreigners, strangers: all a chat between interpreters, and – there must be flowers. And chairs. Ride a chair, Amina, forget the horse – unless you're on the steppe, the barbed wire stops you riding on: or it's the ditch, the waves.'

'I wonder,' Amina says, 'when they drove the quadriga in the sea at the feast for Apollo – did they really let the horses drown? There seems a contradiction – darkness, or light...?'

'Sacrifice,' I say. 'If you don't do it by yourself, they make you.'

'I didn't mean that,' says Amina. 'What taste the gods have, to get off on burning flesh. They could try a Montecristo, smoke something for themselves....'

'I told you, it's performance,' I say.

'You reinforce legitimacy, Parviz,' she says: 'You make real; make flesh, the image, and the state. Without a perishable body in its cloth of gold, there's no mystical body, no eternity, no state incarnate and reborn. If there's no chief of state, there's only an idea: no abstraction that lives on. Without you: – it's holey socks and streaky underpants, a group of bums with spoons and bones – no Aida trumpets, no bombardons ... only a failing, then a non-existent, state.'

'You're wrong, Amina.' I say, aghast. 'I'm furniture: no more responsible for Babak than the guy who shines his shoes. If shoes he wears. I carry hods, I'm not an architect....'

*

'God invented everything,' she says. 'The universe, infinity – and reason. Reason was his limit, his weak spot. Our universe is bounded by reason. Circumscribed by laws and rules, it's an infinity that is no mystery, infinity that replicates the known, the knowable – yes, infinitely. It's all predictable: God gave us understanding, and a dying body. Reason is our prison, Parviz.'

'I've heard that,' I say. 'God invents, becomes, reason, and must disappear. He makes his obsolescence – and all the ceremonies set up to magnify Him, his spits and spats, unreason – all that becomes a void. Reason reigns, God's unemployed, redundant. Let's leave Him out. Babak's taken over. *He*'s worshipped and adored. He hands out cash to people who don't expect it, don't deserve it, and who love it, and him. They need it, cash. Everybody does. We have no souls, and anyway, they're valueless. We don't sell anything precious, we've nothing: humans have nothing, nothing at birth or death. Or? Ignorance and incoherence, nakedness, incontinence. We take the treasure Babak offers, though.'

*

Why bother, Babak? All you have is repetition: meetings and protests. Celebrations of nothing in particular.

'It's the spirit, Parviz,' Amina says. 'You're walking in the woods – a spirit catches you, climbs up your nose, sits astride your brain, bestraddles it: and you must dance and sing until you die, you're hunted and you're killed, the sacred stag is you. Before your end, you're cemented in the role. You must take it with whatever humour and invention come to hand.'

'But that is reason,' I say. 'Calculation, resignation. We're asking if Babak is an alternative to God, if he's the first, the primal one – a reborn God who thinks more deeply of His role, what he invents, what he instructs – maybe making just one world, no stars: and stopping there. The universe, infinity: recession eternal – what a swank! Vainglorious, don't you think? As for Babak, maybe he disinvents Reason. Saying things that are not true – that's the actor's trade, much envied and admired. It's not unreason: Babak isn't in the old God's shoes – if those He wore. Calculation, aspiration – that's why people love him ... and they do. They may not burn with passion, but they're loving partners all the same.... He can do wrong, and so can they: it's of no consequence.'

*

This leads us nowhere. For the moment – we're in work.

Babak savours, gloats – Amina might be his. Maybe he practises the moves he thinks aren't necessary, but it's important for Amina that he keeps his passion for her, if there's to be shows, long runs....

'There's celebrations coming, Parviz, let me sing a song,' she says. 'But not the local stuff – it's difficult, and they all laugh at me.'

*

None of this is true – or, it isn't relevant. Babak is not reason, nor unreason. The anthem I commission is a flop. Amina's passion for young Musafar infuriates Babak. He turns against us both.

We run.

Very slowly, on our own feet, we run. No problem. Let's say I never failed. This is art we do, and that means sometimes a guard faints, lets off a gun, a horse craps in the minute's silence.... For Amina – a snotty dottle plugs her topmost note.... a breast flops out her diva's costume.... We're not rehired? – that is the game. Money and luxury melt away.... Sometimes the spectacle is good, sometimes a catastrophe.

Prudence makes us run, not persecution. We've been rich, so we don't need shuffle, carry bundles. It's nothing, retrocession: like leaving the collapsing bank, or being fired, bearing your past and future in a cardboard box....

*

'A pretty pickle, Amina,' I conclude.

'They're vindictive,' she says. 'We should trot faster, Parviz.'

I don't believe in her. Off the stage, she's not authentic.

*

We look out, over a vast plain. There's black empty chimneys, towns with trolleys crawling round, some kites with human faces, some scrubby grass, old bull rings....

'Let's think again, Parviz,' Amina says. 'This is infinity. Probably it expands. But it's not reasonable, no one who had invented reason would invent this scene, would think of infinities of acid rocks that fly for ever in the dark, as if a chem lab had exploded and gone nuclear....'

'You're right,' I say. 'I trusted too much what I'd read. God – if He has sometime been, has not gone unemployed, vanished from creation. He's much reduced, reposing in a back seat somewhere. Babak – could be God, could be unreason. He's the new kid, the brazen boy – he loves this landscape, it is his, and he wants ever more.

'You, Amina, when you ask me for your personal grade, I say "B query". Dull and ungenerous. There is a spark when you chime with a band, or spot a sponsor, and give your spirit to them – otherwise, it's B without the query, I'm afraid. Babak's amused. He loves buffoonery, with him the ring-master. Without his sense of humour, no one would make a court of B-types, loutish *ados*....'

'It's his cosmology,' Amina says. 'This is his point – it's all creation: the repetition, the climbing up glass walls like newborn bugs, and sliding down again, and being killed, little unique things, without a name, you and me, an unknown species with no reason to have lived, except to fill a space in sequences of arbitrariness – rungs in a ladder ....flea circuses, a nullity.'

I say, 'It's trite. And – those can't be bull rings down there – maybe for baseball, or for opera....'

'Should we go back?' Amina asks, quite hopefully.

'They're not called fascists now,' I say. 'They lack enthusiasm. They have to watch the markets. It's a formality, the prejudice, all that.'

'Ghosts, zombies,' says Amina. 'Ghosts love a joke – they spring out and make you fall downstairs – hundreds of you, hundreds of stairs, like Odessa. Or when I found it worked, got sympathy – falling off the stage or collapsing on it, lying inert, then heroic – standing, and being brave. Ectoplastic. A grand old trouper!

'Zombies though – they're different. No sense of humour, none at all.'

'If you're a hegemon, even of a zombie army, what war do you want to fight?' I ask. 'If you're a soldier, what does winning mean to you? Armies are inert, Amina – no invention, no imagination: that's the recommendation...'

Before I can decide – what are we for? offence, defence, parades? – we're back again.

No one has missed us.

*

'We are his soldiers,' says Amina. 'All soldiers wonder about their general – that's their life, present and future. You can forget the past. What matters is what kind of hegemon he, she, is. Does he know strategy, objectives? Does she know you? – that your life is your most, your only, precious thing; that usually life is dull and aimless except for keeping it alive – like a watch that must be shaken constantly to make it tick along ... a life is scrabble, or free choice: consumption of a withered fruit, stuff to be thrown away: or stuff that's never quite, or ever, enough. But – the universal, all its soldiers, has always been hunters and the hunted. We are eternal corporals and sergeants, the PBI, the *soldato semplice,* the *poilu.* The Staff is guys in suits who sit on chairs in rows that I've set out.... Forget them. What matters is the campaign: attack, or digging in.

'It explains the mounds of bodies in their bags: and it explains the flags.'

'It explains my parades,' I say. 'And you, Amina, you are the band, the forces' favourite, entertainer of the troops. I set up the march-past, victory parade: muster the trophies and the captives.... You – are the R and R, before the pub crawl and the brothel. And of course – a soldier's life is dull and trivial – even now, when every bullet has a billet, guaranteed.... You don't need conscience, and if you don't get paid, you steal and loot, you pillage. And in the end, you sometimes get to kill the general.'

'We've been lucky. When we two deserted,' Amina says, 'We didn't see the many doing the same thing they always do: they run. Usually, if there's a few of you, your side just catches you and shoots you, and that's that. Change sides? – it's a gamble....' On she talks.

*

You spur yourself with triteness, these worn tropes. All's war – trade, culture, sex and class, north and south, for thirty years, a hundred years. The world is ending under you in twenty different ways, you thought them up and now you struggle with them, trying to wake, go back to where you were. Still you wear the uniform and do the drills and bull your boots....

You must believe in it because it's so, and if you try to get away from what is true, you're blind in a blind alley, holed up with creatures you've invented.

*

I'm thinking of how to organise a good escape. A reasonable, painless one. I say,

'Amina, we go back, you and I. Back a long way. We're bound together, we are one....'

'I know,' she says. 'Everybody is. We're like the blackbirds – they always sing the same song, and if it changes, it's because another blackbird's changed. We go back, yes: we think that Hindus have a mystic tinge, with their aeons, eras: – but we have scientific ages: stone and iron and bronze .... and then the silver and the gold. When it was gold, we ate caviar and died of syphilis, spoke French in Jaşi, lived in New Caledonia. But if you say as much – they lock you up and tie your arms and legs,' and she laughs. 'Too much sex will make you mad and eat your nose – it's joy, and then you die. It is our classic trip. We humans always sang and danced, buried the dead and spoke in metaphor, and deferred to ghosts.

'We always hunted, waited, temporised, and knelt before the boss, and were complicit in the frauds and massacres. They bring us sacrificial animals to roast, we think we're safe when gods applaud. But priests and seers – they're killed the first. Those slaughtered beasts are all the butchers' meat you get: the tenderloin from sacrifices. Everybody envies you, and wants revenge.'

We laugh. It isn't humorous.

'The place that's hard to cross – must be the frontier,' I say. 'We should find somewhere we're less likely to be caught.'

'Babak might turn against us, but we'd live,' she says. 'We'll each accuse the other ... Or there might be a coup: for us, that's worse.'

The choice is being accomplices or renegades, traitors or spies.

We leave it there.

*

Intimate friendships – those are the dangerous ones, where confidences make you vulnerable. They're typical of decadence. It's weakness, shuffling off the fear and the responsibility: looking for comfort. This regime started original. One person, recuiting others, pointing them in a direction ... and now it's just another one that lasts and lasts, and twists and sloughs its skins and underneath the new one is the same, same colours and same length as what has been grown out of, and cast.

*

My friend, a chamberlain, an upper servant serving as a counsellor, or turn and turn; always a servant: – my friend and confident, Yoann ... fascinated by the ceremonies, what he thinks must be the art, the arts, the culture. Culture for him – is sitting quiet. Here – it used to be just treachery and bullying, and making bucks and sounding tough. Now – it's a canapé ... where to line the chairs and pin the medals.

I say, 'Amina suffers for her intellect. It's bigger than what she knows or needs to know. I'm something fraudulent – I remember what I read in books: most people don't... So, I repeat, with flourishes. Superficial. It passes off as genius. It's a decadence.

'Amina – what she does is artistry, but she's convinced: she'll never be an artist.'

'Amina isn't that at all,' says Yoann. 'Not like you think. I hear a different story....'

I cling to my idea about her, and the role that it assigns me.

'We have to ask,' he says, 'since democrats don't ask at all: after democracy, what next? More democracy? No, that's not the move, the answer, that the game requires. And if we ask – after our despotism, what comes next – democracy? Perhaps: and after that? What next? You see, Parviz – we cut the problem down to time. For democrats – it's terms. They're canonical – four years, two terms maximum. The despots: – it's a human life, long, short, or in wheelchairs. For us, in despotisms, how do we live in this uncertainty – our body teetering, and another's – bigger, stronger, more vulnerable ... standing over us?

'An answer's the wistaria. See how it winds around, and knots, seems ancient when it's in its youth. Love, Parviz: 'love', that is.... What lovers do. Wistaria. A family is a treasure here – but it's a prison. Lovers – they don't pull you down, like fathers do. It's flesh, it's foibles, arms and legs – no blood's involved. Amina's arms ... see how they twine, Parviz, and grow, and twist around the bamboos supposed to hold them up. You were her prop, Parviz – and now she's grown up, out of your sight, you don't bear her weight....'

Amina – lovers, gossip, intrigues and factions?

Yoann's my friend, he is agreeable. I don't believe him, not at all. Love is his illusion, it's 'courtly love', here in our court. Titillation, provocation, trysts, obsession.

The system runs on cash and favours, just like all the rest. It doesn't need be called capitalism – cash and favours is enough to build it, prop it, and bring the world to boiling dry around us.

'Just watch Amina,' says Yoann. 'Don't try to theorise. Remember you used to be much more intelligent – think what you could have done at eighteen if you'd not been thinking about sex.'

*

Who? Who whom, Amina? Who's on your side? Not a groom, an ostler, a horsey knight – nothing vulgar, and nothing physical... Who do you love, if it's not me?

*

'Yoann,' I ask. 'Do we have slavery? And camps? Perhaps they're universal. I've never seen them, but I've never looked. I know this is a business, and we must compete with friends and enemies around the globe. We always need new clothes and stuff. At least the pants and socks are nearly free.... When it all falls, when people can't make money from how it is – who'd represent me?'

'Everybody asks that,' says Yoann. 'It isn't difficult. Rich countries – they have parliaments, so do the poor ones.'

'Force is the midwife, Yoann,' I say.

'Words and things,' says Yoann, waving me towards the panorama – green and yellow, tranquillity, a bird placed on its own patch, singing its ancestral song.... 'The corporation's magic. Dig a hole – and out comes cash. Let's stick to words, let the unfortunate deal with things.'

'If there's a camp,' I say, joshing him along, 'Even if Babak set it up, the day I'm out is still more joyful than the day I'm in.'

We laugh.

'Some places,' Yoann says. 'They make the cons, the lifers, stamp out license plates. Now, that's a torment – all those journeys they won't make. Slaves – they get sent here to work for us. It's not so bad....'

'We have a difficulty, Yoann,' I say. 'Amina's a native, but she's a foreigner too.... She can't sing the local stuff – and I am worse. Born nowhere, everywhere a stranger, protected only by my non-existence....'

There's nothing to be said.

Yoann says, 'You must tough it out, Parviz – that's been the culture here.'

*

'The story going round, Amina,' I tell her, cautiously, 'is, you're in a fronde. I know that's useful. Even so....'

'Oh Parviz,' Amina says, laughing. 'That you are in a fronde is widely known. Impresarios – they always are a fronde – it's old as melodrama and the claque. A dutch auction, trading in flesh. It is your trade – it's of no consequence. Babak's people – all were dancers, like him, in the troupe. Now, it's just dressing up – the frogging and the osprey plumes ... all dance ... and family, the bastards too ... all branches on the tree – it all goes back to primal tents, the groves – thronging with dates and assignations....'

'You make it sound an idyll, but, Amina, you must hold tight to your independence, to your little liberating voice,' I say. 'Think! A hundred years ago – those marriages! the snuff, the mustache wax, your wifely task, to varnish his teak spare legs....'

'You should never varnish teak,' Amina says, quite overwhelmed. 'Aside from slavery, there were expeditions, little wars, continents subjugated and painted over, the standard shade.... Remember the spats, the blanco – oh Parviz, must I go back ... however many generations?'

'No problem, Amina,' I say. 'We're talking universes, and this one's got much bigger since we came back here.'

'You could be a help, Parviz,' she says. 'I'll grasp the universe, but you, instead of empty ceremonies, think ritual. Ceremonies come from dance. Rituals place us, and everything, in an order.'

'Help me, Amina,' I say.

'Help me, Parviz, if you can,' Amina says.

*

'My fronde,' Amina says, grinning as she says the word. 'Has relatives and men of science. The cousins – men of faith. The scientists – men of hope. The other frondes – there's not a dancer close to them. They don't grasp how things work here....'

'Now – no fighting!' Yoann says. 'A war will throw things down. And if you leave, what will you do?'

'There's lots of science here,' Amina says. 'It doesn't help my act. Doctors and rockets – I'm a refugee, Yoann, this modern stuff – it doesn't help at all. I'm for travel, not for settlement.'

'They say your trade goes down all over,' Yoann says. 'Songs. Titillation. If you go somewhere much more modernised – you could be an expert on us here. Sell things too.'

'There isn't much that can attract,' she says. 'There's that sort of lokum, with the prickles in. I don't even know its name.'

'Dig!' says Yoann. 'Find the roots. Travel! We, the court, go everywhere.... Love us, hate us – mostly there's fighting, places rich or poor, we don't take sides. It's transition: if you look around, there's a new centre. Ah, China! They're cool flames. They burn and they are not consumed. We're glued here, but one day we'll be unstuck....'

'Some people came and took away my shoes,' says Amina, starting to shake and cry. 'I can guess what it might mean....'

'It's Security,' Yoann says. 'A sign you're not to leave – but the only course for you, is – Go! You're not a stable element. That's good, that's very good – but if they take your document and you can't leave ... the message is: get out!'

'I never understand a paradox,' Amina says, brightening, 'But understanding isn't necessary. It isn't what you can, it's what you must.'

'Exactly so,' Yoann says. 'Whatever confronts you – you must make poetry from it. If necessary a hundred thousand lines. What matters is – your heart. You must know those lines by heart.'

'Shoes, Youann,' Amina shouts. 'My shoes!'

'I stand by my advice,' says Yoann, quite suave. 'When we were young, the movies told us who the bad guys were. Who they had been. Everybody tortures and assassinates. Fights wars you see and those you don't, has – is – a proxy, fights wars you never know there were, stands back and let it happen – torture, assassinations, makes what kills and makes the tents for whoever's left. It's like they say – there's rich and poor, there's us, our side. You don't need an agent, a fixer, to explain all that.'

'We all have one or more of those,' she says. 'Without it, we should starve. and many do.'

'Once,' says Yoann, irritated, 'There were cities everywhere. Then the deserts came, the nomads took over, and everywhere became sand, scrub over-grazed, abandoned.... Now, there's nomads everywhere, like you, Amina. Of course, there's poor souls, like Parviz, but mostly they're ambitious, nomads on the make, the march. Tourists at first, then they are settlers.'

'We always thought of you, Yoann, as a poor soul,' she says.

It doesn't matter. 'I live in the court,' he says. 'Not in these cities,' and he holds his throat, puts out a purplish tongue: 'Quite unlivable....'

'Shoes,' says Amina. 'And I'll be off. No horse. I'll leave everything as it was.'

Yoann does a pirouette: 'I'm back,' he says, 'into dance. And Parviz?'

‘Oh,’ says Amina, losing patience, ‘everybody’s into culture now. Solo acts, putting the beat into old stuff. Parviz has turned to mental rehab, confessed his scepticism, earning benevolence from the great. Acquired a kit of drums.’

Yoann twirls on. ‘It’s dangerous to have a friend,’ he says. ‘People are vindictive and perfidious. Parviz – such imprudence! And all these statues! And parades! Everywhere is mobilised.

‘Remember Erbil – a magnificent city – the new astride the old, as it should be.... The latest is sat firmly on what was the head, head on head – a totem, the walls surge higher, ever higher.... A pueblo, citadel, Jerusalem and Mecca – bound into one heap, as they should be.’

‘It’s all the dance,’ she says. ‘It’s hard to grasp – it’s all more folksy, yet it’s all more complicated: invented. And business and security, Yoann – they’re one.... Selling plastic stuff – it’s a skirmishing, a tussle to the death.... And – what do I have to sell, and is it worth a mortal thrust?’

‘Don’t bother to tell anyone about the city,’ Yoann says. ‘I drop in Erbil as a bait. It’s a place that lots of us don’t go – although it’s true: it’s quite magnificent. But – don’t trouble security with my gossip – I am security. Don’t try to sell me. *I* sell contacts, influence, and info – but I don’t take cash. I’m into options. And the dance – what do we want from it? To go far far back, to when we were just bodies. Bodies in the garden: we rejoiced. All the rest is building on the primal scene, the ur, the “what we were” and “what we want to be”. All colours, like a water-colour paint-box, all gets mixed and ends up brown. All religions – back to the boom-box strictures of that old zoo-keeper – that bodger! Supreme improviser....’

‘Parviz, then,’ Amina presses on, ‘was just a trader, selling me?’

‘We knew that,’ Yoann says. ‘If he could, he puffed you up. But – lustre fades. We all start geniuses, but as we age, we stumble, we slip off the glitter ball.... The young must infiltrate the foutons of the old ... us whiteys must make compromise....’

'You're not at all a whitey, Yoann,' she says, chucking him under his multifolded chin: 'Unvarnished teak, I'd say.'

'We could have cities of different kinds,' he says, not listening. 'Cities where you want to stay, cities where you want to leave....'

'And cities where you can't get in,' Amina says. 'And I could provide security against Security, Yoann.'

'Or – stupidity against Intelligence,' he says, quite sharp. 'No, Amina, dance, dance little lady, just dance. Or sing. God's mother taught Him how to love, and she was black, original. But reflect, Amina. The mother of God is God. Her mother....'

'I love you, Yoann,' Amina says. 'But enough of motherhood. Wherever I can stay, I'll keep chickens. Eggs and plump thighs, Yoann – that's what keeps a species going.'

'The circle, Amina,' says Yoann. 'Never interrupted. After Babak – another, more, Babak: more, or less. After war – the peace: sleep and waking, sleep again. City on city, chickens, eggs, and chickens.'

*

Amina thinks – I don't believe in this at all. 'Do not preserve things intended to be smashed,' create to destroy; don't think continuity, or you'll wish for horror after horror. Not evolution, but metamorphosis. There's movement, to and fro, rest and flux, then rest. Make the bowl so it will be broken, smoke the joint and throw away the ash, eat the food and clean the table, live so you can die. Someone else will come, perhaps. The earth is born in water, fire will clear it all away. It's good.

Sacrifice; more will be born.

She doesn't tell this to Yoann. There is no sequence, no low to high, no vice versa. Time happens, it always has, there is no cause, no other cause: – Chaahk, lightning, that's what shamans need: lightning in the blood. The divine leg, electric, charged and stamping – flash! the energy – the god throws the thunderbolt, you leap and babble, you hallucinate: – and then it's gone. No trace.

The song comes out, that's that, it's over, it has no store, it's in no place. Then – out it comes again: no cause, no sequence. We can't live in science, it's around us, but not in us, and we're not it: we live in our design which is the shape we see in us, our world, the body, the universe. Mathematics tell us when the world will end, and we're indifferent. It's reason – something we don't invent, quite alien to us, to our finitude.

Signs and designs, and we are born to die.... It's comforting. It's frightening. It's good, she thinks.

Domitilla, travel agent

'Dear Amina,' Domitilla says. 'I didn't know there was a country where you've come from. You seem – well, quite like me.'

'Do you mean a country with a name?' Amina asks. 'Or that there's not room on your map for mine?'

'I only have a little map,' says Domitilla, tying her foulard tight around her head, like a bandana. 'Enough to get me home – though my home's not on the map.'

'You could get a dog,' Amina says. 'They don't have maps, but love to go back home.'

This goes nowhere, though it seems logical. 'Your country,' Domitilla carries on. 'I hear it's blown clean by the winds – the pointed mountains, like starched sheets or napkins – but of course, we're all dirty beasts, like dogs, when it comes to it. Proud and perfidious.'

'Oh, those are proxies,' says Amina. 'Soldiers are sent in to spruce them up, and soldiers are sent out: wars and humane missions, and then there's fighters – some who go, and some who stay, terrorists of different hues.... Proxies who fund proxies.... There's lots of people put into the "fridge"....'

Domitilla signals with her eyebrow that she'd like to hear some more: good explanations, or she gets bewildered.

'It's an isolating place – like a fish tank,' Amina says. 'There's a joke that goes the rounds – that people are sent there, they crawl around like *écrevisses*, and then the jailers come when they are cooked and bright, and bite the heads off.' She pauses. 'They're very red, the *écrevisses....*'

'It isn't how I know the world,' says Domitilla. 'People are so taxing. They run like ants. What can we do? – shut them up, or have them rampage in the streets, or have them plot – one thinks of Ravachol, Peter the Painter.... I wonder what his canvases fetch now?'

'We toy with all those sides,' Amina says. 'At least, we think we do, but really it's quite clear, it's best that others take the risks. We're rubbery. You adapt. So, you see – I don't believe in futures. One day it all will end, we might be there, or maybe not, but you and I'll for sure probably be gone ... and so....' She lets her voice, her little voice, trail off, she widens her big eyes, and Domitilla says,

'A little voice, like yours, Amina – it's quite in fashion now. You need an agent – or a person that protects.'

Amina laughs – 'Oh, I'd an agent: Parviz. He's in the fridge, or maybe honoured internationally. And an old guy, Yoann, a pluralist – he keeps a dossier on everyone and their cosmology....'

'It sounds an inconclusive kind of place,' says Domitilla. 'Like a book without a plot: with an occasional narrator.'

'You learn to navigate,' Amina says. 'You aren't allowed to keep a dog in town, so you must draw your map yourself.'

'It seems to me,' says Domitilla, 'you think some wars will never end, some hills, streets, cities – last for ever, whatever carnage they must bear, there's no way, no reason, that they end....'

'Oh yes,' Amina says, 'I'm convinced. Some impresarios will never have a client. Some chamberlains will draw up dossiers on everyone they meet.'

'I think I know all this,' says Domitilla. 'It's not the history we did at school. That always ended well....'

'We could try separating,' says Amina. 'Each population, all the different partisans: staying a country in the atlas, all grouplets autonomous ... though there's not many each of us could live with. Or then again – everybody could escape. There's horses, natch, but they are difficult. I had a coachman, but you go nowhere without a coach to match....'

'And a map,' says Domitilla, unconcerned, frustrated even. 'And so we're back at the start once more.... This tearoom – would you call it fashionable?'

'Ah,' says Amina. 'Fashion! We're back into my songs – what I couldn't do, the folklore, things that pleased the president. He'd been a dancer till he stuffed and boozed. It made him human, some would say more *sympa*, though those terms are not the same. Parviz, my ex-agent, when he started drumming, he drummed dirty – rimshots and dropping sticks, setting skins alight. It wasn't fashionable to be a snob, but taste was much fragmented: say you were a Darmstadt fan, the furs would fly....'

'I meant something quite different,' says Domitilla. 'This place, run by Madame Hong – it's not in line with tax and rights, there's cockroaches, I hear; if you come here at night, switch on the light – it's Matisse! *La danse!* And yet they say this here's the favourite haunt – for the supreme crust, the cream: pouring the finest gunpowder or lapsang ... to the new and fresh. But my! how they're dull and ignorant.'

'Don't mix fashion up with taste,' Amina says. 'Fashion is dead leaves dropping on the forest floor. Beneath, though, there's networks, meshes of roots that power up all kinds of toadstool, agaric or puffball – some will kill you, others make symphonic stews ... and that is taste.'

Domitilla leans forward, excited: 'I've got you, Amina!' she says, delighted. 'You're into systems! No start, no end, no purpose outside themselves.' Amina sees how Domitilla, leaning forward, wears a vest. 'Domitilla Palegreen' the label says, like in the fifth form, and Amina sees right down to her old friend's breasts, light freckles, flecked like tapioca pudding ... soft, grainy – texture acquired by bathing nude, or undergoing infraviolet treatment, on a bunk ... accompanied.

'You must do something with yourself, my dear,' says Domitilla, pulling close her underwear and leaning back. 'Walking down the street's becoming difficult – imagine singing to a country! Especially yours....'

'It's a throwback,' says Amina, remembering, crying; wiping her wet nose on her shawl, leaving a snail's trail, silver and straight.... 'Babak wouldn't let us make those spicy gingerbreads, effigies like himself, his belly like a cauldron.... Tradition. So much fun...!'

'They decreed like that,' says Domitilla, trying to ignore her friend's distress. 'In the Enlightenment. *Noblesse oblige.* What a hard life you've had, my love.'

*

Outside, there's a crackling, *tric tracs, cipolle, petardi*, stun-grenades, compressed-air hooters, a rushing to and fro.

'That is my cause, or one of them,' says Domitilla. 'A big manif. I fear – I confess – I don't join in, save with the spirit. I'm afraid of being hit!' And she pulls a mournful face.

'It's causes here,' Amina says. 'Back there – it's the elections. Joy and contestation. The rules decree – it's elections, fixed and bent.'

'Ladies,' says Madame Hong. 'Pay the bill, then wait until it quietens down outside.'

Domitilla pays. Madame Hong swats at a roach: 'I'm clean as the sea,' says Madame Hong, 'Those fucking beetles are just natural. I despair....'

'My partner disinfests,' says Domitilla. 'We're both for clean environments.'

'Oh, it'll take much more than that,' says Madame Hong, despairing.

'I'll find employment,' says Amina, suddenly decided. 'I shall tell the truth, about whatever I feel like.'

*

They climb a mountain of stairs to sleep – the elevators are being disinfected. In the morning, the pair watch the exercises – so many people, wavering, bending, waving invisible ribbons. They are flames.

Domitilla's partner? Not in sight.

'The blossom,' Domitilla says. 'They're remembering the blossom. Poor dears.'

'You don't exercise, Domitilla,' says Amina. 'It would make you clean.'

'It's a battle,' Domitilla says. 'But the sparrows have come back – look!'

It's true. Not what Amina means by truth, but all the same.... 'I could do what you do, Domitilla,' Amina says. 'The job.'

'Exactly,' Domitilla says. 'Anybody could. That's why I don't want you to, my dear.'

She sells tickets – everybody feels they'd like to see where Domitilla comes from. Not so sure about Amina.

'I like to see policemen wearing those white gloves,' Amina says. 'There's an aspiration to be clean.'

'You don't have the right documents, Amina,' Domitilla says. 'You could end up anywhere. Even nowhere.'

*

'I have a tiny problem, Domitilla,' says Amina. 'Parviz – when he was my agent, we signed a document that says I'm under contract with him for all time, and all my earnings too.... It's more a father-daughter thing, you see....'

'Oh that's quite void,' says Domitilla, wanting her friend to find her feet and leave on them.... 'No one will honour that.'

'That's reassuring, Domitilla,' says Amina. 'As the contract's registered in every country and whatever happens – it's good for when the world ends, and if we travel to another world, and then another, on and on....'

'Well, yes,' says Domitilla, thinking of how the universe gives endless possibilities for ticket sales, and she could run an office where they serve madeleines and vol-au-vents for tea.... And not have to say to Comrade Chu, 'Yes, it's a system, sending people here and there, it's hygiene, fertilising, like nightsoil disposal, nothing to do with civilisations and comparing except it makes the people come back refreshed, exhausted, frustrated and bewildered too, and keen to be at home. System, comrade, nothing more.'

'You mean, I can buy out of the contract, Domitilla?' Amina asks, quite eagerly. 'Except I have no money, but I still have my little voice and shimmery clothes....'

Neither knows what's next. Best to keep quiet, and hope time drags its harrow over every word sworn and personality pledged, like breaking up mosaics with the prongs, making new furrows for new kinds of seed, or setting straight lines in older faces, more mature; brains blotted and forgetful....

'Of course,' says Amina. 'If Parviz is in jail, the contract's void. For extremism, or by mistake; or by association, or for the question of his passport. Who he is, or was.'

'Don't get obsessed,' says Domitilla, irritated and at a loss. 'In the face of great injustices, people are induced to be, well – unjust. Of course, you can't believe in guilt, Amina, from what you say. For you, there's no sequence of intent and consequences, no law to break – even if you're justified. I'm not sure there's an answer to that one: no right, no over-riding right to defend, nor to be insane, excused. Provocation and retaliation ... they happen. The thing is, to be on the side that wins, like here .... Not that you know at once who you should back – especially when you're foreign, amid foreigners. And of course, there's what your agent is .... The rituals.'

'He is a drummer now,' Amina says.

'I meant, the hold he has on you,' says Domitilla.

'Mostly they don't have a trial,' Amina says. 'Old habits – they're worn out. Some places, some cities, have been so destroyed, the rubble's higher than the buildings were. They cart the dead off with the landfill: – the cement is made of desert sand, that doesn't stick like seaside sand....'

'You could try real estate, Amina,' Domitilla says. 'Construction. But there've been bankruptcies. It's hit or miss, like singing songs. You'd need an office, but you don't have cash....'

They look at each other, forced into silence.

'Americans come here, but you can't get in over there,' says Domitilla. 'They have to be so careful, just like here. And you're so complicated.... Your documents, I mean.'

*

I want a place that is predictable, even if it's tough, Amina thinks. Places resemble each other, like people: the people Domitilla fears may hit her. Many things become the same all over – the buses and the food.... You'd never know the diff.... And Domitilla's right. You can be hit anywhere at all, or worse. But even if I find a tranquil place, predictable – all the rest is unpredictable. People especially. A place without people, now – it wouldn't be a place, it would be a fiction, like the love that travels on my little voice – '*Voix de notre désespoir Le rossignol chantera....*'

'You should go back and have it out with Parviz,' Domitilla says. 'It's the only way.'

'I'll settle somewhere,' Amina says. 'Not here, not in the centre where there's everything, but a place distracted – those rural towns where it's tranquil, boring, and there's goats and chickens in the cellars.

'And we wait for it all to end. It will come; the conscription; the trucks; prophets and ambassadors tearing up the stony roads. Eternity chopped, and changed.'

*

'You don't need go there, Amina,' says Domitilla. 'You can call Parviz. On the phone. We're fortunate – with our network, you don't need go anywhere. It's in your pocket.'

'You're right,' Amina says. 'And you should mean more than you say. When we leave the land, or when we're driven off it – we're animals no more. We're something different. Unnatural. No habitat. So many people have swarmed here, so eager to be that something different. Except, in the end, there is a paradox: we'll be the only ones who're left. The land will be ours alone.'

'What did Parviz say?' asks Domitilla. 'Don't go through these wrenching tales of yours: it's not the time. I think you're over-sentimental. You like the prickle of nostalgia. It's not decent to be post-colonial, and think "recessional", and so you shift the scene and empty it. It's the same sentiment, you know. Lost empires and lost lands. Regained – the savour's lost.'

'Parviz said he'd stick to what we had agreed,' Amina says, not listening. 'But I can think again, and so will he. What's his is mine, and mine is his. And he has nothing. For myself, I'm optimistic....'

'It's all ridiculous,' says Domitilla. 'But at least you know now how things stand.'

Working the land is terrible, Amina thinks. Maybe the herders, nomads – eating, drinking, wearing your animals – it's acceptable – but the rest! ... rice-paddies, ditching, winters, rain, the ox-plough ... blight ... the fief, rackrent, land-registers, and *corvées* infinite: the clearances....

'Your partner, Domitilla?' Amina asks.

'Oh, it's not sex,' says Domitilla. 'Maybe you need that, but it's so ephemeral.... We want to denounce our Comrade Chu and run the agency ourselves – she's "partner" in a business sense. And you, Amina: trail your cloak for Parviz, have a fling with Babak – think of them as sturgeons. Don't try to eat the flesh, scoop out the black gold in their guts....'

'I get a rash from caviar,' Amina says. 'But – I could do business like you do. It cancels out the landscape, that's for sure, but it's the way to find a space.'

'You're missing out on quality, Amina,' Domitilla says. 'You've no family, you're not in love, you don't like anybody much, your songs were written by old guys long ago – and you're in legal mire. The artistic world would not admit you – you're a monster. I know what you and I should be: we'll never get there. Will anyone? I send the groups to Paris to find romance, but they're in clumps of sixty, counted every hour....'

'Paris is vinegar,' Amina says. 'The kind that smells of sulphur.'

'There's too many emotions in the air,' says Domitilla, stamping Amina's ticket with a home-made exit visa. 'You can't enter in them all. It's enough you've seen people twisting, snared in them....'

'Enough? Enough for what?' Amina asks, intrigued.

'Enough to be equipped. Like a vaccine that brings you gripes for days, and glad you didn't die,' says Domitilla, kissing Amina goodbye.

*

'The blossom will be out,' Amina says. 'Then it will fall, and for months the trees will be bare. You ought to leave, like I did. We could sort things out. Maybe like before, Parviz ... though with more equity....'

'There's never a before,' I say. 'You can't remember it, still less have it reproduced. It's not a good to time get out here: it could go either way: the same,or worse. My job got bigger. Easier in a way, but quite beyond me. And so I lost it. There's generals who set up the parades now – I didn't know what all those soldiers do, or what those tanks and things are for. Why do they celebrate with missiles anyway? It's a sign that someone will retaliate. It's quite perverse.'

'You should re-write our contract,' says Amina. 'It isn't valid. Neither of us profits if it's dud.'

'So it makes no difference if we leave it as it is,' I say. 'Unless you think I'm trying to cheat you. But you don't earn, Amina. Why do you doubt me?'

'How is you new activity?' she says. 'Parviz the drummer....' and she laughs.

'Drumming,' I say. 'It was the way you talked, communicated. What they talked about has long long gone. Drums were a language binding us. Now, it doesn't mean a thing ... the noisiest way of being silent. At times you riff, frustration without words: mostly, you keep the beat for stuff that's in 4/4. Who cannot understand? It ridicules our history, the species doesn't need to hear a beat, another one.... For me, it's irony: we regress. We cling to a grey noise. It has nothing to say: like train wheels, or jet engines. Passing time; and time is space and space is distance that you can't enjoy, you cannot stop in space or it becomes quite something else, and more expensive too.'

Where is she? Maybe she's already here, I think, quite fearfully.

'I'm in transit, Parviz,' says Amina. She cries. 'My ticket's stamped, my passport couldn't be, because I don't have an exit visa from where we were, I was, before. I can leave where I've just been, perhaps. Indeed, I have, I have to, but I couldn't leave where I had been before. I can't go back to anywhere I left illegally, of course. Even my passport: without stamps – it isn't worth a bean.'

'Then start again,' I say. It's clear.

I think: she can go where she can't want to be.

'I can't do anything about our document,' I say. 'The contract's good until I say it's not. A minute's work, for sure! But wait! You might tour everywhere – your little voice is fashionable. It could be magnified to fill a continent. Small things have taken over once again, we hunt and gather in small bands: like chimps – we do not share our food. I am your friend, a lover too. Something, quite small, is owed to me.'

I'm desperate – things may get worse here. If they stay the same, that is already worse.

'Come back, Amina, ask for dispensations from our chief, our Babak,' I say. 'Remember, though, my music, yours – it doesn't go down well, not now. My theory is, the future's ours: the music must be national – crossing-over from the regions: with an electronic beat. It's a hybrid, a dragon on wheels, that cannot fly, with snot like candy-floss.'

'I'll put some lyrics to it,' says Amina. 'But no one will carry me. Not even to the dragon's nest.'

We laugh. We're comrades, mates.

'Your music, your politics – is there some principle?' she asks. 'As an artist, you're not getting far. Like art, the despotism you are in is arbitrary. It's with you always, not just when you pick up your sticks....'

'Those are different kind of principle,' I say. 'Though how many kinds there are – I'm rather vague. Maybe I should leave it to the personal. Free will? Though you will say that's where all principles must lie.'

'I don't have a principle,' Amina says. 'I'm worse placed than you. I speak freely on my little telephone to you, but I am stuck. It's a right, to move. Maybe that's a principle, though what I do about it, I'm not sure. There is the law – but just a little law, it seems, that circumscribes the rights that I may have....'

'It's natural justice. To move, to appeal a law, to have your reasons reasonably expressed, and not be persecuted for them,' I suggest. 'That's universal. That's for sure.'

'Your contract, Parviz. It binds me – and you – in unjust ways,' she says.

'I take your points, Amina, and I stand by mine,' I say. 'Some are trite. If we forget about the principles, would everything be the same? Maybe anyway – we have nothing, like when we're born.

'It's like they say – regimes degenerate. What does that entail? The fridge? I'll put all this to Babak. I know, Amina – dangerous friends! Friendly enemies. Babak gets lonely, he's too old for dancing. He'll never be a warrior again – he's delicate about himself. He mocks the generals, all that – he thinks they're thugs. They've taken over from him. They'll keep the show going if he doesn't make it....'

'Dying?' she asks.

'We're like that,' I say. 'It's to be kept in mind.'

'You're faint, Parviz,' she says. 'You come and go. It can't just be the line....'

'You're perched on the judgement seat, Amina,' I say. 'I'm passionate for you and your plight – but you're not in the game. You have to buy cards here – you want them free and not to pay your losses. And I'm the *maquisard*, not you. You're the singer in exile, and I'm here! Fixed. I protect myself. It's my adventure, my big mistake, my crime. I'm cleverer than Babak, he's on the slide, I'm watching him go down, I'm riding on his shoulders, ready to jump off and be anonymous. And you're my only client, Amina. Today, no one likes your music, your little voice, the international style. I love what you might do, and you can't do it if I'm not there. There's a glue sticks us together....'

'Nonsense!' she says. 'You're too late. You're a deluded patsy. You think you're a bully, alongside the assassins and the fixers. Instead – you don't count, and no one counts you. When it all changes – how will you go on, the new world, and you're a dinosaur? Dinos don't have masters, don't need ceremonies. Even if you've survived the fire – the fire will come for everyone.

'And money, Parviz – watch the money, not the cards! Cash is what they're taking from the table. You've no idea, Parviz. You enjoy corrupting yourself. You're rotten, and you've come to like the smell....'

'Well,' I say. 'I've said my part. You could have saved the cost of calling me, Amina.' And I hang up on her.

Earth

Silvain's scenario and dig; Svenja: agent; Damien: critic; Jamela: executive and lover; and extras.

'I have clients, geniuses, whose talent and fame would make you foam with jealousy,' says Svenja. 'You're all alike, of course. Authors: would-be and shouldn't be ... loved and lost ... just lost. You think you're liberals because you don't believe in killing rivals: you're indifferent to people like yourself. You can't wish them harm – you'd be wishing harm on to yourself. You care still less about anyone who's not a rival, not competing with you, not having anything that you can steal.

'Only the rich, the patrons, buyers – they attract and fascinate. You hate, despise, them if they don't bankroll you.'

'My work has legs,' says Silvain. 'It strides away without you, or anyone.'

'Now, instead of sex and madness, or family eccentricity, you want to write about philosophy!' she says, ignoring him. 'You ought not. You think you are a communist, and that it is a higher state. You're wrong. You see the flaws in liberalism, the narcissism, acceptance of inequality and suffering. That pretends we're all the fittest and strongest: let those who really are, stick it to the rest. And so, it dresses up despotism in scarlet robes and judges' wigs. There's not much philosophy in that.'

'If there's disaster, and there might be an answer to it – you can't expect soft paw remedies from me,' he says.

'If you don't want the despotic version, there's the anarchic, and the libertarian,' Svenja goes on, not listening. 'The despotism of peers. Of everybody against each.

'Liberals start from the individual, then trip over the other people – there's no way forward. The communists start from societies. Society is a bundle of wet sticks. It's a false opposition: we are individuals in societies. The century when philosophy came to an end got stuck between these premises. We've not moved on. Perhaps a communism will save the world. A reprieve. It's temporary: the suicidal urge ... beneath the dream of perfection, of immortality, of everlasting profit – there's the saviour's sacrifice, the illusion of omnipotence.'

'You should write it down,' says Silvain. 'See if it makes sense.'

'So, what are you inventing now, Silvain?' asks Svenja, quite amused. Silvain is lively, quite affable when he's drawn away from money questions.

'What binds people,' he says. 'I have in mind two young, youngish types – know everything, have experienced all life has, their own and others. What keeps them together? Not sex – the more you have, the more it is anonymous. The less you have, the less its hold. It wouldn't be a moral tale, but a tale with a moral. Quite against the current. Not naive, not worldly-wise – but puzzled. Mature.'

'What's the moral?' Svenja asks.

'Lies are stronger than the truth,' he says. 'I have in mind something like the best of Truffaut, the worst of Godard.'

'The new wave?' she asks. 'I wasn't born then. You're a film buff – you're a throwback. What binds characters? The plot. Even a cadaver. Wise people who're naive, and are driven apart by some intruder even more naive.... Serious spoofs made by far-out perverted people who can't hold their drink.'

'That's not it,' says Silvain. 'I'm serious. Our life, our species, everyone, flirts with being separate; free will, the individual. But really, that way we would die. We're social.

'Perhaps I'd set it in the States – Americans have that awful history – militias and terrorists, private armies, gangs and mafias, the war of all against all ... but it's completely social. A *noir*, dystopic. The destructive mode. Genocide. Yet people flock to get in there and live bad, real bad....'

'I'm sure you think these themes are new, because you've just come round to seeing them,' she says. 'But I'm here to be honest with you. I have to truck your stuff around to monsters, get them to feed on it. Your ideas – are worn thin, tired. Giving them an intellectual spin makes them sound antique. Stick to your love story.'

'Love is the sign the pirate ships sail under,' Silvain says. 'It doesn't mean a thing. Better, it's a travesty, a false flag.'

'If you mean, between people, lies and truth are meaningless, I'm with you,' Svenja says. 'If there was meaning there, we'd not be where we are, where we've been heading from the start. The bible, the Odyssey – heaven and hell – the theme is classical. "Seek truth, get lies". But your pirates don't come in. The idea of a flag inspiring trust – no one believes in that, not now. Perhaps that is the only sign of hope – that delusion's dead.'

'Let's scrutinise you, Svenja, just a little,' Silvain says, despairing and irritated. 'The politics – it's the snide talk that parents have. They were or aspired to be – bourgeois in a state that didn't favour them.... It needed them, but didn't give them the rewards and space they thought they merited. And so – out come the labels when they've fled – liberals, communists, bureaucrats.... It's infantile. Read history, Svenja, don't just imagine you've experienced it....'

'Do me a synopsis. Show you're serious,' she says, dismissing him....

*

Fuck it, he thinks. More unpaid work and insults, working for Svenja, my own future as a slave to unknown cynics, purblind, frivolous. *Neinsagers* and indifferents – readers who don't read.

Filmakers who need a hundred hands to film a simple tale....

'I'm postponing everything, Jamela,' Silvain says.

Bed with Jamela should be good; probably it gets boring when you're slept right out.... She wants more of me, he thinks, because what she has is not worthwhile....

Every end must have a beginning, Silvain thinks: it's ancestors who give you pessimism and frigidity – there must have been a first cause for it.

'I strongly advise against you reacting,' Svenja said. 'There's readers leaving messages. Don't respond – it's depressing, and they may want cash, or selling you ideas.'

*

If you're an artist, you must be interested in everything ... your nose must capture every smell, yours too – if someone leads you down a tricky track by it, your nose – go with it! it's your profession.

Listen! Listen to these characters, their precious talk, their airs. They're nothings, nobodies, how they repeat.... But – they have plans, they try, they take the bus, go to inhospitable places. Most people don't, just read about it, do nothing. Are not interesting.

*

'You're interesting,' Damien says. 'You know so much and don't expose yourself. How to smuggle, how to corrupt the cops, how to leak and launder stolen stuff in auctions, how to find and how to hide.... How to mediate, how to start wars....'

'I'm a writer, I must know everything,' Silvain says.

'I'm curious,' Damien says. 'I'd like to know how to do these things – it's the detail that you don't set out....'

'You could be anyone,' says Silvain. 'Tax, cops or rebels. I wouldn't trust you, whatever you might be.'

'Oh, I'm a fan,' says Damien. 'I'm sure you could go further down your road, elaborate a little .... Help me – us – feel involved. There's aways sequels, when you have a brand – the name's enough to cement you into history....'

'I'm not sure,' says Silvain. 'I thought a lot about the book....'

'Well, surely you didn't just jot down about the fiddling, the crime, the going free. The being free,' says Damien.

'You have it,' Silvain says. 'It's about freedom. If it has a price, like they say, what that might be, if it's worth what it takes. What it is.'

'Give me a title that it's like,' Damien asks. 'Usually there's a betrayal, a comeuppance, turn of the screw. Here, there are no screws!' And he laughs.

'There's no literature, no fiction, like it,' Silvain says. 'I told you, I thought deeply. It's not about shouting, screwing, crying and coming good. It's not about criminals getting away with it, it's about seekers. Philosophers, if you like – not the old type, into their inkpots, but people trying things out....'

'It may not go far,' says Damien, wisely. 'Hard to film, too....'

'It takes hundreds to make a metre of film, and the actors are dumkopfs and need paying their weight in gold,' says Silvain, quite bitterly.

'Your characters commit crimes, but they're not criminals – they want to be free,' says Damien. 'But they cause great suffering. Is a dictator free? Or a president elected? – they cause suffering. They act as if they're free, even if they say they are constrained, somehow indebted to spectral shadows massed and waving banners....'

'That comes in too,' says Silvain. 'But politics has got banal. People want the basics for themselves – then glory. Parades. Rhetoric. I prefer straight fraudsters and crooks, without pretences, who get to feed and clothe themselves; without a contract, laws and rights.'

'That's where we started from,' says Damien, brusquely. 'It's the "how" that interests me.'

'I don't know you,' says Silvain. 'If I had the answer to the "how", why should I share it with you, and not use it for myself?'

'You haven't understood,' says Damien. 'No one reads your stuff. No one, probably, will take the step I have. No one will offer you to try it out – the remedy, the freedom, following your path. You can take whoever you would like, your woman, your editor, anyone you like. And I the same.'

'It was an exercise,' says Silvain, impatient. 'In fact, I don't think this freedom means much at all. There's a something you don't have in jail, impossibility of "getting out". There's fearing arbitrary restraints – a despot who stops you saying what you want, or meeting who.... And stops you, perhaps, dong things you did before, or they do elsewhere, or are stupidly restrictive – but in fact, the universe is bounded by a host of rules, not all understood, and things you cannot do – fly, using your arms and legs like birds, reproducing yourself by thought, visiting the dead, bilocation....'

'This is prevarication,' Damien says. 'The guys you write about have clear and modest thoughts – "free" is for them quite defined, and circumscribed.... Free must be modest, not some right-wing spoof. Things that you were unable to do, and after following your prescribed procedures – you're able now to do. No absolute, Silvain....'

'You miss the point,' says Silvain. 'Though you've said it. People, you say altruistically – do things they want and couldn't do before. But is that being free? Or freer? Let's say it is, but can you add and add to what they have, being more free, come what will – and is that desirable? Does it fit some plan, some natural objective? Animals have terrible lives: they die young, some eaten in the nest, the seasons kill, the hunters too ... food's scarce, the habitat's destroyed, or slowly it erodes ... free? Who is free in this set-up: the ant, the bee? The meteor? "Free" in the universe – does not exist, does not compute at all....'

'Sacred questions,' says Damien. 'But all I want is what your charcacters have – something more desirable at the end than when they start. Call that freedom, if you wish: that's what I want, and can't obtain when things are what they are....'

*

That's what I want, thinks Silvain. And Jamela too. Svenja's too arrogant to say there's anything she wants: she knows too much – so much the worse for her.

'All right,' he says to Damien. 'I'll join you, show you how it's done. But beware, you're simplifying my simplification. I'm flattered by your attention, but you've no idea what I was doing. Do you grasp "taking the result as the path"? A flat design you must enter into? You'd maybe mock, and call it a mandala – but what I invented, is what you read. When you close my book – is it still there? Or is it in your head? My stuff's not clutter – but your brain is blocked, a sink, a sewer, with detritus, every shape of crap.... Remember, I don't do keys, I do doubts and criticisms. That's what you saw. But the design, Damien. That's the centre of it, and you may have missed it, missed entirely....'

'Well,' says Damien. 'I'll be satisfied with something simple.'

'Do you know what you want, Damien?' Silvain asks: 'Really know, and know before you set out to achieve it, knowing that "knowing is having". You should become wholly what I set out for you, which isn't my invention, but a universe, and has no parts, but puts them, the disparities, the contradictions – together....'

'Yes, certainly, of course,' says Damien, interrupting. 'I always start from there.'

*

'It's a big test,' Jamela says, 'to make concrete what you just wrote.... It goes further than you can, I fear. If you fail, these guys, your friends, could do much harm to you. And remember too, a failure means the state will hunt you – be more aggressive if your little band succeeds.... I'll take a chance with you, the first step.... But you are superficial. You say what can't be shown to be a possibility, or even making sense....'

‘It’s fiction,’ Silvain says, much annoyed. ‘That’s how it is. You’re never called on to distinguish true and false, or in between. Fiction’s mostly in-between....’

‘No,’ says Jamela. ‘That’s part of your cover. You’re so prudent – you write like a criminal – afraid of being found out, or sued. Or both. No country, themes not explored, a narrator who wavers, disappears, changes personality and body, sex and age....’

‘Well,’ says Silvain. ‘That may be so. We need to go where no one in particular can be fingered, no one leads, and it’s a country more or less anonymous, but like all countries now has people of all origins, beliefs and architecture. A realism that isn’t fixed – or fixities you can find anywhere, and so don’t fix anything at all.’

‘That’s your way out,’ Jamela says. ‘You never tell the truth. But is there anything that’s real, that’s really what you hide?’

‘Oh,’ Silvain says. ‘There’s cities, and their treasures. The Turkmen have always kept their secret – so have many many others.... Who wants their history dug up and filched, or sent abroad, or turned into a potash mine? There’s animals that quite invert the ideas of evolution – very good they are, they taste of chicken, you’d be foolish if you sent them to a zoo, a lab.... There are beliefs, and passages that lead you to the universe of dead and never lived – how it would upset if ever they were free to roam, to eat and vote, and having died, not be exterminable; confined in camps, not counted in the census.... All these instances, and more, I have in mind. You see, they are in the shadows we create to hide what we want hidden or not exposed, half-way unreal, embarrassments. Those, you don’t need to smuggle through the customs. You can sell them – slaves, antiquities and maps of treasure troves – no one will ask you, no one arrest you for what does not exist, is ephemeral.... There’s millions who believe in things that clearly don’t exist – it isn’t hard to think that hidden things are not believed in, but ... there they are, and you still don’t see them or believe in them....’

'Maybe,' Jamela says. 'But that's just monetised. It's stuff that shouldn't be, and that you sell. It doesn't make you free, it makes you rich.'

'Or round about,' Silvain says. 'Perhaps it doesn't make you rich, it makes you free. You're rid of it....'

'To wander? Extended world, like what the animals see, whose sight is wider than our spectrum's band?' she asks.

'Rather it's when you see parts of the universe the others do not see, or haven't yet espied,' he says, 'a sighting of what's hidden. That would be history – the past, of course, but the future too. The future's part of history: from delicacy and laziness, too often it has been ignored. Science has taught – time is a concertina, fold on fold....'

'Oh, you're so tricky,' says Jamela. It's not a compliment. 'You're not trustworthy. That guy Damien – he'll have you steal the rings, he'll take them, and let the dwarves have vengeance on you. You're a sucker, Silvain....'

*

'It should all be here in my Lemprière,' says Silvain, waving the dictionary. 'It tells you where the cities were. They already found a big one, here in the Karakum – it's the sand hides and protects ... or rather, it's the sandman, sprinkling forgetfulness, preserving and concealing....'

'This is insanity,' says Jamela, gesturing around – the desert, a road. 'These sites have all been looted, and besides, it's grand theft, stealing, trading, antiquities that no one knew exist....'

'Don't be afraid, Jamela,' Laurel, Damien's assistant says, handing her a spade. 'Those cities hypothetical – they may be here, piled on each other – or lost and wiped out completely: it's the unknown. That's rare. Enjoy it. You're an explorer, take all the time you want. Lie about it too, unchecked: where you were, what you took – just start to dig. It's history....'

'No,' Jamela shouts. 'It's folly. I was not made for this. This leads to no enlightenment....' and she scrambles up a slope, on to the road.

There'll be a rundown bus, for sure, goats on the roof and chickens on the seats ... but no!

A coach, full of Austrian ladies all asleep. On the side – 'Hippy Holidays' with flourishes and arabesques ... and up goes Jamela: and she's off!

'Seleucids? Qarakhanids? Alexander's prefabricated towns?' Damien is keen, and on he goes: 'Intensive urbanisation,' he says. 'Almost anywhere will have been built, inhabited, destroyed – each settlement may have had messiahs, texts and prophecies, a message.... As it happened, unavailing: cast aside, but nonetheless – an inspiration for one who searches.... And here at last we come! We seek! Who's there? Who's in need, who's listening? We who understand – we are the revelation! Piercing the veil, it's called....'

Silvain says, 'I thought the revelation was hidden, unseen....'

'Knowing what you're looking for,' says Damien. 'Is the first step, of course. It could be books – on skins, on birchbark or on reeds: tablets: or golden plates. It could be stones....'

'Why here?' asks Silvain, though there is nothing you'd usually call a 'here'....

'They were all here and prophesied or made the rules,' says Damien. 'Nestorians and Zoroastrians, Manichaeans, Jews, and Muslims of all schools ... Buddhists and animists – waves of inspiration: and alas – it didn't last. This is the navel of modernity – this desert, and the others, further West and East. They drew a bad card. Wrong kind of weather, wrong kind of agriculture, wrong kind of invasions, of irrigation ... but seers of every stripe.... That's what we're looking for, Silvain, old friend,' he hugs Silvain; and Laurel for the first time smiles.

'A sect?' asks Silvain, disappointed greatly. 'Another guru milking the gullible, talking banalities....'

'That would be repetition: and mechanical,' says Damien. 'You don't get free that way. No – it's inspiration that we're after. We hope to find a source, a hint – good, if we do, and if we don't. That means we reject the past, all of it.... We're slaves, Silvain: we're free only if we sell ourselves over and over....'

It's triumph.

Silvain is unsettled. 'Those are bleak words, Damien. Remember, Jamela dropped out before a grain of sand was turned. We are not charmed.' He's sad, abandoned. 'We miss her terribly. Laurel is not the chiliastic type – and nor am I. We could spade up some jugs and mugs and waft away, sell, and hide the secret of their provenance. But – that would not be what I want, nor you, Damien.... We'd be at the start again.'

'Oh, Damien has a map,' says Laurel suddenly.

'It must be false,' Silvain says, after a moment of surprise. 'A desert has no maps, it shifts its shape; it's empty, it's a dry jelly, a dessicated polyp: it sucks you up and leaves you flayed and parched, a skeleton....'

Laurel

The sun goes down. It's cool, after a while. We are not fooled – the sun will rise, and burn all day, it will consume you, if you let it. There's no shelter, the wriggly beasts bury into the sand. That's it. There's no amusement, no zoo creatures prowling, looking for food and wondering if you are.... You need inspiration. Damien is right – inspiration's a necessity here.

The dark's an effect, day into night, as if a filter's fitted on a lens.

'Silvain,' Laurel says. 'When Damien sleeps, I'll leave our tent and come to yours. It's terrible, that your Jamela left, and you sad ... and sceptical.'

'That's good – remarkable – of you,' says Silvain. It's an offer, a project, quite unique. 'But you are Damien's....'

'It isn't like that now,' says Laurel. 'Maybe that's what your mother said – that women and princesses, and you men are the throne. It's not the case, it never was....'

'If I wanted that,' says Silvain, 'I'm not sure it's a good idea. For anyone.'

'You'll like it, when it's under way,' says Laurel. 'But you can of course say "no". There'll be no punishment for that.'

'I'd have to think,' says Silvain.

'That's not what to do,' she says. 'But you're the judge.'

'Maybe,' he says. 'And so are you.'

'Yes,' she says.

*

Damien is tall, much taller than Sylvain. He has a black and russet beard, carefully nurtured and curated. He has a scholarly mien – 'the Macedonian obol': 'modelling five card stud poker' – he could talk on either, quite convincingly. It's a surprise, that he wants great power and presence, to be a prophet, splitting seas and drowning armies....

Silvain has dark receding hair. You see him first at lunch in restaurants, waiting for his company, old friends usually male, university, rarely lycée. He's so early, the waiter thinks he's a bum sheltering, scoffing bread sticks ... but he's not a bum. He is unemployed. He looks unemployable, untrustworthy. It's not how he talks, but there it is. He doesn't graduate, he writes, instead. He's a genius. That doesn't help, not a bit.

Laurel's an inspiration, though not the kind Damien and Silvain are waiting for. She aims to please, and usually she does.

Jamela is a well-known executive. That's how she got time off to go to Turkmenistan with the loser, Silvain. But she got rid of him and the others – a lucky shot – and the Austrian coach is well-appointed. She's no Cinderella! She made a mistake taking on Silvain, but she's corrected that....

*

'People have got here before us,' Damien says.

That's obvious! Then, 'You're right, Silvain,' he says. 'I should have thought – inspiration is your bread. What are we doing out here, thinking about digging up the dead? I feel the spirit, the spirits – I've drained them, eaten them, sucked them like withered figs or dates.'

He calls the guy, the garage, to pick them up. Silvain folds his tent. The sand as far as you can see is marked out, like the archaeologists do – with staves and string. 'Pegged out,' he says to Damien. 'That's what you've done.'

Damien says, 'The guy is late. Do you say Turcoman or Turkmen? Turkman?'

'He's Kazakh,' Laurel says. 'It's their desert too.'

That's not quite so, not so at all, but who's is it, anyway? Who made it, what happened to all those people, swept away, assimilated, driven off?

Damien is bright with afflatus. He looks eccentric, possessed. He has the face for it, he doesn't need to change an attitude. He must have read the scientific literature, and with his map – he shows where all the cities ought to be.

They travel as a threesome. Damien is possessed. Does it mean he's complacent about Laurel, sharing herself with Silvain? You would guess yes: he cares a lot. He's a boss. He's like that: sensitive, a narcissist. Laurel wants much more than Damien or Silvain – they're not in her strategy. But Damien's not thinking about Laurel, or Silvain. Silvain can think about Laurel, and a book he might start, an idea that runs and dies before it comes even a long way before THE END. The end – it frightens him. He's never got there, not anywhere near. It's cheering.

'Do you like me, Silvain?' Laurel asks, 'Aside from all the rest of what goes on?' She doesn't think she's sharing anything, certainly not herself: she's all of a single piece. 'Go on, Silvain. You. Like me?' It signifies: Jamela wasn't liked, she left. You need to ask.

He doesn't answer, doesn't know, or care. What difference does it make? Yes, probably he cares. Not saying – that's quite smart, from someone who usually is not....

It's quite a normal world, to Laurel. A disordered man who thinks of writing books, and a disciplined guy who thinks of being something absolutely different from what he is, being a sage, a guru, an inspirer – and avoiding the martyrdom; the disappointed disciple who murders you – from craziness, fulfilling some wild story's theme, or from being disenchanted. Or paid.

Some people – maybe they're police, or tax, or special somethings – they want to know what Damien has found, what he and Silvain have discovered, tried to smuggle out – have already done do, passing it on, laundering it through tourists – maybe Russian or Chinese: and filling in the holes.....

There's nothing. Not a clue. They are not satisfied. That's how it's done. By night? Using someone like Jamela to carry the stuff out, not worth a search, and the buyer has been found, and if you have a lot, you tip off a friend: a bent auction and a provenance established.... Something like that – except, of course, there wasn't anything.

*

'What am I doing!' Silvain thinks. 'In the train of a visionary, when it was me who set the vision up. And my thesis – that what holds people together is the lies – banal enough, but when Laurel asked, I gave neither truth nor lies. I sent out: silence. I must get out of this, this three-way lock. Be myself.'

'Trust,' Damien says. 'That is the vision, and what lacks. Not belief: that's run its course. I must offer myself as universal intermediary. The problem-solver. My transparence – like a creature living in the deep which gives out light, a phosphorescent giveaway, but you can see its entrails, the busy anus, through and through the packaging. I am a light bulb, offering myself to settle arguments, disputes.... My inspiration – from the desert: the peoples settled, swarming over, the customs, faiths and fears, then driven off, becoming other, changing language, art and destiny.... I've seen it – the flowering of the desert, the sand in bloom. That is the lesson of the past, not shards and rust and noble femurs....'

'That's wonderful,' says Laurel, 'though maybe it is harder, Damien, than you think: to find solutions, be a trusted friend of enemies, both sides, of compromise, of drastic vetoes....'

'Hey!' Silvain shouts. 'This isn't me at all. I don't believe in compromise – I believe in truth and lies. Trust is not justified – you must find out first right and wrong, not in the religious sense of sin and rectitude, but what's the truth, what's not. Evidence, falsifiability. The past gives us examples – but that is all. A mass of instances – a plenitude no better than a single case. The path is politics, the solution ... who knows? Anyway, you know, when you set the problem, if it can be solved. Mostly, it's maths – set down the workings, that shows if you're a genius ... nothing more.'

*

'There's Laurel,' Silvain thinks. 'Everyone's unique – so, finding another one like her – it might be better, but for sure, it would be arduous. Besides, it's clear that I was found ... I'm not the finding sort. I don't impinge on her, and Damien impinges even less on her and me. He is the wife, and me the lover; Laurel's not into that scenario. But – if Svenja knew, she'd say that Damien was my perfect book. It writes itself. My inspiration – it's enough to cover writing down, no more's required.'

*

For Silvain, there's disappointment, that Laurel is not more interesting. That she doesn't find Silvain interesting. So, there's no development, no 'je suis l'autre'. Disappointment that whatever Damien does, he is the book, where Silvain writes the judgement, that may never reach THE END because

... because Silvain is flawed, because Damien gets nowhere, throws in his hand, fails, freaks out, is bought and sold ... is never more than an unfinished book, a comic book, case book, footnote in the history of two countries, each acting the part of vanished peoples, epics too long and incredible to be remembered by one person, much too long to have been devised by one, or fifty ... and all about what's long long gone, the language too, the heroes borrowed and invented, their deeds unlikely, impossible, their virtues quite disgusting to new sensibilities....

*

Damien has a call to intervene, almost at once. A territorial dispute. Countries not of the first order, as they say, but bristling and determined.

The mediation's not a success. It is a failure.

'Yes, Damien,' Silvain says. 'You show how, in a way, my idea was right. You're free, you want to make your freedom work and spread. You are above the fight, and yet – involved. What does not emerge is whether your freedom has some power, involvement, persuasion, clarity.... It's just a state: like something might be beautiful. Then not.'

'They thought I was a crank, Silvain,' says Damien. 'And then – they ignored me, and they prepared to fight, and behind them, each had a train of medium powers, alliances; and then the big ones woke from lethargy, and in a moment all were ranged behind the one or other.... Religion and trade, history, regimes and loyalties ... all were brought in – and my freedom or my suasion had not the slightest leverage....

'I showed them what to do,' Damien goes on, disconcerted. 'They wouldn't set a price to buy a piece of land. I showed them maps – how once it was, when they were one; or before, a place unknown: divided now ... but the people's different: religion, regime and loyalties that change, transmogrify, metamorphose with every season.... I remember guys who mustered with their flags and guns in every square, then wept when they were rocketed....'

'You muddled up the cards, Damien,' says Silvain, 'and the rules. You made the point that desert's useless, whoever helped to make it so – but what its value or its underside might be – you didn't know. A surprise package, as you said – and they weren't buying in to that. And you were wrong to say that making deserts dated back by centuries. There is the now – the melting pot where we all are ... you said it was a process where we all assist: the powerful states for sure – the most. You brought the others, the world order, in. Stasis. No one would sell, evaluate, or cede ... nor make a neutral space....'

'There was no game, there were no rules, Silvain,' says Damien. 'Not reason nor unreason. The quarrel could be resolved in just one way – the will to fight, broken by the fear of what that would involve. There was a weighing up; no mediation, and no peace. There was a calculation of the benefits of fighting or of backing down and saving face. There was no room at all for me to intervene.'

'That's it, Damien. That's what I thought,' Silvain says. 'You're free to walk away – whether they think you crazy or a cosmopolitan, an apolitical who doesn't understand what countries are.... Walk off, Damien, and disappear. At least – you're free! The idea, anyway, was mine. And Laurel – she's another, free and with the idea .... We're free musketeers – disarmed....'

That's the end of that.

'Give me some money, Damien,' says Silvain.

'*More* money, Silvain,' says Damien. 'Why not, while it lasts, and there's always more, from somewhere? Does it come from the working class, do you think? Do they mind, if it does? We float, Silvain, and if we sink, it's to be expected: but while our buoyancy persists – and of course it always will – we can live the kind of lives we live.'

'What kind is that, Damien?' Laurel asks. Usually she doesn't bother with their conversations, but this intrigues....

'The best kind, is one with a beginning and an end,' says Damien. 'Svenja will have told you that, Silvain. Not that it will apply to us – or if it does, it's not what gives us what I say – our kind of life ... as if there could be others living the same thing.'

'In the Karakum,' says Laurel. 'Apart from the garage guy and Jamela, there was no one else at all. You, Damien, said we'd have to do all the digging ourselves, in case we were reported.'

*

'There's a kind of philosophy there, Silvain,' says Svenja. 'If Damien tries persistently to walk on water.'

'I think you're pleased you won't have to sell my take,' says Silvain. 'Damien will run until he's emptied out: I'll follow him.... All philosophers see one thing: how they'd like to live, in a world they'd feel was theirs. Not where they are. They ignore the things we'd notice now, that they decide to push out of the frame – slaves, crusaders, the guys dismembered, women raped, the work, the death, the sickness and the fear. The rest, the hope, the daydream, order; that is philosophy.'

'You and Damien,' Svenja says, 'Are quiet, pacific. There's no drama, and no quarrel. Bland as a raspberry junket. This planet's wrong for you – you won't accept you're out of time, and out of place.'

'If we were pugnacious,' Silvain says. 'We'd lose. Where there's conflict, people are wild, they're beasts who rip you open, out of nervousness. They don't aim – they fire off every round they have – you'd be insane to tell them 'Stop! Reflect!''

'Well, Damien thinks he can do that,' says Svenja.

'Mine was an idea,' says Silvain. 'It doesn't mean it was a bad one just because no one can make it real. People, ideas – they fail and decompose in different ways. Quite soon, the people die, and that is that. Ideas are buried, but rise up and haunt the cemeteries ....'

*

'You did much of what you said,' says Laurel. 'Damien is free. He knows how to smuggle and dispose of loot. But – what does he have? He has cash, but where's it from?'

'He lends to me,' says Silvain. 'Gives to you, I think. But how? We didn't dig, Jamela had no hidden goods.... In order to be great, you need an army, or a treasure. Preferably both. Damien's financed. But how? When will he come out the red?'

'The red and black – they don't mean now what they meant centuries ago,' she says. 'Or when people still kept their accounts. Now, it's spend and spend, and something will turn up.... It's our discovery, salvation, our miracle. I love it. Credit is trust, Silvain – and trust is all that's left....'

'It doesn't work for you and me,' says Silvain. 'We don't have a bean....'

'It can be your task,' says Laurel. 'Your next exercise – to find who's backing Damien....'

'I bet I know,' says Silvain. 'It must be a cartel, a syndicate – Damien describes his scheme, after a while he pays them off – they make a profit, and they're free.'

'There's no gain to pay them with,' says Laurel. 'The machinery – it doesn't interest me. I'm not a party to the scam. You are, Silvain ... so I suspect. I'm not. But you are both in peril. The investors will have their revenge....'

'You miss the point,' says Silvain. 'Damien is free, and so he can't be caught or touched. That's what "free" means. It's true, Laurel, that you are not involved. But Damien – he is *free!* He doesn't hand out cash, pay dividends: he shows you just one thing: how to be free.'

'Hmmm,' says Laurel. 'There is an air of casuistry. Damien and you, Silvain, should take great care. Be very very prudent, both of you.'

'If it wasn't so, people wouldn't want their freedom. Some put security before their freedom – that's their choice. But others....' Silvain says. 'Like Damian and me, put freedom first, for always, even if the earth should heat and crack, the magma spewing out, the oceans boiling off....'

'A terrible solitude,' says Laurel. 'And peril.'

'A disappointment too,' says Silvain. 'Though success was never guaranteed. Anyway – Damien has you.'

'No one has me,' says Laurel. 'Surely, what you have, Silvain, you don't think it is possession? Even if you were free... But clearly you are not, since you must borrow money....'

'Damien....' Silvain begins.

'The cartel must have made a deal,' says Laurel. 'That he can spend their cash, and pay them profits – times, times over.'

'You've lost me, Laurel,' Silvain says. 'The idea was mine, but I've no notion of where it leads, and how it grows, distorts.... I take the cash, because it serves: being free is not a part of that, or, rather, it's the opposite. You were right....'

'Well,' says Laurel. 'You like me, no? We all like what we can't possess. You're the philosopher: you even call that love. Love of beauty, of the good, the freedom....'

Silvain's confused, and angry too. 'It's not the same, Laurel,' he says. 'I like high-flying birds, and myrtles, but it's not philosophy. Don't ask me questions without futures, without pasts, without criteria.'

Laurel doesn't listen to this stuff. She has her own ideas.

'And, Laurel,' Silvain says. 'I meant more and less than you might think. Peace or war – how might it end? Us, I mean, we all. Is fragmentation, conflict more propitious than the opposite? I have no theory to cover this: my argument was as you knew it at the start. How to achieve a freedom in the world – as it is, through the best means and strategems, and not be caught. All the rest's beyond me, dreams and rhetoric. My thesis was strong, and limited, magnificent, subversive. Damien achieved his freedom, and used it in a hopeless enterprise. No one suggested trying mediation no one wants.'

'I don't believe you,' Laurel says, amused. 'There must be more you left unsaid. How to resist: capitulate. What is it fires you up – your obsession? What's the fuel in your motor? Obsessions of your friends? Rewriting history, freeing the slaves, dethroning God and making colonies?

'You didn't start from freedom – you began with ties. Ties and lies. How you do terrible things, see others do them, have them done to you....'

'That would be ties, not lies,' says Silvain. 'That way leads to everything. I refined. The result was Damien.'

'Yes,' says Laurel. 'Damien is the end. Part of the end. Happy Damien, quite unsuccessful, melancholy Silvain....' She pinches Silvain's cheek: 'Enough of Damien anyway. Where's he's gone to – there's no sparkle....'

'If you're powerful,' Silvain says. 'That's what counts. Freedom doesn't come into it. You can be slaves or warriors: but you can't stand someone else giving you commands, telling you this way or that. That's how we are, the monkey way. Being warriors is risky, but at least you can desert....'

'You're an awful tory, Silvain,' she says. 'A coward. Blind, indifferent and uninformed. Digging where nothing grows, digging to feed no one. You're a worn-out boot. It's not surprising we all leave ... you give us bunions all over.'

'I work for Svenja,' Silvain says. 'It's a torment. It never ends. Everyone gets tired of me, it's a fixation.'

'It was an adventure, Silvain. For a while it filled our lives, and now it's over,' Laurel says. 'That's very good, something else is waiting in the wings. We came to know the earth, we had spades, there was sand unlimited, riches hidden like Easter eggs. I read a book that said that when you work the earth, that is the source of freedom.... It's not what I had thought, but there it is. Believe it if you can. At least, there's no time for much else: no dirty tricks.... Remember that!'

'The earth was different then,' says Silvain, as Laurel waves farewell. 'That was agriculture.'

'Property!' she shouts back.

High-flying birds

Sergio: a writer; Jana: an interlocutor

'Sergio,' Jana asks. 'Why do you write about Americans? You don't know much about them.... You're born a journalist, a false naif. Writing for movies now instead – you don't have a hope.... They're all a con – not your game at all.'

'It's interesting,' Sergio says. 'Americans are masters of the world, but my characters don't know it, or can't live up to it – they complain because they're poor, sick, or discriminated. Or their parents were devils; or they dropped out of school. That's the juice, the lymph. All we hear: – complaints. And the world? What's happening there? Who'd care, or be engaged, if I were creating Africans? These personages, they're homely shadows of our dark side, our vulnerable imagining.

'The movie guys, they think these guys are class! The States – they have all the robots and the plagues, spies: and millionaires ... common as dirt, that you wouldn't find anywhere else except in China. And they have millions of actors too – whistle, and they're round your ankles.'

'It's a waste,' says Jana. 'Your bluster. You could be original, my dear, if you just dared. It's true, no one else but them, for now, can be lords and despots of the universe ... unless you write it down for them, they don't do interesting things.'

'Power. You can't make a distance, not from the US: that's not "us",' he says. 'We're still subjects, even if the goths are everywhere. We're docile, broken horses. We stamp and snort, but in between the shafts we go – it's become our nature.... The sun is setting, Jana – another one is ready in the East.... But it's our day that dies. Maybe the truth's too large to tell. Anyway, I'm not bitter, I'm frustrated. I despise success, but I hate failure.'

'We understand each other perfectly,' says Jana, trying to touch him as he moves away. 'We match.'

'Perfectly,' he says. 'Fucking you – it's like fucking myself in a mirror.'

'You're a nasty person,' she says. 'You don't deserve to live. Think of all the nice people who die.'

'We've been in a nasty place,' he says. 'I caught the nastiness. Not that I'm sick. War is normal – but so's dementia. You remember something here and there, but being terrified – that stays.'

'Yes,' she says, 'but that is no excuse. Humans were sometimes full of fun and joy. Remember that, when you add up their bill.'

'Oh,' he says. 'I shan't collect! Not from humans. When there was the war, it was like eye tests – trying out different lenses: those colours; the orange and the grey, swirling and misty ... look! high-flying planes, condors in the clue. Look! tread softly – castrating bomblets a silver finger long ... graffiti on everything, broken insults, fractured cheers: God is great, God's an executioner. And the people who'd never seen, never thought of seeing, that what they saw now for the first time, would stay on their eyeballs always ... they're Adams taking the first walk in deserts, on volcanoes, on slimy seas.... We stared at them – people who'd seen their houses and their towns fall down, to nothing, to grey dust: shouting, dumb-mouthing, digging like devils on speed. People they'd never seen before, looting, crying, hugging them and showing them the dead ... seeing the inside of private things, bedrooms, sewers, humans, dogs. Fantastic. An experience like you were Satan, setting off the end of the world, torture refined, indifferent to confessions: people on wires like galvanised frogs, cartloads of monsters, some dumb, some shrieking, unloaded into cold perdition....'

'I was in a hotel,' says Jana. 'Making up the story of what happened. Working on a switchboard in a colony of bats People making obscene calls, hoaxing and trolling....'

'You don't trust anyone unless they've saved your life,' he says. 'Then, you get reprieved, organised, and you're in a pack of crows, led to gloat over rotting cadavers. The snappers going "peck peck peck".'

'Do you think about what you think, Sergio?' Jana asks. 'That's the world you're in for ever, but it isn't there. It ends.'

'I'll have to find it, then,' he says. 'Fighting is everywhere, you can hear it, you need it, it's a guy selling crack on the corner ... that's my country, it's in my heart, I'm its loyal citizen, my passport's tattooed all over under my clothes, my number's on my prick. It's an end. Like combat. An end that runs for ever, till it's over.

'I like ends: beginnings make you tremble and emote, you sob over kittens in their death bag going to the river.... Ends are unequivocal. There's no judgement around ends – they *are* judgement.'

'There!' says Jana. 'Exactly. I wouldn't accept your copy, it's not trustworthy. You took your maelstrom with you, and found a whole country was a replica. You were in your home, it was a prophecy coming real. You knew nothing of it, you'd always been there....'

'That is what it was,' says Sergio. 'And here's your problem: you. I saw what I expected, and for sure, it was me, myself. I was the missing jigsaw piece: I fitted perfectly. But why, then, Jana, why are you here with me? Not the same maelstrom, certainly.'

'No,' she says. 'Mine grew inside. I had no books, no pictures that my dread resembled – that would have been relief. Wars end, horrors go back under the skirting. I and mine – we don't end or melt. We are unique, too deep in our dry well to be hauled up – there's no rope long enough. If only there was solitude. I am two. I – we – hate my other....'

'Yes,' he says, 'and I am a place, a somewhere else, a place you've heard about, wouldn't want to see. You two, Jana, you're an unlit box. Boxes don't have windows, or surroundings. You're worse off than me.'

'You think you're a good soul, Sergio, by misfortune in an awful place. That isn't me at all,' she says. 'I'm the exact opposite. Bad soul, bad place: maybe everything else – is good.'

'Self-pity, Jana, self-absorption,' he says. 'My universe is man-made – they could have done it, could even now be doing it, quite different. Making it woman-made, machine-made.... Anything else you want. You're sealed in for ever, Jana. Being with you is a waste of time – and imagination.'

'White men,' Jana says with determination, resignation.

'Of course,' says Sergio. 'You're right. Greatness and squalor of their domination and their privilege. White men won and lost in many recent wars: we know – it's history. Maybe white men and history are wrong, should be rewritten. Then – start on the rest, the other colours, other conflicts ... causes. Where do I start? Psychology? Having God on someone's side? No, it must start with the writing: writing itself is where I'd start; and screw the history.

'I speak as an off-white man, from the swamp and forest and the steppe; a hunter, warrior, despoiler of the species and the habitat. It's evident – it's what I just said, always said, and what you're saying of me now. I'm not even in between. I'm not a tragic over-trusting Faust, riding to the abyss, I'm the coachman, chained to my seat – I go down into the gulf with the horses: the rich passengers, however, are still carousing, back in the inn. We're victims, Jana, we see too clear. I chronicle the history: you, the inside of your box. *Ahimé*....'

'I don't believe we've lived in illusion,' Jana says. 'I think we live in truth, and always have. What now? Truth is no help: it happens, is where we live, whatever we do. Sergio: what would Herzen say? Or Chernyshevsky? Lenin? Gogol....'

'We should invent something, Jana,' Sergio says. 'Something of our own.'

'You see?' she says. 'It's like I said. We're lucky to have each other.'

*

Sergio and Jana – pack their separate bags. It's easy. You wouldn't want to steal these travelled bags, nor what's inside. They've always done it so – not to separate, just packing separately, to leave together.

'Family. Rooms, parks, streets, gardens,' Jana says. 'We've had our interaction with all those long since ... the little that we can recall. Anyway, it's gone. We're settled now, and in control, we don't need props. We've seen all we remembered scattered, junked, like dolls-houses under steamrollers.

'What we knew first hand – it's been muddled into what we've seen, but we weren't really there, or we were alone: or sat with victims who we couldn't touch.... What we didn't know from way way back, we saw later on, and knew how to behave. How to eat strange food, to kiss, drive dangerously, shoot dope, shoot a burglar, shoot a lover ... if it wasn't part of our surround, we could cope if ever it arrived. We'd seen it done by experts.

'Things – expensive, decisive things, are even easier. They've been done for us: cool, cold, frigid. History.'

'Most people now are modern,' Sergio says. 'If they don't *do*, if there's no urgency, they still know *how* it's done: quite painless, mostly. What's more interesting – is believing things that you don't need.... Why? Finding room for abstract things that take a lot of headspace.... Religion, patriotism. All things that get you into arguments, fights ... that occupy spare ganglia, and time, but haven't been experienced, and probably are false: abstracted abstractions. Believing without checking; assuming an atmosphere – the silent rhythms of a church, a mosque – and hearing spirits, rules and histories, extrapolated from a void....

'We're full of what has been, is not; and what we're told. We're full of substantial nothings – we can't get rid of them, we add more, contradictory, until life ebbs, they pull away transparent, fluid, like water falling off a rock when the tide pulls in reverse. Is it the moon calls, Jana? – there's parking up there for milliards of ghosts ... thin as candy-wrappers....'

'No, no,' she says. 'That's the wrong way. We'll never move, if you think that. Just say – we've planned ourselves, been planned....'

'If you had a mother,' Sergio says. 'That's what you'd tell her. You'd leave out the dope, the idleness, the beatings and the running from the cops. Your lies are bigger, noisier, than a turbine hall.'

'We two never took a side. We observed,' she says. 'We were conventional. There were no battles, no movements, no betrayals, no delusions and no suffering for anyone. We don't recognise the colours of the present, its moods and moments. Its clans and tribes, its families, its tamgas and its ciphers.'

'You have to do all that when you are much much younger,' Sergio says. 'We thought our truth would have two sides, and we would turn them to the light. It isn't so. One side's a lie. We must be born with a trimmer's notion of the double truth. It helps survival. It doesn't work. Throw it aside.'

*

'We won't change. We're old rocks in the river bed. Nothing moves us, no flux, no flood,' Sergio says. 'I've always hoped to go deep. Deeper than what I see: alas, that's invisible. It's logic – the deep's unseeable. All I've had to do is to stand back, report, and give credit to whoever I found credible. It's worked for everything.... How can you find a place in this that's safe? The middle? Above somewhere? Not possible – of course, you're in somebody's pay, didn't you realise they were spinning you your tale?'

'The fighting?' Jana asks, not following his talk. 'The emotions? – we don't touch those. Do they matter? It seems to me it's all loss. All grief, and fears justified. What does it signify – to lose, to inflict this loss. Is it a lesson? What does it mean, who, what, is it supposed to interest, to educate.... It's punishment, of yours or theirs. I'm not a pacifist, I think,' she says. 'You resist. What, you wonder, did you do to cause it, the loss?'

‘What then?’ he asks. ‘Defence? You protect what you value. It justifies. To be a principle, defending must have a chance of winning ... and you don’t know ... there’s risk in all this. Why risk? Why attack? Why exploit? People do – they have chains, custom, greed, plans ... an armoury.’

‘When we find the motivations, we can live closer,’ Jana says. ‘Us two.’

‘You know why we shall not, not ever,’ he says. ‘Let’s try solving you. I know that many women – when they seek knowledge, take courses, take degrees – and they’re a target. A sexual prey – a saint, a false saint, to be punished, broken like a steppe horse, bridled and fed, and gratified – the nature changed; to release an energy, inflame the appetite, and have an everlasting hunger ... or maybe satiety, emptiness as a ship has a gaping hold to carry any merchandise, here and there, never at rest. There’s gangs who will break you, who have broken you: men. Women perhaps as well. The sexual body, made addiction, made repulsive, making you incapable of constancy, of judgement, attachment: they took off your brakes – you can go faster, always faster. You can crash. Often, you do.

‘There was a movie when some gangsters took the star, Delon, and gave him alcohol and *héro*, to break him, made him dependent, a puppet. And he had a cure. Of course. It was a movie. I often mention it, it’s my fixed point, a talisman. *You* have no cure, there is none, Jana. You’re spoiled. A sport for men. You have a hunger eternal that they gave you, a disappointment and a bitterness I can’t accommodate. You have to stay where they left you, corrupted and insatiable, the lust and the emotions twisted like iron bars around a tree, it’s growth forever compromised, deformed.’

‘That’s it, Sergio?’ she asks, angry and amused. ‘The analysis? That’s me – a sex slave? How wrong I was to seek enlightenment, when it can end so bad ... Or even make a choice. What I want, what pleases me. Or a constraint – to be condemned. Or just life, not stright, not bent, just running on. The purpose of intelligence: to cause loss, disorientate, to yield, be ruined and corrupted, is that it? My punishment heavy on my head. Is that all?'

'You could say it's only sex,' he says. 'And rock and roll. That moment's passed. The clay is fired, the form is fixed. They call it a disorder. It's incurable. A passion, like for chocolate bars. It's not my trip. It's a perversion I can't share or cure. It's yours, only yours. You should have been brought up differently, less trusting, less sincere. Your judgment! Cracked and shattered – no one can trust you, you lie and steal, betray; you forgive yourself until you can't … and on and on, life sentences. Your victims, friends and lovers – you and they fall silent. They're bewildered. No, not for me, no thanks.

'This solitude? Is it war? It's normal, has always been – does it mean it's good? Of course not – normal is terrible, you know that, you live it, can't endure it.

'You sought a skill, knowledge: instead, you've fallen in the tar pit.'

There must be a different way of seeing it, he thinks. This must be how the humans are? But my vision – it is misty and obscure? What does it take to be convinced, accept that someone's spinning out the truth to you, truth about you, you alone.

'There is,' she says. 'Another way of seeing: my way, my side. Wars are all different, they say. We could start one, examine what goes on, the emotions – what fires them up, what it means in the universe – as we experience it, are living here. Not a universe designed for us, but this might be our war, our demons, victorious or scared away.'

*

Who, then, is the universe designed for?

No one.

*

'It's nonsense, Sergio, the old nonsense,' she says. 'You cast me as the slave of passions and of men, men who are not you. You're the good analyst, psychology is made for women, men made it but they don't need it, it doesn't fit them, nor they it – not at all.

'It's rubbish! A myth that leaves us all incurable. You know how lonely countries are: your places.... Reflect! You can't bear solitude....'

'You have the wrong history, Jana,' Sergio says.

'You're jealous: acquisitive. The old story. And you're not a country, Sergio,' she says, 'No one's waiting to set you right.'

*

'When you stop inventing me,' says Jana. 'Run through your argument again. Instead of loss – think "justice". It will all turn out quite different. Then try greed, pride, and so on. Keeping sheep: it's violent, though it doesn't look like it. Dogs, wolves. Shepherds killing nearly all the time.'

'You have no friends,' says Sergio. 'So, I can say what I like about you.'

'I have no *other* friend but you,' she says. 'I don't believe you, so I have to disappear.'

'It's what they taught me,' Sergio says. 'It's the antique stuff: they use it to justify. Slavery, madness – those interested them: as illnesses, quirks like cramp, or stammering. Ideas? Magic or Bolshevism – they could cure those too. What they devised, it was unanswerable, a tapestry. They said they'd worked it out, elaborated the unseen: they were the best, the pioneers.'

'If you don't know,' she says. 'The best is nothing. Best do nothing. Best not do torture.'

*

They're comrades. They help each other, within the limits they both know. Those limits are all you need to know, about your comrades.

*

'What a find!' says Sergio. 'All these houses are empty. Left as they were used – fresh bread. We can camp out here: – see, the living things, humans, beasts, have left – these poor houses.... Abandoned. People driven out or run away.'

'We can't ask, find out,' says Jana, picking over stuff. 'If there was somebody, we'd not learn much.'

She peers up the road. 'No!' she says. 'I see them, all of them – gone up the road to dance, to dance in the big space – where the buses pull in.... Every villager, every one of them!'

It's wonderful. Sergio has poor sight, so he can't see the crowd – 'Leave everything as it is,' he says. 'We'll wait until they're done, welcome them back.'

'No,' says Jana. 'We'll go up, join them, and I'll dance with you.'

He looks up the road. He has binoculars in his bag, but doesn't take them out.

They can't hear music. It's very quiet.

'Come on,' says Sergio. 'We were misled. There's no war, no fighting here. Just people so trusting they left the houses unlocked and warm.... Went to enjoy themselves, for sure, or at least – give each other courage, joining together. Holding each other tight.'

*

'I'm cured,' he tells Jana, as they take the road that leads away, away from the village and the few straggly trees. 'Some places there's peace, and living as we should. I regret all the throwback talk about you, your hang-ups. My fault, my obtuseness.... I invented everything....'

* * *

'I was cured,' he says aloud. 'Driving a truck – it's exhausting and frustrating sometimes, but on the road you get a sight of peace, and you can work things out, between yourself and you; your interlocutor-self. Or just drive and see time pass, either side, under the wheels.'

Sergio fixes on the thought: that Jana enjoyed his company, knew exactly what he was: and then, he started to apologise for it. He'd changed, become uncertain, wavering, a penitent, a pilgrim starting on a long long trip to being something else – maybe to something unreformed, or wobbling, unlikable ... changed completely into another personality, introspective, questioning – a bad professional, obsessions brought out in the sun and left to dry ... a new man, a construct, up to the minute, instantly becoming past.... In search of lost innocence – good for a column....

Suppose they're wrong, wrong about their own ideas, about their own discomfort, about why everything has happened, happens, what you might do about it, why you don't, you can't, you've no conception that matches anything....

The idea troubles him, because he's found no way through. All's clear ahead, on the road, and Jana's nowhere on his route – she is indifferent, indifferent to the relationship they'd had before – both reporting war, and so, in a limited way, locating themelves outside the violence, confusion, loss and anguish, and yet faithful to all of these ... emotionally in charge – of nothing but themselves.

*

Sometimes he has mates – a Fausto, or a Vito. 'You're not a proper trucker, Sergio,' says Fausto. 'Trucking is work, not thought. The cab – it's your fiefdom, not a refuge.'

'A trucker has a house,' says Vito. 'You roam inside your shell, but somewhere there must be a nest. You live in the truck, Sergio: that's not the way for us.'

It's true: he sleeps in the cab, his bag – and nothing more. Like a soldier – advancing, chasing – does he regret leaving somewhere he has been? Or anticipate a home – still someone else's, a language not understood, customs not decipherable arriving disoriented ... or missing, uselessly, where he once was; almost a couple then? Neither. None of these. The road throws up its problems, and the rest – ceases to be problematic. The places – are fluid, cloudy. Post-stations, you would say – requisitioned temporarily and at times – occupied.

'Look!' says Fausto, winking at Vito, and taking a photo from his wallet. 'This is what you need.' There's a woman, high slav bones cambering up her ruddy cheeks, a raw mouth. Two kids....

'Yes, absolutely normal,' Sergio says, at a loss.

'They're all Germans, where Fausto's from,' says Vito, leading Sergio on. 'He's got used to it.'

'Why, do you expect they'll come and take them back?' Sergio asks, not understanding where he's being led. 'The provinces? The empire's gone, long ago. Karl – abdicated, you recall....'

'Or look at this,' says Vito, showing him a picture torn from somewhere – a magazine.... 'One of these....' he says. It's a guy, a body built, re-built from scratch: sporting a guru's loincloth ... unlikely, unlikeably muscled, oiled.... 'If you're not up to making kids,' it says.

'You guys – kidding me,' says Sergio, trying to raise his smile.

*

The trips are long and heavy. If the despatchers know you, like you, they put reason in your route.... They don't like Sergio. Load him, one day he'll break, with doubling-back, working to the limit always; if you're not bright, clued up – over your edge you go....

Taxi

They gather in the square, when there is a lull, the tourists and the wanderers flocked somewhere else.... A good glass.... drink the new wine, always, a ritual, then the old.

Taxi: ...the booze has gotten to his legs. Like Sergio, he finds a car to sleep in overnight. You usually need to break the window to get in. Colonel Zero, who did tortures somewhere, a rat who's lost its appetite, not its glare... Mister Blanc – a gentleman who specialises in visas – outside the Brasilian consulate, he'll wait in line for you for hours, but must be away and on his pitch by seven.... There's many more. None of them's a criminal, they're not single-minded, not impulsive, they're too identifiable – but all their life is casual, bordering crime and fiddling to stay alive. They're not attached too much to life.

'It's getting dangerous round here – festivities,' says Taxi. 'Wild boys. I'll tell you guys the lesson.... You have a bat, a baseball bat – the next guy you cross'll have a knife.You learn to use a knife: the next guy has a gun. So – what's the answer?'

And he waits. It's good that no one but him sees his legs, their state. He has in mind to take a trip, to take a cure, no booze, maybe over the Himalayas, seeking a bonze who'll take him on.

There's guys from human pyramids, fire-eaters, jugglers drop by – not highly rated in the evening meet ... their girls are virgins, so must be twelve or thereabouts, and even then there are no guarantees. There's jealousy – perhaps a homicide. The girls are small enough, you leave the corpse somewhere if it's come to that, jealousy's an inextinguishable flame, the girls are fluid, carefree – they are slight, really small and with the months, the dessication, they're smaller still, and no one wonders where they are ... the circuses ... the last nomads: those caravans. In this continent, the rest have been exterminated, or settled somehere where you wouldn't want to be.

There's not much Sergio could work on, or work out here, if he could decide he had a pressing something to investigate. It's fascinating, it's the city, it's the safest place to be.

'If you're armed,' says Taxi. 'You must be prepared to use it, and know how. Otherwise – a weapon's a liability. Me, I don't carry anything. That way, you've a good chance you'll be ignored, passed over, or made harmless at the most. If you carry, you'd need be eliminated, disarmed and taken seriously....'

'I don't represent anything that needs to be beaten, killed,' Sergio says. 'I'd not interest Colonel Zero: I know about the mysteries, but did not get anywhere with them. I'm a blank page. And – all that sitting, driving everywhere – it weakens you. I'd not be sport for him. But – I believe all of us, we have a load, we must deliver it, and take another one until we quit....'

'I share that,' Taxi says. 'If I find someone from the right school of ancient thought, they might save my legs. My hope is, it's all so enlightening, up the mountain, I'd not need to booze, and chat to guys like you, Sergio, who haven't got a clue....'

They laugh. It's isn't humorous.

*

When we seek knowledge, is it to find something we don't know, or to explore the depth of our own ignorance?

*

Taxi and Mister Blanc – they must earn, sell, to eat. Most people used to do that; then they needed more when they were lifted out of poverty. Mister Blanc and Taxi sell. They sell their time, standing in line for you, minding your stall, selling what you can't, or carrying it to where it can be sold or where it was before. Selling souvenirs, or info, tips: selling a picture they have found. Taking things, taking the brass letters off mausolea and *loculi*, selling them as scrap. Selling scrap. Odd jobs and odder jobs. Sleep is free, but they wouldn't have paid anyway – lodging, dossing down in archways, in buildings being worked on, being destroyed or being built.

It's harmless, and you see them when they're up or on a roll, and no one sees them when they're down.

Sergio has cash left from his good job, but also a bag he has to park somewhere, and pay and risk for that. He's safe: just don't make enemies, don't steal from enemies, don't steal from friends, be reasonable, accommodating, argue from a basis in your rights, presumed, but don't hector, don't harangue.

Sergio gave Taxi a great favour.... He asked Fausto to give Taxi a ride, to set him on his way. The Himalayas. Without Taxi, Sergio is lost. He lost his ally – the gesture is magnificent, and Fausto risks much, giving Taxi that ride.

'You're a good trucker, Fausto,' Sergio says. 'You live a chaste and useful life. I hope – where Taxi's gone, those groups of exalted pilgrims ... they don't corrupt. It's knowledge, false knowledge. He may be cured, but – it's like Jana, he won't live as he should, as he can.'

'Who's Jana?' Fausto asks. 'Taxi seemed to me a poor soul. Maybe it's your imagination, that sees him better now than what he might become.'

'Taxi was innocent,' I say. 'Like Jana.That's attractive, but it doesn't make you stick to them. He could do little, and had nothing, he grafted and he schemed, and he survived, but still had nothing.... Now, perhaps he'll be a millionaire, a prof, a footballer. Those legs – like oak roots.... The innocents – they see what we are, pass by, look for an innocent who also knows how the world is put together. That's some task!'

We laugh. 'I guess a trucker doesn't have that much, not much of anything,' says Fausto. 'Your life, like mine, and Taxi's – it's difficult, but it's not complicated....'

'That's what I looked for, Fausto,' Sergio says. 'Have done with the complexity. It's what I've tried, but each has an absorbing search, takes all their time and interest: Taxi – climbing the Himalayas to be cured, and Jana, trying to make the truth from scrums of liars, spies and traitors....'

'You're better off here,' Fausto says. 'You can't live too near to people, Sergio. You'd think after all the travel, socialising, hiding out, you would have learnt ... but no! You can't live satisfied, not even on your own. You couldn't even be a trucker! Couldn't figure it.'

It's true. They don't, either of them, find it satisfactory.

'There's always guys that come from other squares, try to take our space,' says Sergio. 'Taxi knew all about rough types, how to confuse them, persuade them to go away. He had friends too – the cops relied on him to keep some kind of peace.'

'Well,' Fausto says. 'There's no quiet lives here, I see: don't call on me, if you're in danger – it's not my game at all! There's jugglers, fireaters – rough, unruly types.'

'They leave when they do really bad,' says Sergio. 'And can't deny. They don't have friends among us, don't wait around for justice here.'

*

It's best, when you have to wash, to use the fountains – but it's difficult. You must be swift, before dawn, keep your clothes on – just profit from what you might call the enlightenment, the cleansing, from mouths of carp and dolphins, from the rivers of the world, pristine – the Nile, the Tiber, the Vistula, the Ob.... Make up more names, join them to the allegories, the naked marble ladies perpetually beneath the stream, the cold rush – and quick, quick, away before you're caught. Taxi didn't wash – hardly at all, and maybe in the little fountains at the corner of the street; you have somehow to use your hands to clean yourself and keep the lever pressed ... it takes a special skill, but no one interferes. They stay well clear of you, and don't go near the fountain either, when you've left.

Sergio – his bag. 'Left in care,' he thinks. 'So, it should come back: and the maps and the binoculars – not of much value, especially the maps.'

'What next, Sergio?' Fausto asks. 'No trucking, that's for certain!'

'There's always been a "next" so far, Fausto,' Sergio says. 'The principles remain. Those are unchanging. We're working on what's next....'

After months, a card arrives from Taxi. They hadn't thought he was the writing sort: 'I'm high, very high,' it says: 'high above the green, here in the white. I know I'm orange – that's the drink, maybe the die from off my coat. Down on the plain – they're magicians of the cosmos, the universe ... they draw you diagrams of all there is, and whether God is cube or triangle, or maybe doesn't exist at all, or's drifted off, carried by the wind.. But here, everybody's climbing, crapping, leaving stuff, some of it expensive – just thrown away without a care. They have the passion, the itch to reach the highest point. Higher and higher: most fall when they're coming down, but I'm sure they've had the wisdom, been on the top ... I'm way above the birds. I see them far below; black, grey gliding wings, arching like eyebrows: spiralling and sliding. No doubt they're at their roof, right at their limit of their breath, the atmosphere, the visibility. There's nothing so high up here, no birds, no animals but us, nothing to eat – unless it's me, haha.'

'He's on the way to being cured,' Sergio tells Fausto. 'He thanks you for the ride,' he lies. 'It seems his legs are safe.' And Fausto shrugs.

'I know I'd never be a trucker, Fausto,' Sergio goes on. 'At least I know how it's to be done. Mostly, trade's pacific. First, you must understand, and travel, the confines of your territory. Then work out what's to be done to live off it. What is the price, the cost. Who pays.

'There's always a destruction where people are involved. I was squeamish; I thought: 'I can't live like that. I'll watch!' I was afflicted: infected, too. What was I passing on? Truth? A snapshot, a morality? I had the horrors, like Taxi has the shakes. The cure is not so hard for Taxi as it's been for me. A negative's enough: 'don't do it, Taxi!' That is all. He can go on.

'I know – nothing is changed. I experimented – I let go, and dropped, left Jana – not worthy of her, and besides, she didn't like me, didn't like my company and nastiness. When you drop, where you land is always tougher. Finding a new innocence, takes more time, more ingenuity. The stronger ones go armed. Maybe I should. I shan't....

'As you drop below your hopes, the reward diminishes, the challenge increases. The trial is always harder, you'll lose, your loss won't be excused. Or rather, won't be noticed. It's a battle worth avoing at all costs – even if meanwhile you've been a millionaire, a president. But it's the hardest thing that you can face. You ought to do it. I promise you, you'll sweat and groan.'

'That's just the start,' says Fausto. 'There's going on, year after year. Not doing things. Not being your first self. And finding no one cares.'

*

'*Messianism*'. *Who will start?*[1]

That's some question! Not a real messiah, that seems sure, whatever that might be, entail, fulfil.

You don't hate, feel contempt, for what's in front of you – the state, the people with the power, exploiters, warriors –

---

[1] Section 8 of the last chapter (7), of the Plan for 'The State and Revolution' (1917) V.I. Lenin (not written).

colonists and miscreants ... but all of that must be thrown down. Destroy it all – not that you think you are the strongest, far from that. You have the strategy, that's all: the eye. Then, when it's down – you have to build it up again, against the odds, against the fears of those who thought the purpose of their suffering was to have done with that, with all of that: the state, the power....

You have to build it up again, your power, and make new men and women to be its citizens.

A new state, new cops, new jails, new wars and persecutions – and the messiah must be followed, whatever sacrifices are demanded, whatever the mistakes they make.

There's messiahs everywhere – you even get to vote for some. Lots have started: some of the most convincing have already finished, burned out like massive fireworks on the cinderpatch.

Making new people: easy. School does that.

It's the economy that's difficult – harder to get that fixed.

Marauders, pessimists – not easy getting rid of those.

And so you stop. Stop bothering about all that. Whatever you've studied – cards, horses, not studying, guessing: sex, avoiding sex – you'll have been avoiding waiting for messiahs. Does that mean all the things, too, that messiahs have promised, false ones and the genuine? – whatever fate we had in store for them ... and better not conclude that there have been mistakes – we'll never know, which was true, which false. You might regret – messiah-watching, – the time, waiting ... a sterile pastime. Best not reach that chapter – the conclusion. The rest, the preparation, is all manageable. Prepare for a messiah, hope one doesn't show – they won't redeem your failure.

The economy .... those fields of maize, the hares shot near extinction, protected and restored – and shot again ... the farting cows and sheep asphyxiating you, drinking your water, rotting your body with their doctored blood....

Messiah watch: you could start a party for it, sell the cards, require discipline: And backsliders – might be shot....

Nino (me), Juno, Uzun

'Come on,' shouts Juno. 'Come right on out of there. Out of the thicket!'

'You can't talk to me like that,' I say, 'We live together, but we're not together.'

'That's a luxury,' she says. 'That shows we're privileged. People oppressed – they live together, really stuck. Slaves protect each other. If they don't, there's money in between: or rancour, fear, indifference. There's none of those here. You're free – I saw you give your clothes away, that destitute – Marva. Now, that's intimate – excluding me. For good.'

'I had my operation, Juno. Now, I can see. With clear eyes,' I say. 'You don't see no messiahs. Some of those old shirts were crass. There's no hostility with you. There's nothing. You're in decline. The dementia-pit awaits. I'll tie you with straw and hide you in a hobnail trunk. No one will find you, you've already lost yourself. You'll go on a bonfire, become eternal flame.'

'Oh, you fucker!' she shouts. 'I can't count your lies. If I cared more, I'd wash your mouth. Go – feed the animals!'

'We're not farmers, Juno,' I say. 'We do anything, to pay the rent. Remember?'

'No use, a cow,' she says. 'You'd not know how to milk it. Nor how to kill it so we'd have some steaks. Keep tigers – then you'd know what feeding the animals really means.'

*

'I understand,' says Uzun. 'You two can't communicate. Juno's touched, I think: not by divinity – in the head, I mean. And you're that way yourself. Don't buy a cow, or sheep. Try to slink away. Don't try to borrow from me, so you can start a farm – you don't know how.'

'It's true we're poor,' I say. 'That's all. We are not good at living in this country.'

'No,' says Uzun. 'You are a warning against all you believe in and you do. I don't mean success or boasting: you can't manage carrying on, and earning a good death. Music at the funeral, all that.'

'Uzun, I say, 'you're dear to us. Placid and determined. You're lost here – where people are the opposite of that: troubled and volatile. You would have been a benefit had you stayed where you came from, but here – you're an anomaly....'

'That's what they say,' says Uzun, 'Of us creative types. It isn't so. Art is universal, or it isn't art.'

'But, Uzun,' Juno interrupts, 'you're here to collect our rent that we don't have ... Not paint us....'

'Don't underestimate me,' Uzun says. 'There's sheep under my family tree, and in the branches, round the edge. Sheep have character, and usefulness, and humans don't, for them there is no need, no purpose. I appreciate you two are on the skids. You should separate – two's more difficult to chase than one. And you –' he points to me, 'Nino! You're near the edge. What you should be is an investigator. They say you would be private – but it's true of us, of everyone. Accept that you're outside, an onlooker; guy with the telescope who watches from afar. You know much less than each of us, but see a broader field. No one will love you, and you'll want being paid. There's nothing else you can do in life. "Truth", they will say, "it has no price." It's so, but doesn't mean it's valuable. Think "gumshoe": find a gap in some reality, where a beam of dusty light seeps in – stick your hand in, out, where it's torn. Wave. Is there someone outside, in the universe of truth? Are they interested in you, in us? They may be krill. Or dead.'

'About the rent, Uzun,' says Juno. 'If you must break legs, I warn you – there's no cash inside. Our bodies are robbed tombs.'

We laugh, a little nervously. It's natural.

'You must be prepared to move around,' says Uzun. 'Be ready, go on the move. If you've no pack animals to help – your backs are strong.... Drop your stuff, and somebody will pick it up; the same for you. We've all been here before. Eviction is the gate to empire. Remember that. If empire doesn't call – weave carpets.'

It's good advice, and we disregard it instantly. Arrive at the same conclusion by quite a different path.

'There's another thing,' says Uzun, taking off most of his clothes and oiling himself, from a can with flowers on the side. 'When I throw you out, I have to break all that you have. And the rest, I steal. It's how it's done. Get used to it. You're not a detective yet, Nino. Or maybe you are. It's up to you.'

*

He throws all their stuff into the street, broken.

'Liberation,' says Juno, still shocked. 'Prison break! We were in prison cells, Nino, non-communicating. Feel the air now....'

'Do we owe Uzun?' I wonder. 'Freedom can't come free ... if freedom's what we have. We can't pay, anyway.

'I have to find a mystery, resolve it. It must be useful in some way, or it's a novelette....'

'There's causes everywhere, no mystery,' she says. 'You can't miss the tragedies, but you can ignore them, every one, completely. Uzun sees you capable of something tiny, really small. Obsessing. A case. Solving a case means filling it, closing it, checking it in somewhere and leaving it. Those cases – they're on shelves, kilometres of them, card and fabric, leather, trunks and kitbags.... What's inside? You never know, you haven't got the document, so you've no access. That's what Uzun thinks you can do: fill one of those receptacles. "The end of inequality"? Did you think that was it? "The end of everything – of all the other species – of ours – of history – of sex ... of doubt ... of fear ..."'

'Enough, Juno,' I shout at her and wave a hand, sort of aggression. Uzun in his wrestler's strip unscrews the window frames and throws the doors and floorboards in the street. It's miraculous, how every habitation, however squalid, has one unique, illuminating feature – a hearthstone with a rune, a roof-beam with a woodsman's mark.... Here come the ones we lived with – flying, thrown out....

If my hand had touched Juno, it would have hit into her like a spoon-bowl on butter. She'd hit back – that steel bar; and Uzun would hug me to his oily belly, choke me. I'd have no response. None of this is happening. The frame that held me in with Juno – hey! Here it comes – Uzun spins it like a hunting boomerang, skims it far off. Those don't come back.

'Too much is going on,' I say to Juno. 'Reflect! Most people can bunk down with anyone, and be content. Then there's the few, like me, maybe like you, who must discriminate, and don't get off with anyone at all. Where does the future lie, I wonder. Round pebbles? Make a beach. Or jagged shards...? Cripple your feet.'

'You said it, Nino,' Juno says. 'Where, oh where? My future – I had one, and the path is blocked: by an oiled rattler, and a spitting mamba.'

'Is that all it's about, all this?' I ask. 'People disliking each other and themselves...? Snakes and ladders – those anacondas take it out of everyone, into the basement: but don't complain? It happens to us all, it's the movie we're all in, unpaid, unscripted – nothing you do disturbs the great, the absent, director; that flicker never will get screened, only he will watch it in his mansion on the Boulevard, giggle at your arms and legs a-flail, your trusts and mistrusts dribbling out dubloons and ducats like a wormy pirate's chest....

'Necessities, decisive actions announced by fleets of battle-cruisers firing blanks that tail away to muffled executions on the cellar steps... All tinnitus. Repetitions you can ignore. A re-run of the histories from Gilgamesh to Stalingrad – spilt milk.

'All trivial? Even clear visions that dissolve the precious *sfumature* of the sages, chase off the mysteries, the wonder, the moral meanders and the certainties?

'There must be something more – a negation, a hidden highway, not stated but implied, even in our pasty faces, torn and bloody clothes, our fusty tattered revolutionary banners, defeats and still survivals.... There has to be a ... something to indicate another certainty, hypothesis at least, maybe dragged from the ancient wardrobe – a cloak of visibility, still wearable but only in days of splendour and necessity that may never come again, and surely never were....'

'It's what you said,' says Juno. 'Disliking. Disliking what there is. Pretending to be something more.'

'Of course,' I say. 'You have to start the action. No one can say you're a messiah except you. Then – you asked for it. Sacrifice. A symbol. Symbols proliferate, like Indian cents – an insult, you might say. Chuck them; or in the piggy bank ... Not enough, not ever, for anything.... A cent won't buy you anything, so what's an Indian worth?

'Remember – Lenin didn't write the chapter about messiahs. You might say he was a bloodless sacrifice – which doesn't count. 'What is to be done?' he asked, remembering Chernyshevsky, who was sent in exile among the Yakut.... That's – to be avoided.

'If you're an opportunist, however brilliant, you must avoid exile, the north. Think Batagaika, the sinking land where the permafrost's in melt, opens up the slimy way to hell, the regression of time, the tepid animals, spectral, lions ... and shall we live to see the dinosaurs emerge? Then, we'll have made full circle. When you summon up my destiny, Uzun, remember – Bolshevism creates a merciless and inefficient state; a mediocrity who doesn't run the show – but down the cellar steps you'll go....

'Ah! you think. If only there'd been anarchy without a boss! And then you think – no! We'd have been gobbled up, sold out. Again.

'And so – it will come to pass...!' And we three laugh. We ought not. Uzun has nearly slaughtered us.

'That's old stuff,' Juno says, although her intellect is tickled by the ghouls.... 'A past evoked – but not remembered: you can say anything you like. And – Messiahs don't set up to cure a melt, a burn. They expiate. No one wants that: what good does it do? We know – what's to be done. There's nothing to be done, nothing, at least, that *will* be done.

'And look! There go my shoes! How will I trek barefoot? And will you leave me here, Nino?' and she hugs me.... 'I'll be your woolly rhino, Nino,' she says, clumsily. 'Just – give me a ride....'

There's nothing for it. She's straddled on my back.

'Hi ho!' she shouts: 'Everyone needs a hobby – here's my hobby horse: old Sticky Mud here – onward! Upward!' And so we go: geeing up.

*

'Lay me down on this grassy bank,' says Juno, giving a last dig with her heels to make sure I've understood. 'The choice was good. Uzun – that bastard – broke all your stuff and stole my money that you didn't know about. The choice is: – messiah? or detective? The difference between imagination and memory – remember? You're lucky, Nino: you have both. Visions and charge sheets; kept separate in your small mind. Vastness and depth on one side – on the other, 'did matter move?' 'Look at me' and 'whodunnit?'

'I know, Juno, that I don't know which to choose,' I say. 'The big or the small. Except – the big ends really bad, with sacrifice. The little – passes guilt and the deed to someone else, so's they can't wriggle out. But – that's trivial. If the universe is scheduled to explode – as it surely is, and surely will – finding the responsible designer doesn't matter much. There is a plan. We always hoped there would be one. That, in principle, is good.'

'Sleep on it, Nino,' says Juno. 'And here's some fun! I saved this from the wreckage....'

'Lethe water?' I ask. I'm exhausted. 'No. Manhattans,' Juno says. 'That's all we had ready when Uzun came – and he is strict. No booze.'

That's how the adventure starts.

*

I sleep, I dream of making novelties, new men and women, equal and free, and with a vision. What could go wrong?

*

'You get in my way, Juno,' I say. 'I'm doing something complicated, yet so simple, that its fundamental structure is the one you wash and clothe each morning, you pick its nose, shave off its leg hair....

'A messiah – may fulfil a prophecy. Eliminate the time that has elapsed between the prophet prophesying, or the stone, the palmleaf, birch-bark – being read – and the accomplishment, the sacrifice. The fulfilment: it's a joke with time. Its denial. We are what we were, what we were to be, and are. We are what we were. It's like the Khmer Rouge – put back the time to 1431, the disappearance of Angkor Wat. Time does not bind, its passing leaves no trace, or need not. We have beaten time. The past, Juno, is encysted in us. But.

'That 'but' is my dilemma. Are we our woolly rhino, warmed up and tumbling from the mud? Has time no meaning and no substance, no purchase? The universe seems careless of millennia, of distance, shapes, of matter; of sequences, existences. It does exactly what it wants with past and future ... they're all there, and haven't happened. And they've gone. Long long ago.

'That's the messianic world, I think.

'The detective, though, sees you and I as artefacts, real things you can put under glass, or formaldehyde, or lie detection. We are us....'

'That's undeniable,' says Juno, 'and it's dull. If that's all you come up with, you've no traction. You're a butterfly.'

'Don't provoke, Juno,' I say. 'You know some kind of communism's our only hope. I doubt that it will work. Seeing how few around are interested, I feel I must approach such questions by another – philosophical – route.'

'I'm sure you're right,' she says. 'Don't mention being right if you are looking for a job. *Some kind* of communism means bits of something else, or bits of everything, or something you call new but just grows.' She peers at me, unconvinced –

'You're lost, Nino, you have no past. It's good. It will help you doing what you haven't been.'

*

I'm street food. A samoza, a clear oil poured over me, in my clothes, and then I'm held in pincers over the flame. In transit – to Venezuela. To somewhere where they're leaving; someone going in attracts only wonder.

Sister, mother, lover: those are no more, they're in the past, the past I haven't got. They've all left, all those Venezuelans, when I'm trying to get in, before it's all resolved, all cured, the oil – flowing all over me until I'm cooked: no bosom for my head, unless I loll my own head down, like the pelican who feeds its young with blood – my blood, my youth....

*

'Hey! Nino!' Juno shouts, 'where have you gone? No time for that! Don't snivel, don't leech on others, don't expect they'll give the sympathy you won't feel for them.'

'I appreciate it, Juno,' I say, 'your honesty. You don't often find a person who is frank.'

'No,' she says: 'You're lucky in me. Of course – you'd like to discharge on me the other emotions that you have: too bad! No hope, no deal. You even want to hog first person, as if the rest of us are objectified – poor "he"s and "she"s, while you swan off the only "I", as if there can't be different "I"s, a platoon of them, a CIA of "I"s, watching and acting, feisty, putting other "I"s and "she"s in chains until they find a judge who'll hear them out, make them safe and in the pokey....'

'In a few years,' I say. 'The reference to Venezuela will be meaningless. You'll need a footnote. Meanwhile, I'll have been there and made a fortune repairing bicycles, and lost it....'

'Nonsense,' Juno shouts. 'We've lost everything here, why go somewhere else to lose it all and not speak the language – we might as well go to Tabriz. That's where Uzun was, not speaking a word of Farsi, but being a world class wrestler. Too good for you!'

'Too slippery,' I agree.

'Now,' she says, 'everyone finds someone, clings to them, love, want, desire, a resting place. Then – it evolves; they separate, then, love, want – all those things ... they find again a someone. With me – it's different. Nothing for you, except I'll be with you always.'

'As my bad side, my cold side,' I say. 'Give nothing, take nothing. That's the sum.'

'Exactly,' Juno says. 'It's just a diagram, but it is the sum, and your two sides – they're the short ones. I'm the long one, with the solution of the theorem.'

'Anyway,' I say, 'after Uzun, we must start to put together some more stuff. Not your or mine: stuff that can be broken and thrown in the street again. And so, and so; until.'

*

'This hotel smells,' says Juno. 'Smells of people quite like us. The desk is where they call the cops, denounce your dodgy papers. And the smell – it's what we'll take away, but leave it stronger than it was.'

'Why, Juno?' I ask. 'This perversity. It's not flattering, you clinging on. We've nothing. Why?'

'Time, metaphor, and gratification,' she says, quick as a ferret. 'Time passing – it's like a harrow on the soil, dragging us millions with it, in its prongs, spreading out, reducing, homogenising, cutting and departing: spearing here, uncovering there. Levelling and polishing ... leaving us scarred and flattened.

'Metaphor: the life-world, the construction of a reality which you find – surprise! is shared by everyone. It's in your head, in everyone's – but isn't real. A construct. We live in symbol, and in metaphor – it isn't life, dear Nino. It's invention. Without it, we're ourselves, our poor aimless brain atop a gangling body. So – be human, join the species; on your own, you're lost, a nullity. Construct your social world, glue yourself in it, find hobbies, lovers, balloons to have your sex with.... Your votes, your demos – let yourself go in them; be bubbles in your national champagne.... Things you'd not considered, never seen – link to other things. By language? or by sight – the pineal eye? Language lets you be the other, anyone you want, whoever takes your fancy: tomorrow, all change! Change opinion, change your flag, your shirt, your philosophy. No illusions – your eyes lie like your tongue....

'The bolder ones among us who create, coin poetry from cinders and horseshoe nails – they pass it on ... the simulacrum of reality and life, that lets us live in something not ourselves, and realer than we are. The real beyond ourselves, our private real. The structures and their matchstick people – they bury us, and we mulch into their soil, the mud of history, the Others, voices....

'Metaphor? Not quite – it's grasping structures, chains of being we infer ... idealizations....

'And gratification. Mmmm! I love it! Sherry trifle with artificial cream, spurting from a can! If I have three coins to spend, I can spoon it down and sit and watch the lime trees on the boulevard shedding their pelts.... Sad: the evening browns, the light fades, hiding away to come back – boo! – to wake us up tomorrow. Tomorrow too – is guaranteed. Work for those coins – but be prepared. You leave, or else they kick you out: – you need the gratification ready ... your trifle.

'Expect nothing except ... that what can turn you on is ready waiting, and abundant.'

'And me?' I ask.

'Perhaps you'll find the murderer, found a religion,' Juno says. 'It's not that you like humble work: reading theology, or having acolytes. You've chosen your dark tunnel, Nino – off you go! I'm taking a ride, just ludic, on your back: – 'tunnel of love'? ... The tunnel's real, the love is not included in the fare.'

'No one looks after us,' I say. 'Here, we are free. Suppose we travel to a despotism, where our questions matter more...?'

'Oh,' she says, 'I stole some of Uzun's oil. We'll slip away....'

And that we hope to do.

Chaghri

'You're stuck, Nino, it seems to me,' says Juno, looking at me critically: 'You're like the bottom figure in a totem, having to support the rest, but with nowhere at all to go.'

'Where do you get these notions from?' I ask. 'This information that we haven't paid for, nor requested....'

'Oh,' she says. 'On the corner, there's a guy who hands it out. They think he deals – but for him, everything is free. He was an addict, went to a monstery for the cure, and found a God....'

'It's good publicity for dope,' I say. 'But I'm a miscreant. I won't deal, and finding divinities – it isn't me. I shan't use. If you might be messiah, those old-established pantheons, however you get access – they are competitors who don't play fair.'

'This guy,' Juno goes on, ingoring me, 'gives you the latest. May be wrong, but it's all plausible, and he's no reasons he should lie, or even exaggerate....'

'Unload yourself,' I say. 'It's clear he's thrust a stick into your nest....'

'It's us,' she says, ignoring provocations. 'We talk of our inventions, all that stuff, as if we stayed the same while all else changed; the animals have disappeared, there are no birds, we have to pollinate wild peartrees by ourselves.... Think! We don't evolve the world – it evolves in us. We've changed, we fill some gaps, extinctions compensated. And we grow monstrously....'

'I heard the zoos are blossoming,' I say. 'Animal sex – explodes. Those masturbating rats – they break the pattern of the family and reproduction.... The pleasure principle takes hold ... each borrows from another species....'

'Oh fuddy-duddy, Nino,' Juno laughs. 'It's us! If you saw I'd a clitoris like a corkscrew – you'd sit up. Now, it's not the time to tell and show ... but we're diversifying, and we're changing shape....

'Behaviour, groups, relationships! Imagine, Nino...! those lady crocodiles ... wow! Tickle your fancy, dear.... Imagine it!'

'I can,' I say. 'But if I'm modified – how does it impinge on me?'

'It opens up what you might be, and what the rest of everybody is,' she says. 'De-miners. Carrion-eaters. Sweeping the battlefield, ready for the next round: cleansing, ready for more dirt. Private armies. Mercenaries who start by filling gaps: recruited, they are devotees of war, and holiness – some guys making millions pull all the rest along. With cash comes power. They mix their motives, they are legions: a hunger for true beliefs, for cash and kids, slaves, women. States and flags, chrism and garotte. See them hobbling out – top guns emerging from their hospices to fly again and make big bucks ... dog-fights....'

'I know all that,' I say. 'Wars cost too much, you buy an army and it doesn't fight – your own won't die for you, nor salute the flag. You must buy more regiments. It's part of strategy, diplomacy. Wars are over, like the song said – but there's extorsion, vendetta, the big Putsch. It won't last, won't stick: the end of war – it isn't peace, it is more war. Mercenaries don't fight each other – they fight *you*! Where do I come in? I'm in no fight.'

'We're back to revolutions,' Juno says. 'All armies become privatised, they roam around, looking for cash, looking for causes. They can be chiliasts, my dear, those sweepers, cleansers – jousting knights, who are the only bands that's trained and quite autonomous.... Marauders on a continental scale, they roam and spar when pros won't go – to central Africa, the Sahel, the steppe – fresh desert brought to desert.... All turned upside down and shaken out – a steely wind. The termite hill is emptied in your ears: ants all over, you and everyone.

'And so the battle hymn resounds, stirring those peoples settled now for centuries but with a geographical imperative: the westward urge, the eastward mission ... north, south... And the mercenaries – unfinished business. They all have lots... there is no time their business can be finished in. The epics – too long to be memorised by one, a hundred, griots. Too long to tell, no lifetme long enough to see the skein unwind.... Savage poetry – like the book, like Rama – don't keep it in the house, all will burn down. Conquest – Kalmuks and Touaregs, the Congo *en marche*....

'China builds a wall a kilometre high, half the world long, a million soldiers on the watch – no use! No use! The fundament is weak, the sand obliterates, a stinging ant sits on the throne....'

*

'What will the guy down there deliver for today?' I ask: 'These insights totally transform my plans.'

I don't know how, but all has changed.

'Chaghri,' she says. 'He's not "that guy". He's our informer: Chaghri. Remember it.'

'It seems,' I say. 'That when we extinguished all those animals, and saved a few, from curiosity, shut up in the zoo – not that we call it so, and "gardens" too have ceased to be a place of frolic and excess; those lilies purple, peacocks with their rose, the cows that browse, the grounded geese – have these all gone? – to be replaced with useful stuff: the cress, the rhubarb without barb nor beard, blood-blister aubergines, the soapy spud....'

I flounder....

'No, no,' says Juno, 'you are drastic, Nino. As the creatures dwindle, we take on their attributes. You can't be messiah to a crowd that simulates, no, that has mutated into toads and otters. But – we're not yet at that point. Relax! There will be wars and massacres – carried out as they have been, since time began, by patriotic soldiers, monolingual and single-minded, paid by the state or some warlord. They're only mercenaries as we all are – our private selves, hired out to someone who will pay. They are the grease that silences the squeaking wheels of modern times. Remember, Nino, and rejoice. Be sure, that in the end, the right side wins. We yaw from right to left, from debauch into austerity – but it's the swinging to and fro that cancels out extremes. Sure, culling will happen, always and more vigorously....'

'Don't get me wrong, Juno,' I say. 'Our species going on will differentiate, fill in the gaps left by the vanished ones. We must expect individuals, groups, to transmogrify, becoming cuckoos and comaro dragons, elephants in must, and wanton foxes. Not "actors pretending to be animals", but humans into animals, gents and ladies: everyone. All creatures, great and small, will have their message: for sure, they don't need mine. Some may be waiting for messiahs. Each will eat all, or be eaten by them: that is the life, the death, we celebrate. No traction, no attraction there for me.

'And – I know, each is responsible for our collective ills. Just select some idling bozo, absorbed in his random being, and you'll have caught another guilty one. The punishment? It may be death – by boiling or by buboes. Or just to live on and on, responsible for everything, not brought to book, and never pardoned.... The ultimate, the penalty that trumps the rest – irrelevance.'

*

'Chaghri's not the mystic sort,' says Juno, shaking the heavy rain off her head. 'Where he was brought up, they don't look kindly on that stuff – the paintings, deities, invented lamas from invented countries – they've been through all that. Or, rather, they haven't – it's ended bad, for those who contemplate. Now they want to make a state that gives them some protection, doesn't sell them, doesn't decapitate, is not a secret service. Chaghri'll tell you what to do.'

'I don't trust him, Juno. Standing out there in the rain – what does he know?' I ask.

She twists away from me, and shows her teeth. A lynx. If Chaghri told her what animal she will become, he's spot on. A solitary cat. That's her.

*

'All the cash, all the notes we have, are false,' says Juno. 'If all the notes that exist were false, we'd be unnoticed. We'd be fine. As it is – it's a problem we can't resolve. This is our obstacle.'

'Do you value me because of the project I might have?' I ask, 'or because of what I've done – what I am, what I might be?'

'Yes, Nino,' Juno says and laughs. 'That's another puzzle. What are you, what you are or what you might become? Like the notes. Do we try to pass them? Or wait until there are concessions, that if they're decent made, with artistry, ink that's fast, and colours bright as *coqs de roche* ... maybe a half-face value redemption fee.... That would be statesmanship. States work like that – they even cut the zeros off, or add some more – maybe they think a zero doesn't count....'

'I'm lost, Juno,' I confess. 'This animal life – it's so baroque: the hunted revive and steal the scene.'

'The documents,' she says. 'False too?'

'They look good to me,' I say. 'Maybe I'm childish in this – but we all seem to need a nationality. A birth date, even a place where we began. It's all there, and the paper's excellent, the places, dates – all tops.'

'Again, you're foolish, Nino,' Juno says, quite affectionate: 'These are not projects, wishes, what might be and what's desirable. In fact, you pose no risk to anyone.'

'Then,' I say, 'why not be a Rusyn, born of a pattern-maker in Uzgen? Modesty should be the mark, the *pinçon.* What attracts the fancy, Juno, what seems ordinary, and yet the end of journeys – mysterious? enforced? a drift?'

'That's it,' she says. 'It's bland. You have no mission, where you might have been is insignificant. No national struggle there – you are a particle, a shard from an explosion. Unserious.'

'Well, let it be so,' I say. 'Ask Chaghri. But – it's not about being born, it's about falseness. Like all the money we have that isn't worth.'

*

'He's confusing different things,' Chaghri tells Juno. 'The falsity of the false. What is the false false to? To live a false life: what would it be worth? Would it have meaning? Is there such a thing, as meaning in a life? Self-delegitimation.... That's common enough: class, colonialism, racism – produce false identities ... but are they false lives too? You live what you're not – where's what you are? How do you know if you're having a false life?'

'Oh, you do, you do,' says Juno, vehemently: 'But the authentic – isn't that a trap? The quiddity of life lies just in living it .... True life – wouldn't that be fine?'

'Real money,' Chaghri says. 'Maybe you have to start with false, and falsify again – and then it's fun. Demystified, even if it doesn't buy you anything. Fun for you, at least – and you can try to spend and spend until it's gone.'

'We need something much much simpler right now,' says Juno. 'We know what's false. Must we believe that under all that's false there's something not false at all? If there is – so what? And if not – so what too?'

'I agree,' says Chaghri, 'There's not time to sort that out.'

*

'Who is this Chaghri anyway?' I ask.

'That's the wrong question, Nino,' Juno says. 'I told you, he's in transit. He attracts your curiosity. When he finds what he can do, when he's bricked in, his niche ... you won't spare him a look. What's attachment anyway? We must learn to break free. Freedom for us, in this continent, is supposed to be our goal. You should reflect on that.'

'Well,' I say. 'He's not from Chekhov, looking to get out. He's out. Is he really trying to get in?'

'He likes a slice of pecan pie, like all of us,' says Juno. 'He doesn't want a job, he wants the money part. That's hard. He's active and inventive – it rules him out of most things.... But he says you're not a principal. He sees you as an impresario: putting on shows. Signing people who do things well – at least one evening, they get through their act.'

'It sounds like it takes capital,' I say. I'd never thought about it....

'Yes,' she says. 'Not yours, you've none. You need a backer. Then you pay them back. Or sometimes not. That's all another science – cash. Finding who's responsible, the bad guy – forget that. Everybody knows who are responsible for everything.

'The same with your messiah trip – all ends in tears. You have to be banal to sway the crowds, and if you don't join with the other messiahs, singing their song, it all goes bad.

'Bad bad bad, just the same, whether you write the chapter, or you don't. Your feathers – lift you up, and bring you down, like Icarus.'

'That can't be all, Juno,' I say.

*

'You have beautiful eyes, Chaghri,' says Juno, drawing his head down to her breast, so she can't see his eyes.

'Leave it,' says Chaghri, embarrassed. 'I've often told you, you're quite wrong, thinking if you ask questions, every question in your head, the answer will come up. Don't you see, out comes an answer, and you have to ask again – every question. Then out comes....'

'I don't want an answer. Nino does,' she says. 'Something to take him away. Then I'll be able to do my own things. With you, Chaghri, if that's how it turns.'

*

'What's Chaghri to you, Juno?' Nino asks, I ask.

'You see him,' Juno says. 'He watches movements. Everybody does that now – traders, brokers, insurers, spies. All the rest is flickers, figures on the screen. He's like the rest, he deals in reality, real movements – then he skims and informs. Some dogsbody carries out the orders that he doesn't give – he gives information, and it's up to someone else.'

'That's the nonsense he's been telling you,' I say. 'A guy like him, he used to be a bookies' runner. Then he was a dealer's flag – you wanted something, and he dipped and waved. Now – he's nothing. Just an eye. There's nothing left to catch.'

'You must present,' says Juno. 'Call it being an impresario – it's a trade, in talent. No one will be loyal to you, but you'll ride them for a while, move on.'

'Like you do with me?' I ask. 'You've got nothing from it. We've been robbed and cheated, that's about it.'

‘It’s true,’ she says. ‘People are greedy. You can’t cure it. That’s why people turn into animals – they eat what you wouldn’t, mostly don’t have pockets so they’ve nowhere to stash the cash they steal.’

‘That’s a start, Juno,’ I say. ‘I guess. Be prudent, be suspicious. It doesn’t get you far. A messiah would have said – “be like the animals, trust in providence, or luck”. That’s finished; and besides, we’re all being animals now, except we can’t live like them, not like they used to – immense flocks and herds, populating the earth. I see what you mean, though.

‘As for being a mercenary – it gives you money but it’s risky too. What’s the risk for? Some interest that’s not your own: so best not be the murderers, but be the one who catches them.... I’m not cut out for that.’

‘Stick to ideas,’ says Juno. ‘Intuition. That is safe for you.’

‘I’d be more an agent than an impresario,’ I say.

‘They’re all gatekeepers,’ Juno says. ‘Chaghri isn’t, but all the executives are also that, like the big bosses. Gatekeepers.’ she laughs. ‘Into the big garden.’

‘It’s not so,’ I say. ‘When you have millions of clients, there’s no entry, no exit. It’s just hordes. And some big guys try to work the lines – spoons and magic. Entertaining those who wait: throwing cash around, showing off.’

‘It’s superficial,’ she says. ‘Doesn’t go deep. Maybe you can’t, maybe there isn’t ‘deep’ at all. I looked to you as someone boring but who knew the next step. Maybe you’re purblind, stumbling like all the rest. Another disillusion....’

Agency

‘I know I’m a tyro,’ I say. ‘I don’t need Chaghri’s comments to tell me so.’

Chaghri’s always round now – he passes off our duff money, brings back real change. Juno can’t do without him, but it isn’t sex, for sure.

'Why do you cling to me?' I ask. 'Not that I mind you being there so much, it's the hanging on. The claws.'

'I'm a cat,' says Juno, 'today. Like you said. Cats don't feel love, they act it. People come in different sizes, that's all. They have different smells. You have almost no smell, Nino, it's attractive. Intriguing. I lie on the rug and look up in your face, and try to figure out – why don't you smell? Even your breath.... Maybe you're dead.'

'I make things happen,' I say. 'I make people meet people, cash rings against the other cash, like when you dropped a coin on the counter to hear if it was true.'

False notes – they need a tuner. Could printing falsities be our destiny?

'When there were zoos,' I say. 'You'd stand in front of an empty cage and wait for something to come out from the back compartment, and do its act. Prowl and growl. Mostly, they slept. Some of the little ones were obsessive, jumped up and down, the same height, same corner. How everybody laughed!'

There's money now, because there's no economy in what I do, we're free, so the economic laws don't count. Even marginalism – it doesn't hold. Senior's last hour? – those Austrians meant that at the end, you'd find that all the while, you'd been a bankrupt.

'I can fix. People meeting people, blowing up little ideas until they're big enough for people who have none to pay the price. Pushing people to do their act. It's the monkey in us all – once again, it comes out in us, and we know it is our home, as if we never left: calling us, but you must never ever say.'

'Now you're arrogant, Nino,' she says. 'And you don't love the people.'

'People know you,' Chaghri says: 'You could be a boss. Go into politics – you know everyone, and they know you.'

'Absolutely not,' I say. 'You enter – and you're humiliated. Every rise will have its predetermined fall. However banal is what you say, there's guys who want a variation. You feed them – and the appetite grows stronger, till they're nauseated by you.'

*

'You spend time with Sonja,' Chaghri says. 'The singer. She could be your front.'

'That's your solution, Chaghri? That's what you've been waiting for?' I ask.

We find a table, and we play a tape. Sonja's so direct, she makes us weep, she must cry a lot, then cleans up, goes to the studio, does a ten-hour session, singing ditties, all tears: I sit with her and maybe we embrace – quite spontaneous – we're nothing to each other... does she prefer Chaghri who's pocked and sweaty? anyway, on the tape she plays us both – like we were a kemanche, or an oud. She doesn't add a gram to what we are or know. It breaks our heart.

'Yes,' I say. 'She doesn't understand, not understands a thing. She breaks your heart.'

'You're right,' he says. 'And that is what they say. Resist! Hearts don't break. They stop, they beat. Millions have stopped and more and more will stop, big felines, constrictors, foxes – their hearts too.... What more is there, what more to know?'

'Everything,' I say. 'She's a sun, a star – light is all she brings. You're right. No one would ever humiliate her, or want to see her fall.'

I don't recognise her when she's off the stage.

We might run her in a race, quite soon. Showbiz, or politics – see if she's quick, or obstinate. If she likes to race, to win, forgets the losses.... Wins a medal? Wins applause?

I love democracy: it's not a sun, maybe a starry night without the moon. I never vote, I never have – democracy is not about a taking of the sides or preferences. It's a system, a gamble where you're all in with a chance. If you're on the losing side – there's big big trouble all your life. You win – it doesn't make a difference. To me, the best is that the game is all, it shouldn't ever end. No winners, losers, just anticipation. Nothing ought to move.

The dream of class dictatorship, new men and women: that was quite other, and now, it makes me terrified.... Did I think that? Was I right? Did anybody question me...?

Sonja wants you to listen: if you know the words, when she tells you, you can join in, discreetly. Performance, though, is about her, not you; and don't forget that what you think is limited. It's timed to fit, pre-planned. It mostly doesn't enter with the show. Sometimes the audience becomes the choir: not often, and never at the end.

*

'Are you a good judge, Chaghri?' I ask, wondering, as I had from the beginning, 'Can you judge singing flesh? The mouth, trachaea, the mysterious diaphragm – a path, descending to the black light we all seek ... the source of enlightenment through song, the closest there is to stable meaning. Not much, I confess.... And you, Chaghri, unlikely and pseudonymous: are you the jockey who can ride our champion, make our Sonja win?'

'Well,' says Chaghri, alarmed by my intensity. 'We run these nags, and see how fast they are. I think you mistake my origins – I know you've taken me for a *qalandar*, mystic and libertine, a wanderer. It isn't so. I stand on the street corner. I don't roam. I give tips: give info: I don't receive. No one bets now – the odds on anything are short, so short there is no profit....'

'You're not a beauty, Chaghri,' I tell him, joshing. 'It's hard for ugly people to be libertines....' and he is stung. 'On the contrary,' he says, 'libertinism rises from the will, not face and body. I've been Juno's lover, as you must have guessed ... for many years. And so you've hung together thanks to me, despite the reluctance of you both ... I am your enabler. I infect you both, and let you grow your lies and fantasies – Sonja's the challenge that we all, the three of us, have waited for, all unaware, and now attained.... A new body, will and flesh inviolate....'

I'm shocked, amazed. Everyone will know, have known, for days that Juno frequents Chaghri for some fleeting sex: for love, for harmony, and so she finds less fault with me, my abstinence, austerity – my contemplation and my exigences, my need to find a series, a completeness, a piece that fits, that shows that fitting is a universal – what? A pattern, or design ... a fit's a fit....

'Of course, Chaghri,' I say, dissembling. 'I knew that you're a bits-and-pieces man, a gatherer of scraps, an interim, a maker-do, the lover 'neath the bed, the dusty trunk or carpet bag that holds a single secret....'

'Nino,' he breaks in, 'this is of no consequence, your innocent stupidity. We must decide – if Sonja can fulfil our hopes, and satisfy herself: persist. That's all. You, me, and Juno – we have tried: we've never won a thing, a race, a stroll, a nature walk, not found the butterfly, the orchid standing rooted in the wood. Sonja – ah! movement! Thistledown, perhaps....'

'So light!' I say. 'So, could she be a cause...?'

'Ah, the cause, Nino,' Chaghri says and laughs. 'The more you wanted justice, the more injustice happened, and when you saw that – it killed your spirit, you had no idea what you should do next.... You were never into realistic politics, and had no means of excusing what you had believed: the cause, and what it caused. It was, for certain, just. You were right, Nino. Where I lived, there was no cause, no justice. No one sought justice. What we were came with our birth, ended with death.

'Anyway, only what they call "God" knows justice and He keeps to himself what it might mean, and why we still believe.

'Sonja's our emotion. We have none. She has all that there is. She has a writer who writes love, suffering, for her. Maybe the lyrics touch her. Who knows, or cares – we don't believe in authenticity, in trusting ourselves, or what we might have done....'

'Oh, Chaghri,' I say, desperate and appalled. 'That isn't me at all. For sure, not you either. We shall be taken up somehow, to do what will fulfil....'

*

Neither of us goes back to this: the reason why we are exactly what we are. There is a bigger problem, no one but us sees it, thinks it's relevant. It's crucial. We don't like what Sonja thinks. It's not at all what we had wanted to support. It's popular as well.

*

'We should laugh more,' Juno says, looking glum.

I have a pit of anger inside me. I'm angry, but I don't know why, how to survive with it.

'It's Chaghri,' I say. 'Down on the corner, that portentous look. What does he know? Any idiot can be convinced of what they think: science and history tell us to wait, accept the being insecure, if there are whiskers, tails, in out destiny, our genes – we must be patient till they sprout. It's good, it's just. It is inevitable.'

Chaghri – is my friend, my enemy. I can trust him, so I tell him everything, except that I don't trust him, dislike him profoundly, he's the splinter, the ice shard that freezes life....

'Sonja,' I tell him. 'As a creature, what might she be? Perhaps – a flamingo. Sometimes, one is separated from the flock, and you see how delicate, particular it is. She won't speak, give confidences, change audiences – she's always worked by rote, rehearsal. She only knows the flock – but, with us, she is alone.'

'They must be very careful with their legs,' says Chaghri. 'They cannot cross them – that's where we are superior. Also the food – those pink scraps – just nibble nibble all the time – no time remains. If we were all flamingoes, there'd be no Comedy, divine or not....'

‘And maybe no book that tells us what to do,’ I say. ‘What troubles me, is that while you and I talk justice and forgiveness – she’s for unity and intuition. I distrust those singly, or as a pair....’

‘She’s rigid,’ Chaghri says. ‘So are we – you, me, and Juno. My flesh is mine, my skeleton’s traditional – I’m partway in control. You are rigid in your dithering, your ambition that one day you’ll see a crest and start to climb up to the top. Your wobbly beliefs – they hold you firm. And Juno – she is satisfied with almost nothing: it makes her strong. She has the little and she’s powerful – she yowls, she prowls, she’s solitary: behaviour you and I reject. We’re wrong. Juno does exactly what she wants – and Sonja ... she does what succeeds, and then – it’s what she wants. Juno’s indifferent to other people’s needs, leaves them alone.

‘Sonja is the contrary of Juno – she’s libertarian and authoritarian. She has no rudder – but the rudder – it is her! You are the shell, the boat – obeying her, just like you’ve been designed to.

‘She’s impatient – if freedom doesn’t work, repression it will be.... Impatient and intolerant. That’s what you are if you’re to be a great success.’

‘Chaghri,’ I conclude. ‘Sonja’s reactionary and radical. Hard to resist. What drives her? Not her audience....? What are we making with her? Exactly what we do not want?’

‘Both of us,’ says Chaghri, ‘are creators – of free will. It’s a great achievement, and it leaves us impotent, outside. You’re an agent, Nino, but you don’t have one yourself. No one does anything at all for you. Sonja has counsellors, including you, and she’s your work, your totem and your tower. She is the monster you create – now you must run after her, as she rampages on....’

‘Flamingoes don’t do that,’ I say. ‘They strut. Maybe that is what she was. Now she’s a pink dino – leather wings, a tail sharp as a scimitar.’

*

'We're responsible for Sonja,' I say. 'She can't be. We must re-draw her.'

'No, no one's responsible for themselves,' says Chaghri. 'Responsibility is for doing, not for being. You need a context ... people you do things to.'

'You love a woman I don't love, Chaghri,' I say. 'I'm in your debt, you bring in love....'

'Love is a flower,' says Chaghri. 'That dies as soon as it frees its scent. Before that – there's the black twig, the fragile bud – born to die. The flowering's not in the tree's mind: it's death, though, imminent. Death's in whoever sees the blossoming. You learn from me – but I do nothing. I don't know about anything but me. Love? What does it smell of? What colour? How long, Nino, do you think the season lasts?'

*

I don't – ever – answer. It's outside my vocabulary.

'Juno has everything that she could want,' says Chaghri. 'It wasn't much – and now, she's fading out.'

It's true. She's hardly here, she smiles, she droops, she is polite. She starves, she falls.

It's sad, I'm expert in it – sadness. For Chaghri – it's regret. They are feelings maybe – twins. At least, they can cohabit.

'If Juno dies,' I say, 'we shouldn't be too prudent with our runner: Sonja our champion. Don't try her out on little challenges. The biggest prize.... We'll have her wait and build. Be known, learn all her words....'

It's ominous. As Juno dessicates, and loses form – Sonja grows, becomes more monstrous. We wonder – what did we procure, what can she do, and why? There was no determining push: no crisis.... No over-population, no insect in the feed, alliances gone wrong – no ... it was us. We fired her from the clay, and then we fired her up.

Imagination – was ours, that made a bond with her, with Sonja's impetus, her charge. Then, we saw her attach, connect, and form a passion with the mass that came to see her, wave their arms, feel good and justified, at least as long as sound and fire were shooting up.... Her imagination, it took hold.

*

'What can we do,' asks Chaghri. 'If Juno dies. She can't stay a cadaver here, we can't admit it, nor truck her out – leaving suspicion, starting rituals....'

'We could suspend her. She'd be here, but nothing more,' I say. 'She's always been the passive sort, quick on defence, hostile to assertiveness. This way, she'd be like in a shell, or underground: encysted in herself.'

That's what we do. It leaves us free to watch how Sonja grows.

*

'No, no,' Juno says, loud as she can – 'I don't want this! It's like I'm in a web, and waiting for a spider – to consume me; or a breeze that snaps the threads and lets me fall....'

'At least you are alive,' says Changhri, trying to caress her as she struggles in the net.

'The people Sonja knows,' I say, trying to forget Juno, her plight. 'Some of them will feel she's justified their hopes. She's a leader of the newest kind. The world's got small, so all the places that she doesn't know, has not been taught about – they will suffer, without remedy.'

'Collecting stamps,' says Chaghri, 'taught you where the places were, and if they still had kings and such. Without stamps, until all everywhere's the same, you'd never know how every country's made....'

'Her team's the same,' I say. 'Stamps were a thing they'd never heard of, not being the letter-writing sort, nor having foreign friends.... We must watch out, we two are anomalous, Chaghri. Sonja will probably want to pacify, using her snarl:

there are no colonies, but the policy we call colonial – that lasts and lasts.'

'We are bereft,' says Chaghri. 'Lost, misbelievers who are burdened with a consequence, a terrible destiny: – belief in our own powers. Fear of what they can accomplish. We have made our desert, and we're lost in it. When we made Sonja – was it for cash? For the aesthetics of a song? A test, a quirk of ours – to see an audience? Doing something, bigger than we could imagine because we'd failed at smaller things?'

'What happens?' I say, wishing I could cry, be more convincing, contrite, wash it all away: 'Who makes a golem? What are they called?'

'Gods or devils,' Chaghri says. 'Now – they're a fixer. An agent in your case, Nino.'

'One last thing,' Juno whispers. 'How long is my last thing going on?'

'Hush,' Chaghri says. 'There's no way of knowing that. Be patient. We've made a mess, I fear. Sonja, your Sister; we set her up, she walks, she runs, she chants.... You don't come into it. And nor do we, the makers: the creators.

'Others are involved. The court, the followers. The suckers. Dogs roused from the dust.'

'They don't enter, Chaghri,' I say. 'They're accessories, no more. The wheel turns. It helps if there are bearings, grease: it doesn't squeak so loud, that's all.'

'In some way, we could have stopped her,' Chaghri says. 'Though – she'd cling to us, of course. Sonja will bring us down, and we'd be nullities, like before. They'd bring our gender in, for sure – colour, religion.... The fact is – she's the normal sort. All special, and all the same. A scarlet toadstool, that you'd love to eat: they die, and others rise up in the night, and impregnate another crew....'

*

'The work,' says Sonja, 'you know – it does not appeal....'

She renounces.

So – it's all over – the disasters pass to other teams and other pushers, other desperates promote their champions: Sonja, the blessed wise one, she pulls back.

*

'I was ready to depart, take Juno too.' I say. 'There's nothing left for us, Chaghri. We're sacked, Sonja will sing on. She told me that insults received and given, the political life, had seemed "no business for an artist!" In the end, the guys in rubber aprons are firing down the cellar steps at enemies, their mates. Your mates.'

'She doesn't understand,' says Chaghri. 'The power. And that's maybe very good. For me – back to the street. For you, for Juno...? Friends, living off them...?'

'Dead or buried, Chaghri,' I say. 'Friends. Long gone. Know your time, your loneliness. You too, Chaghri: your spade is ready. Do it yourself, or have it done – our rivalry ... ends in a burial....

'The past – ceases to exist. Juno hangs on her bough, like a frozen apple, waiting for the Siberian bear. Who will that be? It's welcome to her, one big bite....

'Sonja renounces formal power. She sings – a voice usually adjusted, sometimes naked: a song from a red throat – most rare. The voice, from limousine and balcony, is a reminder of what the wheedling voices, or the barking ones, can do. Send us to war, Chaghri, that's what. Or to bed with inappropriate people, that we spend a lifetime trying to have them love us.

'Like they said, the transformation takes us one step forward, one step back. Or more, or less.

'No! Remember what Juno said: find laughter! Every laugh is different, without melody and without a harmony. It's good!'

'Leave me then!' says Chaghri. 'You've told me the little that you think you know.'

'Don't leave me, Nino!' Juno pleads.

I tell Chaghri. ‘I’ll see you all in twenty years. Juno – has too little to say, I exhaust her quick. Best leave her to dissatisfaction.

‘You, Chaghri, have as much to say as me – you’re a river, then an ocean. What use if you tell me all the mysteries of life ... what shall we do with revelations? What would we talk of next? Suppose we agree on what the mysteries are? Or disagree? Sonja is right – each person is a drum, a bush piano – each has one note, we play that till we’re rich or chased away.’

*

Ah! Imagination. That thick volume, the atlas: – maps of countries that require no passport, don’t have conscription, don’t tax – wondrous places, and yet, they pall.

The sage said we are either rats or mice. The mice are feeble, but they furnish their small homes with divans and cosy kitchens, places to pass your time away.... The paw and its claws is always at the door, but you can make the entrance small: let no clue escape, don’t fart; and eat cold greens as dangers grow ... hush, hush, and quietly pass away, unobserved, steal your brioches when it’s dark and lonely in that immense outside....

Whereas, the rats: they live in broken spaces, carouse and throw the bottles out into the street, they wear cheesecutter caps, bermuda shorts, and smoke cheroots ... the males, the rest, they do the same. They die by millions, but they fuck all night and in the morning there are legions more. That’s imagination, and we reach its limits. We know everything: it is embroidery and arabesques.

Then, there is introspection; the alternative for rowdy rats, when they slack off. It’s grey and shrouded, probably, but there’s no fear, no need to take your shiv when you slink off to the bar.... What you espy – your inspirations and your influences: they’re irrefutable. A little dull.... Just you.

I tell this to Chaghri.

'Nonsense!' says Chaghri. 'I know your vacillating kind. Forget the mice! You're an explorer, adventurer, Nino. You live in imagination: and you are a rat.'

I think he's right. The world was created by one of mine: an ancestor. A rat: with no fear, no bones to leave. Our history? – suffering and conquest. I'm in it, though I could prefer not to be. Rats: the deserters.

Farewell, Juno.

Me, I'm an imaginative type. Better than the introspective mouse, I'm sure.

*

Chaghri, falcon. He's hooded. I can see him, hood drawn over his eyes; standing in the rain on the street corner. Must know where I am, where I will go.

*

'I'm well,' says Juno. 'I'm just fine. It's you, Nino. You don't move – you just repeat what you don't believe, not quite; what's plausible. I've said before – you're a broken butterfly. I'm cured – my sickness – it was you.'

'With all the fearsome things around,' I say. 'I'm insignificant! You're disproportionate, Juno.'

'I'm in a pause,' she says. 'You haven't happened yet, Nino,' she says. 'I laugh! I'll stay obedient, wait to see acts three and four, and maybe leave before THE END.'

'And have you changed, Juno?' I ask, with anticipation.

'We set ourselves on a board,' she says. 'We make stilted moves. Once in a while a king dies, a queen is crowned, a horse bolts, a bishop's caught in flagrante, a simple soldier makes a leap. Eternal conflicts, red, black, white. No one gets hurt, not for ever. Then it's over, back in our boxes. Our history. Go away, Nino! Do something off the board, break a rule, a limit!'

'Sonja climbed up – and then climbed down,' I say.

'She's had the view,' says Juno.

'I forgot, Juno,' I say. 'How facile you are. You're your parody.'

*

I ask Sonja, 'I'm interested in your success – maybe ... if there is a secret ... I'd not want success like yours....'

'Oh, you don't have a hope,' she says. 'Not of my success. Singing – you need high notes and low notes, and you have to think of that. Think all the time.'

'I'm not equipped,' I agree. 'But I think a lot....'

'Oh,' she says. 'I think of the song. It's over quick. You may not like what I think of, all the other time: I think exactly what my mother thought. I don't let it much impinge....'

'The qualities....' I start.

She laughs, 'You and Juno – you are hopeless. You're a joke. And that guy Chaghri – the beggar on the corner, when he gets a coin, he gives a jujube in return. That's his philosophy.'

'You think we've been pretentious....' I say.

She laughs some more. 'If you'd spoken ten times less, that would be the maximum of pretentiousness. You and Chaghri – have broken records.'

'The themes are of significance,' I say.

'Do you ever think of what you say?' she asks. 'Try it. You'll have a laugh.'

'Juno recommends that, Sonja,' I say. 'A laugh.'

'If the Great Khan had left a record or – since they say he was illiterate – an account made by someone else, or hearsay – whatever he said about the world wouldn't register beside his deeds,' she says. 'Was it wisdom that he offered? Those piles of skulls? You might investigate – I shan't.'

'Really, really, ludicrous? That's me, that's us?' I ask.

'Catastrophes,' she says. 'You first, then Juno, then her mate.' She doesn't smile at me with kindliness, still less with respect.

'Well, Sonja,' I say. 'Each has an opinion. 'That stays with us, until we cast it off.'

She hurries away.

Haste is the characteristic of success.

Start again? From somewhere else?

Surviving

Projects

'The Furies – they weren't furious, certainly not as much as me. I was in the fiery pit. Lots of us were jumping in, all colours burnt to crimson, yellow, white in there. The few who can climb out again – they are like nails: – black, rusty. Silver steel. Doesn't matter how you went in. Most melt,' I say.

'You seem so controlled....' says my aide.

'That's because I'm out,' I say. 'I'm in purgatory, out of hell. I could have gone to jail ... or the asylum. Or have my brothers chain me in the donkey's stall, depending on the country. Most places, when you're in flower, your head in bloom: mad rage – they kill you, somehow.'

'Anger? It's around, I guess, but big annoyance – it's an emotion found in myth. Breaking things, shutting people away ... disinheriting.... Olympians do that,' he says.

I tell him, 'You're stupid. That's what we're best at, us mortals. Destruction. I lost my lover and my work. What do you do? Crawl? It makes things worse. 'Fault' is quite irrelevant, a niggle, an hypothesis. Fault is everywhere.

'Anger – hitting out and hitting those most close: that's the sane reaction, reasonable. The human one.'

He doesn't reply. Perhaps it's impossible. I go on, 'I come on a bit strong, I know.'

'It's inevitable these days,' he says, preparing to leave. 'We all paint ourselves up. We use our monkey's tail: – we used to write with it, even scrawling down those taboos ... de-naturing ourselves. Now – it's anger: drawing on a frightening face. Imposing yourself; the scary mask.'

'History made you angry, now it's nature too. There were endings available once, tranquillity – everybody happy, hares in the cornfield doing leaps. People want to live with animals now,' I say. 'Animals are supposed to have no moral intention. We're animals! Do people want to live with them, live like them, or be like them? Or unlike?'

'It's another thing you probably can't do,' he says.

'I'm old enough to turn towards a fundamentalism,' I say. 'I have big plans. I need a helper, naturally.' I mean him....

'We all do,' he says, and leaves.

I could have shared the project with him, but he might have climbed on to it, and shared it. Stolen it.

*

When colonies became independent, they displayed the flowers and colours that were hidden. It was a hatch of butterflies, dragonflies: new ideas, new forms. Festival and revolution. Then came the mafias, the bankers, the thieves ... the dust, the bidonvilles, the sicknesses. Skycrapers like a box of crunch.

I am selfless. My project – a centre of enjoyment, creative spaces. Start again, re-create the first post-colonial day. Get it right. Roll the road flat this time.

'Anger without hate's banal,' says the minister, Marcène: 'Spread out your idea. We're not corrupt. Just put your money in my Foundation – and it's safe.'

'You're full of wisdom, minister,' I say. 'The money is real, but not concrete. It's in a bank somewhere.'

'You mean, belongs to someone else?' says Marcène: 'I'd like to think that when it comes, it belongs to no one but myself!'

It's a joke.

'That's a beautiful dress,' I tell her.

'It's not a dress, it's material,' she says. 'I'm wrapped. And watch what you say here – I might have to take it off and give it to you....'

Another joke. At the time, I don't know.

'I don't stereotype, you know,' I say. 'Women, colour, power ... not me!'

'I do,' she says. 'It saves so much time.'

There's a silence.

'While you're here, perhaps you'd like to see some animals?' she says.

'I thought I wouldn't have the choice,' I say. 'They'd be around. If there's a trip involved – let it rest. Don't disturb the personnel.'

'No disturbance personally,' she says. 'But maybe the animals....'

'Look,' I say. 'About the Foundation. I could borrow cash, for sure. But what I've got – it's only the idea. Paper.'

She's very brisk: 'We all need ideas. Our brains, without them, crash: who knows? Become polenta? Anyway, ideas arrive willy-nilly. Absolutely to everyone.'

I look for a place to leave my papers. 'Yes,' she says. 'Right there.' That's it.

*

This was when I knew: all my life I had been wrong. Too slow. Catching up the baggage train when the vanguard was far far ahead, making peace or massacring, and I – was nothing. A straggler. To be appeased when I had some position, a tiny power; ridiculed at all other times.

'Too late, too late.' It's a quote, I think. Probably the punchline of a joke: from a music-hall.

*

Marcène sends a document. 'You think you speak in pearly oysters,' it says. 'Really, you speak in snails.' It goes on to talk of silver trails.... 'You can build your idea, but there's no cash. You say you'd start afresh from independence: "as if". As if your project settled with the past, set an agenda.

'Now, you must do the work. Do the physical labour. Dig post-holes, stick the timbers in. Find a spot, construct. You seem the lazy sort....'

Another joke.

It's hot there, very hot. Foundations – you need help, my plan is huge. There's no point in digging, without the cash.

I'm a success – the plan is brilliant, and liberating too. Marcène acknowledges it – but all's in vain. Nothing. Nothing will be built – and I'm responsible, for the total failure.

The first step – that's the lesson. With no first step, nothing has moved.

That's it. Finished.

*

The central square is round, a twister – a dusty roundabout; shy of statues, those don't last.... So, now, it will stay a dusty roundabout; no groves, no grasses, no nymphs and griots, shamans and warriors.... No imagination, no titillation, no provocation. Dust and traffic.

Marcène sees all that and smiles at me, and wags her finger. That's a link, a kind of intimacy: not personal. What could we two have? A fling? A compact? Between us, there is understanding. Nothing more. Besides – moving up a scale, there's attraction, affection, need, and fantasy. I'm in love, for sure, and she's beautiful, if it's permissible to say....

Passion? I don't want the emotion, not again, the waste of aspiration: self-deception, or involvement in a difficult – what? Dalliance? Pursuit, where the object of your hunt plans every step and leads you on, directly to the pit that someone long ago has dug on spec, hoping for a catch of elephants. Instead, it's grassed over, doubly concealed, a refuge for a nucleus of mice....

'We might talk, Marcène,' I say. 'Of something more immediately practical, and smaller, a symbol – not for me, but for your story.... An installation that celebrates – what, an anniversary? A tale?'

'Oh,' she says, 'there's lots of stories. It used to be our export, everybody hoped to make a living spinning them, light, bright like my clothes, the draperies....' and she laughs.

'It's true,' I say. 'My plan's a kind of stereotype, a *forma mentis,* a concrete abstraction distilled out of my head, lying bottled on your desk. It imposes. It's not interested in a justice or a truth; a history.

'"Drink me", it says – of course, you can't, it's one-dimensional, it doesn't pour.'

'It pours when bankers pull the cork,' she says. 'When we were occupied, in someone's empire, we were in jail. Then we got free and could begin to commit the crimes we'd never done before....'

'Oh, I'm perverse,' I say. 'Crimes, historical and not? I think if somebody confesses, a pardon's automatic. The end. Do what you like, and then perhaps repent. What more can there be?'

'"Perverse" I like,' she says. 'Naive, like you – I don't.'

'There!' I say. 'You're on the way to inocence, just like I said.'

'Oh,' she says, 'I'm all for fun. Laughter. Everybody wants to start again, with innocence. Power – even if if it's thrust on you, comes with percentages of guilt, of things complicit, things suspected and committed.... It's like this absolutely everywhere, so confessions from a power are ritual. Right from the start they point to peccadilloes. You've power? Then, you're in the stream ... So, don't own up. Imperial people don't apologise: the losers may.'

'Anyone with power – you don't confess. But you're complicit....' I say.

'You mean you're guilty but can't be condemned,' she says. 'What the cops do, the army ... the corruption, things done and not ... all that you know, keep quiet about. Or you don't care.'

'I believe you, Marcène,' I say. 'You know it all, you're wonderful.'

'I'm on my own,' she says. 'Once, we'd have come to you for an indulgence. Now, you are here, to plead. That says it all. Don't trust me, I'll cheat you if I can, like you guys cheated us.'

*

It says nothing. Nothing comes of my plan. The money that would come to me – it would have helped.

You find reported two contrasting tales from former colonies: one of violence, one of unearned wealth. They're bookends – fake books supporting all the rest; you can't read them, just intuit – moral imperialism! Out they come, ghosts of empire in their shrouds.

People protest, are sequestered, killed, raped, driven off, expropriated. A scandal, political disgrace, the personal state: grand theft.

People steal or skim – the sum seems immense, but almost everyone plays poor, keeps schtum, some run or go to jail, and some hole up in luxury.

There the threads end: frayed, forgotten, left unwoven ... Maybe there's a trial, a hearing when the incident is ancient. There's no follow-up.

*

She beats on my door. Back home.

'I need a shelter,' Marcène says. 'I remembered you, and your address. You sought my help, now I seek yours.'

'I was mistaken, Marcène,' I say. 'I admit it: my stupidity.... Trying to give your place a different past, a different starting-point. Everything done was to be cancelled, as if it had never been. No witness, no guilt no sacrifice, no benefaction, and no slog. No suffering, and no accomplishment.... Nothing usurped: no justice and no consensus, nothing ...'

'Forget all that,' she says. 'There's something new. When there's a slide, we all go down. Surrender or resist? – it's better far to run; to walk at least.'

It's all she will explain. She stares at me: 'Let me in.'

*

It's too strange to talk about. There's some music playing. 'That's perky stuff,' I say.

'Those Brazilians!' she says. 'Our drums, their electronics. It's for dancing to.' She sways a little.

'Are you known about, Marcène?' I ask. 'Journalists? The cops, assassins....?'

'Everyone knows everything,' she says. 'Don't fret. I've nothing, nothing damaging. I'll rely on you.'

'I've lived from idea to inspiration, Marcène,' I say. 'I've no job. If the wealthy ones don't want me – I'm alone. And underfed.'

'You were so big,' she says. 'You spoke of millions....'

'There's your compatriots,' I say. 'Try them. Everybody talks of the communities....'

She does some steps – the tropical beat is going on. It sounds like pebbles bouncing in tin cups.

'Marcène,' I say. 'This is no basis for relationships....'

'Well,' she says. 'That means I don't want one. I need a stepping stone to help me jump to the next stone.'

*

'What do you do here?' she asks, exasperated. 'Nothing?'

'If *Rollerball*'s on the TV, I watch it. Otherwise,' I say, 'I wait for paying inspirations.'

'Like Columbus?' Marcène asks. 'The letter? Then an island, a continent? People to trash?'

'This place, Marcène,' I say, 'is depressed. You add to it. Go to a rich district, show off: pay me the rent you owe.'

She ignores this, says: ‘I believe the girl downstairs does prostitution.’

‘She’s quiet,’ I say. ‘Don’t boss, Marcène. About most things you’re right, of course, but don’t insist. I don’t defend – not anyone: not me, not you.’

‘You were so keen,’ she says. ‘You thought I was the powerful one. And now – you’ve nothing for me. Not a thought, a present – even a joke. You don’t know how humans live, they climb up one another like monkeys climbing trees – and lick and sniff, poke paws in pockets, paws in everywhere. You must support each other – didn’t you know?’

‘I know it all,’ I say. ‘I can’t. It’s not for me. I need my distance, my little power. Stay here, Marcène, but it’s not for long, and I can’t give you....’

‘Anything,’ she finishes for me. And it is so. Passion – is nothing: air.

*

‘How would things change,’ she asks, ‘if I told you I was victimised? Punished for my rectitude. Or said I was a thief: or in a losing faction?’

‘Change? Not at all, I guess,’ I say, irritated. ‘I like big moral questions, the future, how we prepare: not ethical conundrums. We’re all corrupt – if you’re an exception, we would know about it.’

‘In the countryside,’ says Marcène. ‘Long ago, you could be honest. There was nothing to be dishonest for. People lived all alike. And now it’s dangerous.’

‘My plan’s about that,’ I say. ‘And I’ve come to think it was naive. Countries, empires, states: how can you be honest in those monstrosities? By starting wars...?’

That’s a mistake. I didn’t think, think about history, about her history. There’ve been many wars ... followed by imprisonments.

She ignores this. She’s right, I’m sure. My, she’s impatient. So am I.

She says, 'You're lucky I am nice. I could say we were corrupt together: implicate you in a conspiracy. Or I might invite in the assassins – or the cops. Bring in religion, separatism.... Shaft you, in a word.'

'You won't, because it would be disastrous,' I say, although I'm sure she won't want to make a fuss. 'You'd be exposed. I'm mister nobody – bringing me down ... no one would give a damn.'

*

She leaves a note – 'Mail: send to PO Paris.'

*

'You missed your chance,' says my French friend, Serge. 'She's history. You could have taken some of hers.'

'She wanted too much,' I say. 'I couldn't cope.'

'You want everything,' he says. 'You should have understood that she does too. Maybe you saw she's full of things you couldn't understand or recognise. Your plan – to show what they had before the occupation ... that was a start. You, of course, are compromised, and ignorant. But – the villages, the stories, you evoked them. True, it's faded stuff. As for Marcène – you show how she climbed up so high that you could see her fall.'

*

'My problem,' I say, 'is style. I'm not attractive, Serge. Not as a body, nor a brain....'

'You're clumsy,' Serge agrees. 'The Elephantine Style? You're heavy. Dare I say – a lump.'

'I'm a pot,' I say. 'That cooks deep, and slow. Most of what is happening today is science-fiction. I take one, two steps back. Maybe – none forward. That way I don't need retreat.'

‘It’s clear,’ says Serge. ‘And you don’t see. You *do* retreat, always. ‘Start off again’, is your order of the day. Get independence right this time, go back and talk of ethics, moral intention – everything that’s been discussed before, conclusions reached, or not ... sides taken, battles fought, most indecisive too. You want to get things *right*! You can’t. They’re not.

‘Marcène wants help – you give her ... nothing much. Think of her – as the present. Even as a future.

‘The world is new and old. The rule is now – invest, if you have cash. If not – produce. Forget the nomad life, lotus positions, the reflective mode. The rich are there to make the others work, turn out the goods.

‘The poor – will have to invent new space for what they’ll call their freedoms. The rich: they’ll employ fewer of the poor, and make them sweat. Society divided into two: the rich, the poor. The giants are makers of invisible stuff to sell – the rest are just inventing fantasies....’

‘It’s like now, but speeded up,’ I say. ‘More efficient for making cash. It makes me feel old and stale. We used run after the new, the latest trick, fashion, the up-to-date. Now – chasing the novel is a ritual. What’s modern anyway? What’s modernity? What’s modernism? No one cares – all’s been made over, given a fresh patina, had an old one rubbed off.’

‘... and what’s new about science?’ Serge joins in. ‘That’s your theme, your one-note melody. Look! Don’t theorise. What exists evolved, was something similar but different ... so much has just disappeared. Much is still too far away, much crumbles while we look at it. It’s all meaningless, just coloured stones and wind. Only what we think and know is new: the rest is magma, heating up and cooling down.’

‘That’s what I think,’ I say. ‘And you, Serge – you just bat my ideas back. Add something! Be new: even, be modern....’

‘You’re a bore, my friend,’ he says.

Probably it’s so.

Serge doesn’t know how to be original.

'Enough, then, Serge,' I say. 'Come back when you have something new, concise, to say.'

*

He's right, though.

Paris. Marcène is my adventure.

I wait for her outside the main post office. She'll come – she loves receiving mail....

*

'Marcène,' I say. 'My ex-friend, Serge, said I had a problem with my time-frames; making connections. In a picture gallery, full of frames – you see people like you know, done by the Flemings or the Copts, you're back with them. Go to today – and the people painted are unrecognizable – structures, or hoglike, limned with a lipstick, grotesques....'

'I see you have no visual sense,' says Marcène. 'You don't grasp how reality, always, everywhere and for ever – is the same. Art changes according to its function, not its accuracy to what you think you see....'

'Of course, Marcène,' I say: 'I know all that, even if I don't internalise – imprisoned in my taste ... I see how everywhere the artefacts are different – I deal in them myself. And, I'm an enlightened soul. If I don't go to the manif here, against the racism, it's because I don't want a beating from the cops.'

I trust her, totally. Not to do so would be – prejudice. Stereotype.

'I'm not corrupt,' she says. 'If that is what you think. Corruption often starts because our wages are not paid. You need the cash to live, and so you start to fish, give favours, accumulate some greedy creditors – and soon you have a debt, a gang, and there's no way to stop. I made a point of all my guys having pay on time ... My cousin ran the treasury, of course....'

'I'll help you, Marcène, if I can....' I say.

'Not me – help some of the many who have real need,' she says.

'I would, I will,' I say. 'But I'm quite broke. But, I have an infinite sympathy for those in need....'

'This is the centre of the picture world,' she says. 'If they offer you some art – don't accept. Don't buy in the street....'

'No one has ever offered me ....' I say.

'I took a picture from my wall,' she says. 'The ministry's. I sold it really well....'

It doesn't seem quite right to me. No, not at all. Property – it has no halo, aura, no sanctity, but still ... belonging must have a significance ... especially if a picture isn't yours....

*

We share a fear of death. She's escaping an extinction. And I'm a dumb animal who faces sacrifice, I'm the zebu whose blood will help to save the mangroves. Or bring rain, stop the kidnappings, abuse of my brothers. I don't believe it, none of it, but I am hobbled, prone, with not a hope.... All of us offering as sacrifices to our fears.

'In another life,' says Marcène, 'I shall go back. In this life – I must stay and make my way here, among these arrogant people. You, my dear, you don't need sell, just bluster. I must sell all that I have, all that is me. Does anybody want to buy? It's not promising.'

'I don't know where to start,' I say. 'I'm not an architect, nor a historian. I do a bit of everything: installations. Spectacles and show, and exhibitions: catch the eye and disappear. Make people talk, and then forget.'

Monsieur le Capital

'You're hung up, like all the rest,' she says. 'On trivia. On stereotypes, and what I did and didn't do. You don't look at what's happening. Remember? The development of capitalism in Africa.... Mossendjo, the Comilog, all that....'

'I've never heard of that,' I say. 'You mean the Chinese form of capitalism? That's not your personal problem now, I'm sure....'

'Imagine that you're wrong,' she says. 'Imagine me ... being caught between two tides....'

'I know,' I say. 'That there's no commercial peace, that this huge contest between powers is set up to destroy us all.... The promise for a victor is ... clearing another path to fresh disaster....'

'It will destroy small places,' she says. 'Mine and me. Without a shudder, conflicts and slavery anew will grow and deepen. With indifference and competition they'll destroy us all.'

'And that's what you are in?' I ask.

'We all are,' she says. 'Except you play a variation on quite another theme: romanticism.'

'My side,' I say. 'It's harmless. You, Marcène, picked the wrong side...?'

'I was caught between some warring states,' she says. 'There are no allies. I am powerless, and I became a casualty.'

*

I am, have been, Marcène's lover. That's the term. The word. Love. It implies no reciprocity, no contact, nothing physical.... It ends with being inquisitive.

'My cousin went next door,' she says, 'like the postman. I travelled afar, to see what was our destiny. Was it becoming like these people? – so different from the enlightened revolutionaries they say they are on the TV; in their prized books. We shall be even worse than them – we've no one to exploit.'

'This is old-fashioned stuff,' I say. 'Like my installation. No riches there, just artefacts.'

'Yes,' she says. 'No hierarchy, no chiefs, no sages: replicas, that's all. Dull and fractious. What do I want? Nothing. I want nothing I shan't get. What's the use?'

'We must leave,' I say. 'There's nowhere left.'

*

In Paris, we see crowds marching, defying the cops, being beaten up, disappearing like a swirl of starlings, then back again, or similars.

'It's about consequences,' says Marcène. 'Living with the future. In my place – you see guys running, cops firing, some to miss, all kinds of stuff, sophisticated ... you don't see what's at stake. The past, of course. People overstaying, refusing to step down. You're never told, never see, what is to come, what's to be exploited, who is chosen to preside, to acquiesce, administer. Probably they – whoever – will try to overstay.

'You know you can't, should not, tell the story of the empire – I know I should tell it, but I know it and I want to do something else. So, what happens? It's left to some historian to ladle out the goods and bads. Quite useless. That's the past – how's the present?

'You never know what a conflict's really all about – guys in the street don't know. All's in the contracts that you never get to read. Who is your covert friend, who doesn't let you stray, or sign? Those are our installations: – our present and the future.... You'd have re-installed the past, except – I didn't have the money.'

'If this were the adventure,' I say. 'Why you left – on principle or because of the plot.... I'd gladly come along.... But – are you trying to expose? Or to oppose? Or maybe you just lost a joust....'

*

'I must get to the bank before it closes,' says Marcène. 'Then we can decide where we want to go.'

'I thought you were without ID,' I say.

'Oh,' she says, 'you don't know Africa. You don't know free women. You're patronising, when you think you are protecting. I have a diplomatic passport. Other times, you are my document. You accompany me – a secretary-bodyguard.'

It's true, all of it is true. I don't know Africa, don't know Marcène. How can I repair, live up, live down, to what I'd like to know...? To what I'd like to do, to represent?

'Do as I say,' she says. 'Forget the destiny that sent me to your humble door. You have nothing I could take – so don't imagine I am robbing you.'

*

'We must pass frontiers in the night,' she says. 'If they query documents – there's no one for the guards to ask, so they'll let us through....'

'If you think it's so.' I say: 'Marcène, I tell you – I'm not interested in chasing through the world, being hunted, and unrecognised. I want to have attachment. To feel my emotions have a sense, a purpose. An object that reacts.

'To know what civilisation means – to me, and my people who claimed it and traduced what is most elementary in it: civilisation, the enlightenment, reduced to a mere culture of the greedy: slavers, rapists, bibliophiles and pious murderers.... I want an affirmation: that it's possible to set something right; to redress, to understand the errors. Like the Russians said, "new life! new life!"'

'That's a lot of things to do,' says Marcène. 'Who knows where you'd start to set that all to rights? I have a small, refined group of people to contact. I told you – it's best that I'm accompanied. A sobersides like you – no one would doubt that I am who I say, and competent to do what I shall do....'

'The conflict between capitals,' I say. 'The trade, the military; wars being waged and threatened – you'd not say "neo-colonial", but rather global marketing.... The world's the market, to be won with goods, with arms, with threats, with smiles.... The capital is one, the forces claiming and directing it are multiple, and you, your little nation, caught – a fly pulled apart by ravenous spiders....'

'Absolutely so,' she says. 'But come with me and you will see how I can sort things out.... I feel secure in all the things you lack. I know what civilisation is, and all the other stuff you're sceptical about. What is important for me – and mine – is meeting with some guys who hold some capital that could be vital to my side.'

*

Planning – prophecy – is a pseudo-science: divination. Reason helps, more than a plan. The future will come in some form, and probably unthinkably long.

Marcène leaves me to walk around the town, the city, while she has her talk. I think there will be a choice. Chinese workers, or an African proletariat. A proletariat that won't do what the past had said it would: it ought.

*

'It's settled,' she says. 'I can't go back, not right away. People like me who've left go back in stages, country to country till we're home again.' She'll be my benefactor, fixer.

'You could re-submit your plan,' she says. 'It has a good chance now.... You wouldn't need to do the donkey's work this time.'

*

A guy called Dietmar – on his shirt – sits at my table, while I'm waiting for Marcène to get her contract. He pours self-heating soup from a waxed container into a waxed cup, and chugs it down.

'She'll get her contract,' he says. 'They won't need you.'

Why would they?

'Where are you?' he asks. 'Spinoza or the free industry fronde?'

'I don't know,' I say. 'None of that. In between.'

It comes to me, if I had a new life, I wouldn't study death, or spectacle – I'd spend my life doing good to people, one on one, no screen. Being loved by simple people. The same I'll meet in paradise.... I say, 'If these developments happen, they won't need workers. Not when the concrete's poured and the postholes dug, anyway. They'll all be cadres, like you, with an infinity of rabbits to chase and holes to go down. There's so much you can know, and so much you need not – best treat it as a game.'

'Like you do,' he says. A provocation?

'You might think my stuff is that,' I say. 'But all my purposes are serious. Not serious games – allegories, more like. Real maps of undiscovered places.'

He grins at me.

Marcène has finished. 'Take me to the frontier,' she tells me.

Dietmar types on a tile: – 'concluded'. Marcène and I see him write and send it.

'You should get a proper job,' he tells me, nastily. 'Then you won't need justify your pastimes. You could have told me what was happening....'

'He can't give interviews,' Marcène tells him. 'He doesn't know computer talk. It's all Dogons and palm trees.... No palm trees where I live!'

They laugh.

'I can't stand people like him,' Marcène says when we're alone. 'Trivialisers. Sellers of info. Industrial spies.'

'This "free industry",' I say. 'A contradiction in terms.... What's it about?'

'About me,' says Marcène. 'Everything. On the ether, it's all abstract, like capital, and all serious – in some way.'

'But surely capital is abstract, and industry now and then must be located?' I say.

'I hope so,' says Marcène, and there it rests.

Free is abstract? Except, the consequences of anything abstract are concrete. I never see Dietmar again, to ask – especially about 'Spinoza'. But he might have clammed up, and anyway it's all there at your fingertip.

Freedom comes from authoritarian situations. You're free to wrestle to the top, then you're free to do anything you want. It's a danger, Lenin saw – but then, he did it, so did all the rest, with no constraints. Absolutely free? Perhaps....

'Yes,' says Marcène. 'Your old installation – Russia. We'll drop in there. They're out of cash, but they have friends....'

'Me too!' I say. 'I have Russian friends.'

*

We're in the old National hotel – usually there's only room for ghosts. 'Why are we here, Marcène?' I ask. 'You have what you need to parley yourself back in.'

'Oh,' she says, 'I have a choice – money or things. Things look good, but money feeds. It all goes through my cousin anyway.... This is a detour, my troubled friend.'

'My friends have been rich and poor so many times, they're either prone or born again – into a world where there were sturgeons, whole, for lunch, and desserts all in French,' I say.

'Russian science,' Marcène says. 'They made the break. It was poor communism, but they broke the continuity – the old philosophy with theological roots, the parts of Hegel no one reads – the ideal Man.... They improvised, invented: brain studies.... Slicing the big male brains as if they were black truffles, to see where ideas come from ... those peas and beans ... magnificent, immense.... Inventions worthy of magicians – all junked when the battleship went down....'

'My brain, Marcène,' I say, alarmed, 'is wizened like a kernel. Fit for toasting, hard to slice.'

'Fear not!' says Marcène. 'It's the principle, not the practice....'

'Our ancestors must have been intrigued,' I say. 'It didn't work....'

'Shit nonsense,' Marcène shouts. 'Think of the centuries spent trying to manufacture gold. I'd bring some science guys back home, and set them up.... Science so far has made disasters, the remedies for worlds' end – they won't suffice. I had in mind a centre – of excellence, turning out all manner of exciting things....'

'Is that the capital you wanted?' I ask her. 'Promoting alternative sciences? Lysenko's grandsons....'

She backs off. 'Only a tiny part,' she says. She lies.

'You should be throwing out nationalities, Marcène, not asking new ones in,' I say.

'Oh pish and tish,' she says. 'The world is round, things are not fastened down – they slip and slide.... Look, my friend,' she grasps my arm. 'Gold is valuable just because you cannot make more of it than what there is – hidden, stashed in the ground by someone – 'God', or 'who knows who'. The same with brains – logic says exceptional guys have great ideas. It's sensible to think – their brains are special. As for beans – it stands to sense, a big bean has big sons and daughters. It's true for humans, dogs, and jackals: why not your pea, your bean?'

'I'm with you, Marcène,' I say. 'I've often pondered just the same as you. The possibility is – the world's not based on logic or on common sense, nor even on our observation. It's all a ball of string a trillion kilometers wide and long....'

We laugh. We're closer than we've ever been.

'This is what the revolution leaves for us,' says Marcène, deeply satisfied. 'This will stop the rich guys using Africa to solve their problems.'

Let it be so, I think.

*

It's warm, warmer as I go up North. My friends – have disappeared, the villages are stumps, a few old crones crawl round like wood-bugs. Nearer the cities, the places that I knew are full of smart habitations, varnished like bonbon boxes.

'Your colleagues of the spectacle,' asks Marcène. 'Lovers and enemies?'

'Gone or lost,' I say. 'What lesson, what meaning, do they leave? I hesitate ... you, Marcène, are full of theories and ideas, set to survive, humiliation, dirty-dealing – you accept life in every shape....'

I could cry. There's lots here walking up and down, full of tears; another weeper draws no crowd....

'Each does what they know,' she says. 'In general, I do good. That doesn't make me good, I know. I've turned everything that in the past would have cut me out of anything significant – turned it to my profit, and the profit of all I've helped, and all my parasites. The others, unsatisfied ... well....

'They say the continent will dry out and singe, turn sandy: – here, it's turning into mud and sinkholes full of bones....'

'I know,' I say. 'It's not primarily your fault, and nothing at all to do with me.'

'They want me to leave you here – as guarantee,' she says.

'I guarantee nothing,' I say, terrified.

'You know the language, everything; you love the north,' she says. 'In the GUM there's anything a living thing with cash could want.'

'That's why I'm terrified. They're good people, great people here,' I say. 'But once they see you are good too, and pleasant to be with, they are attached to you. Besides, a guarantee works only if you promised them a something, Marcène. You've nothing, and they've given nothing.'

'That's what I told them,' she says. 'You're worthless, and I can't keep my promises.'

'The wrong way to do a deal, Marcène,' I say.

'You're an interesting piece, my dear,' she says huffily. 'But whichever pan you're in, you don't stir the needle of my scales.'

'It must be a joke,' I say, desperate.

'Of course it is a joke,' she says.

If we – we humans – weren't so fragile, degrading, degenerating as you watch – the need to make a structure, cling to it, advertise it, might seem perverse, exaggerated. A structure? Any structure – a signature, a document, foundation, testament, a tombstone, ledger entry, a distorted kidney in fluid in a flask in a Humboldt institute somewhere, forgotten beneath the stair or in a line of similar, like skulls of Capucins in a catacomb, monks or monkeys – time blends and shuffles ... emotions, they homogenise ... death scares us, and the dead we loved – all waiting for us all in a somewhere we shan't go, no tickets for the ghost train, no, not one, not for you, nor me!

'Of course,' I say, 'another joke. It's just – not funny. It raises spectres of when peoples tried to seem dissimilar and incompatible. Now we say we all believe the same: our likes.'

'You're fluid,' Marcène says. 'Talking left, but hanging on to me, who's powerful and wants to turn the power to cash – it's easy done; but where does that leave you, my dear? Another renegade? Wanting sex, you end up carrying my bag! Me: the opportunist with a clan dependent!'

She laughs.

I guess I laugh as well.

I have some truths I could expound about the Revolution here, but they're well known. What matters is what you do next for centuries when the transformation's over, failed, like France. Napoleons tucked away in matrioshkas; republics and restorations imploding like receding thunderclaps.

'I don't waste myself,' says Marcène. 'I've completed two of three: the projects I've travelled to secure.... The third's twinned to the other two: the one that's sacrificed so that the other two inherit a sufficiency. You, though –' she turns her bullying gaze on me, 'The installations. How many planned, how many actually set up?'

'I have a principle,' I say. 'The May Day celebration – I'd do that if it was not so gross.... In my shows, only weapons you can heft by hand....'

'Oh crap,' she shouts. 'Go back a handful of seasons – history, the shows, are all wars and incredible religions. You can't have principles! Not when you're showing history!

There's always slaves and prisoners, big guns and ghastly priests.... How many have you done?'

'I cannot disagree,' I say. 'I planned some hundreds, executed maybe two or three.'

'I thought so,' Marcène says, her face bursting with derision. 'You exaggerate, no doubt, but you're ridiculous....'

'Sure I exaggerate,' I say. 'I've executed two or three, but planned some thousands....'

'It's crazy,' Marcène says. 'Fabergé was sparing with his golden eggs. Sappho left broken lines and glyphs – but thousands of poor scribblers and smiths ... like you, they lay a plenitude of sterile eggs, exude a cumulus of spores ... Detritus, my poor friend. Useless, de trop – nature with her over-egg and surplus-hatch obsessions, pointless insurance against death....

'You're sex-mad frogs who crawl to splatter on a motorway ... indifferent to uselessness, millions of you, virgin sacrifices, wired up by instinct to pursue, to procreate....

'No room, no room! Full up! But you don't heed. The traffic – watch the trucks! but no! Snap landscapes, paint those crusts, hum roundelays – fill discs and boxes with the stuff, unread, unheard – all genius maybe, but no one cares....'

'In all us frogs,' I say, stung by her scorn. 'There is a prince. It's not my fault if I'm not kissed.'

She laughs, and kisses me. I'm not appeased.

There is no metamorphosis.

*

I push ... to see how far she'd go – not to humiliate, to win a hand, a petty victory. No. I get the truth this way.

That's worth it: know what she thinks, but also what she knows. Everything about her. Nothing about me. You're supposed to tell the world what it is you represent. I am not interested. I don't tell anything – I make frames, and other people stand in them, gesticulate.

'Your luck,' says Marcène, 'is that you can float. Pin you in some dreary work, enough to live on, not to prosper – your lyrics change, for sure they will.'

'Those are your wisest words, Marcène,' I say. 'You ought to live according to the truth you know.'

There's insurrection in her homeland. Questions of language ... pastoral rights. Getting rid of nomads. Privilege, beliefs. Refugees. Moneylending, cops and market-stalls. It all comes apart – you have to run, no one tells you you must stay – how could they, it's not safe....

'It won't last,' Marcène tells me. 'You stereotype. Most places are secure.'

Her projects – they don't look secure.

'Me stereotyping doesn't mean a thing,' I say. 'You climb too high up on rotten ladders.'

'We must be visible,' she says, preoccupied. 'You sidetrack. You see folklore – it's a mirage.'

'I don't count,' I say. 'We know it, and you've told me frequently. Crazy or sane – I make no difference. We modest people – we're all like that. Psychiatry was invented for us – our story's dull, you pay a guy to give you a quite different version....'

'Wasting time,' she says. 'You don't know anything.'

They move us to a different hotel – it's modern but not finished: we're in the part that hasn't quite been built.

*

'If you could write it up,' she says, 'you'd see and tell – how heavy is my task.'

'You're always out, Marcène,' I say. 'I've seen the galleries, walked the Prospekt many many times, travelled the metro at all hours. It's heavy for me too – passing the days.... Tell me, Marcène....'

'The Russian project's dead,' she says. 'I'm not secure. Not viable, they say. Creative science won't be housed. So now they want to buy a part of what I bargained for in Germany.... I'll sell....'

'You can't do that,' I say. 'You'll lose the lot....'

'I know,' she says. She seems exhausted: maybe it's all the drink. 'The Russians say they'll do a deal and get some robust guys from China. They'd do the work – it's guaranteed ... maybe they'd be Koreans.... It was my hope to give the jobs to local people, but, you see – all skitters off, and my interpreter, Mikhail – I don't know if he's trustworthy.... He suggests more than he translates....'

I don't feel sympathy for her, though she's my guarantee.

'I'll talk to Mikhail if you like,' I say – it's not at all my thing....

'Only the poor can afford to be in love,' says Marcène. 'The rest, who have more – a pittance even – we must marry not for love, but for economics, calculation, procreation. Family alliances.... Continuity and a sufficiency, for most, remains the most that is desired. Very very few, and many of those lie ... are by love inspired. Temporarily, at least.'

'Mikhail?' I ask. 'Are you in love with him?'

'Russian men?' she laughs. 'They know they're rubbish. They drink and lounge, so's they go quickly off the scene. Then *smert'*! No – Mikhail's daughter – a person rare and selfless.... We need a nation full of them.... And, naturally, she despises me, thinks I'm a waste, and rotten....'

And she weeps.

*

'Lost in translation?' asks Mikhail. 'Not at all. Marcène's a difficult subject. I don't trust her, sometimes I must paint around what I take to be some dirty deal she plans. She wants to make me complicit. What is her substance? Her authority, her powers, her contacts?

'Is her backing from relatives, or the regime? Is she in flight? I know I'm stereotyping, but it's the country that she's from.... Other places are known for their probity. You should tell her – negotiate with openness, and we'll get on. Otherwise – I have to soften what she seems to want, or the other side won't bargain.... They'll just throw her out....'

I see his daughter, Cooky, in pyjamas, contorted on the floor. 'She's trying out a dance,' says Mikhail, fondly.

'What do you want to be, Cooky?' I ask. She's very young. And chubby. Maybe fifteen at the most.

'An astronaut,' she says. 'If there's a big ship going. I can't stand tight spaces. Or a model. Maybe both.'

*

'I tried,' I tell Marcène. 'Cooky is sweet, without a clue. Mikhail – is under orders, you should be firm with him. Make clear what you want.... There's one side, he's on it, you don't have a side.'

Normal life is this – I never managed to be part of it.

'Happiness – is a long shot, Marcène....' I say.

'I don't want happiness,' she says. 'I want sex.'

I pull a face, screw up my eyes and wrinkle up my nose. 'Nothing doing' – that's both our messages.

'The vital spark....' I say. It's gone.

'I'll tell you true,' she says. 'I was excluding you from the beginning. That ratlike eagerness ... and then, you are mature. Your conversation's just like mine, dull and besieged with cares and trammels. Who wants an Echo post-coital on the couch?'

I know that's how the powerful discharge their load – the leaders all have sex abundant, hugger-mugger with each other, indiscriminate, with semi-friends and enemies; then they make war and deals. Keep schtum. It is acknowledged, but not written down. Rumours – turned to fantasy ... the Empress Catherine with her horse....

'And your walks!' says Marcène, laughing, stroking her nose. 'Like a tart, a novice to the game.'

'I'm bored, Marcène,' I say. 'I want to leave. Let me talk to Mikhail, I'll resolve it all for you – Cooky too. People here –

they want to keep you talking – maybe to do someone down, maybe to see how things turn out, it's their work. They don't show their interest, or who they are appeasing, screwing, trying to humiliate. They won't deal with you: break! ... Let's go!'

'You know nothing of finance,' she says.

'I know all history,' I say. 'Trust me. I have my principles – they won't get in my way.'

*

'In confidence, Mikhail,' I say to him....

I tell him how Marcène procrastinates – not to gain advantages in Russia, but to keep her other offers on the boil. 'Finish it, Mikhail,' I say. 'She's wasting time....'

He's pleased to have a resolution offered, given to him to manage, as a confidence.... He'll dress the story up.... He's probably the one who can decide.

'Cooky,' I tell him. 'I'll give her an invite to a breakdance festival....'

All is resolved. This is how the great ones of the world behave.

*

Marcène and I – we take the train. And no one loses, gains – except to move surroundings. I change from an Enchanted Wanderer to irresolute *flâneur*.

We never met Mikhail again. Marcène never saw the principals behind her talks. We guessed we knew which other countries played their hands .... the middling paternal one especially....

Cooky says, 'My mother was anomalous. She wasn't around much: now I'm an anomaly with Mikhail. Fathers don't stay with daughters long.... Maybe nothing will ever ever happen to me. I could hope for that.'

*

'I could have been of use to you, Marcène,' I say: 'But you are slippery. Today, you're flush, with an army, bought, not paid for, and disloyal – the best arms that rich countries could sell to you on tick. Then – in the afternoon, you're in the forest, a fugitive.

'You are a stereotype, Marcène. Survival – that is what we want. It's right your guys should have their moment, even long lives with plans. Some manage it, some places might work out like that.

'Keep trying. This time, you can't produce. Step back.... Do not insist....'

Marcène doesn't speak.

My tricks, my interventions – haven't helped her, nor me. I'm a romantic, once again, without romance. I can start over, or try another path. Forget the people's history – it makes them horrified. I've lost my anger. It was mine; now, it's universal – there must be a stratagem you use to temper it.... Not just being stupid.

Marcène, though, can't desist. She can't step back anywhere without a tumble down the cliff. She knows it all; what's done, and who'll do what.

Re-running history, fired up by anger – that moment's passed.... I'm an optimist. There's better, but not good. There's worse, but not quite despair.

That's my judgement – it holds good for everyone alive, everyone I've met, who's doing deals and trying to survive. Avoid despair, or you won't get taken on the trips.

*

She doesn't travel home direct. I see a picture: there's a crowd, men mostly, running and under threat.... Just pictures.

I recognise the draperies, flying out behind her like a flag.

About the author

John Fraser lives near Rome. Previously, he worked in England and Canada.

www.ingramcontent.com/pod-product-compliance
Lightning Source LLC
Chambersburg PA
CBHW020550310726
48979CB00008B/1163/J

* 9 7 8 1 9 1 0 3 0 1 9 3 7 *